DR BRENDAN QUAYLE is an awaı
and film maker. He is the author (with]
England's Last Wilderness and the semir.
  Scots Irish of Manx ancestry, he
wood in the North of England.
Trained originally as an anthropologist, he studied amongst
shamans and real-life sorcerers in the mountain tribes of the High
Himalaya. His extraordinary experiences there, together with his
lifelong interest in the myth and folklore of his Celtic ancestors, provide
the inspiration and much of the source material for *The Shining Stone*.
Find out more at www.brendanquayle.com.

THE SHINING STONE

TALES OF THE Q'ALIX #1

BRENDAN QUAYLE

PART 1 OF THE TALES OF THE Q'ALIX SERIES

SilverWood

Published in 2023 by SilverWood Books

SilverWood Books Ltd
14 Small Street, Bristol, BS1 1DE, United Kingdom
www.silverwoodbooks.co.uk

Text copyright © Brendan Quayle 2023
Map illustration by John Booth from original artwork by Brian Iley

ISBN 978-1-80042-229-2 (paperback)

British Library Cataloguing in Publication Data
A CIP catalogue record for this book is
available from the British Library

Page design and typesetting by SilverWood Books

For Niamh, Pads and Max

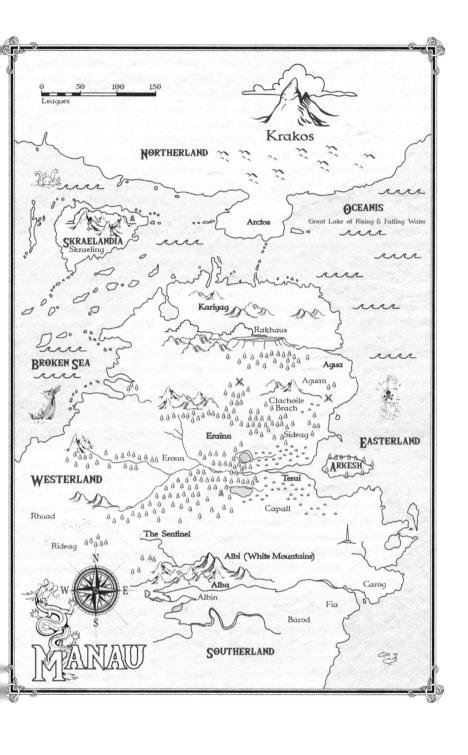

PRINCIPLE CHARACTERS AND THEIR TRIBES

Osian, Albin Otar*; a hunter.

Caryn, (f) Eronn/Albin Otar; Osian's daughter.

Drion, Eronn Otar; Caryn's guardian.

Tiroc Og, Catton – Wildcat; shaman, warrior band chief.

Bran, Brach – Bear; warrior.

Gimin, (f) Ruadh/Rideag – Red Fox/Red Wolf; hunter-warrior.

Reyn, Ruadh – Red Fox; son of their chief.

Romi, (f) Tarsin, Flying Fox; an old pirate.

Lakon, Eronn Otar; Tiroc Og's first lieutenant.

Ganoc, Catton – Wildcat; Tiroc Og's second lieutenant.

Log Marten, Pinec; name unknown.

Cana-Din, She-Eronn Otar; priestess-warrior.

Gwion-din, Eronn Otar; an elder, her father; a ferry keeper.

Yamis, Barod – Beaver; warrior, boat builder.

Bron, Brach – Bear; Bran's twin brother.

Aridh, Aguan; Sea Gypsy, mercenary.

Garidh, Aguan; mercenary.

Iona, She-Eronn Otar; warrior.

Pone, Rhuad – Red Fox; warrior.

Ranig, Sideag – Grey Wolf; elder warrior.

Aehmir, Lepoch – Wind Hare; seer.

*Otar are a group of tribes whose totem is an otter, but of different types (e.g Albin Otar – Lake Otter; Eronn Otar – River Otter etc.

The Morok

Morok are a force of outlanders of unknown tribal origin under the control of the Ferok – Polecat tribe led by Kahl, a skryer and prophet, and Krachter, a Ferok, Kahl's lieutenant. They are allied to the Skraeling tribe whose totem is a shark and whose king is Iskar.

Iskar, Skraeling; ch

Note on Totems

The tribes distinguish themselves from one another through totems deriving from mythological ancestor animals, e.g, the Ruadh totem is a red fox, the Rigead totem is a red wolf, the Lepoch totem is a hare and so on. Totemic animals can be seen on warrior sword hilts and staffs, in their cloaks and head-dresses, and in body paint). In some cases, members of tribes display the physical characteristics, talents, abilities or attributes of their animal totems, e.g: Albin Otar (otter) are slim and are great swimmers and fishers; Catton (wildcat) have nightsight and curved fingers like claws; Brach (bear) are huge and thick framed; Sideag and Rigead / Rhuad (wolf and fox) are slender and swift-footed; and so on.

PRELUDE

CARYN AND THE JAR

Across the Broken Sea a shaft of sunlight glanced off a distant floe, the sea ice glimmering iridescent like a summer sailing ship. And I thought of *his* boat, gone a full fifty moons to the day, and no word. Nothing. Sighing, I lifted my burden and turned for home.

Caryn, sitting at the table, arms folded, didn't look up when I struggled back through the door, barely able to open it, my fingers so chilled, the arms of my robe stiff with cold. A fresh ice storm was screaming in from across the bay, battering the wooden walls of the cabin and tearing at the roof thatch of this, the only home she, his daughter, had ever known. Dropping the wood bundle, I shouldered the iron latch shut against the blast, double bolted the door, and thumped the axe down against the frame. In easy reach. You never knew who – or what – was out there.

'Never seen first snows so thick,' I said, stamping it from my boots. 'Good thing I got those stores in before thon storm. Fishmeal porridge tonight – what do you think?'

No response. She gazed at the shelf above the fireplace, absently rolling a driftwood ink-pen in her fingers – her mind clearly elsewhere. 'We can eat when you're finished that,' I added, nodding at her writing pad as I loaded up the log basket.

'I hate *Askrit*,' she exclaimed. 'Why do I have to learn it? It's not as if anyone speaks it anymore.' In a sudden move, she tore up the page she was working on and kicked it under her chair.

I shrugged. I understood her rage. We'd both looked at the wall calendar that morning – the first of the Moon of the Snow Bears, the same day Osian, her father, had taken the sea crossing to Erainn. Only he'd not returned; maybe now never would. She was hurting, taking it out on herself – and out on me, her guardian. The mood would pass. She was a good kid, mostly cheerful. 'We'll maybe go over to old Yamis's steading tomorrow – snow's permitting.' She smiled thinly. It would cheer her. It was always fun over there. Yamis joked over everything and, as with all Beaver – the Barod tribe – there was always a lot going on with the goats, ponies, cats, not to mention that his steading had the biggest roaring fire on the island.

When I'd warmed up, I poured meal into a pot to simmer over the fire. 'It'll be ready soon.'

'Not hungry.'

'*We* didn't always have food,' I said, remembering the Long Winter. I added more water to the oatmeal. Caryn didn't like it too thick.

She sighed and tossed her hair. At times like this I really felt for her, stuck here with one of the Aged Ones, having to learn a dead language, and him with the one arm and the greyed mane always harping on about old stuff. But the *Askrit* was important; not just because it was our only written language, it was the root of all the tribal dialects. Though she hadn't ever spoken other than Albinese, the dialect of the Albin, of her father's family, knowing *Askrit* she'd find understanding Ironese, the dialect of the Eronn, mine and her mother's tribe, as well as the dialects of the other Manau tribes, a lot easier. Should she ever be able to leave here, that is.

In the end, she ate supper when I served it; silently though, wrapped

12

in her own thoughts. As I ladled a second helping into our bowls, a sudden burst of firelight bounced off the window ice and caught the jar on the mantelpiece. For a second, like that ice floe at sunset, it glowed. Caryn noticed it too. I saw her eyes widen. I wondered if she also saw the way the jar glowed when the light caught it – the fleeting impression of a silvery quarter moon with a golden sun in her crescent arms.

A trick of the light maybe, but strange, given the date. I'd longed to get rid of the accursed thing, but of course, I couldn't. It wasn't a decision I could make. I'd seen her in the deep night, holding it up, rolling it around, looking for a way inside. There wasn't one. I sensed she was going to question me about it, maybe ask what was inside, so I immediately busied myself clearing the table. But she didn't – not yet.

'You'll be wanting a story?' I suggested when we sat later by the fire with our books. She nodded. Anything would be better than studying. So, I picked up my story stick, looked at the totem carvings for inspiration and asked, 'How about the black wolf of Omark who wanted to be a red fox and set fire to his tail?'

She looked at me without a trace of a grin.

I tried another. 'Well, what about the toothless squirrels of the Stone Forest, who tricked the beavers into cracking open the acorns?'

She shook her long hair, the glorious tricolour mane of the Eronn, and sighed.

'The red stoats of Gor who waged war on the blackthorn bushes because they were fed up being pricked and thought the thorns were alive?'

'I'm not a kid anymore,' she said, folding her arms across her chest. 'Why d'you want to tell me fairy tales?'

'Hmmm. Actually, Caryn, none of us is too old for a fairy tale. After all,' I said, laughing and flapping my arm like a wounded bird, 'we're all fairies really.'

She winced, suppressing a smile. 'Fairies aren't real, Guardian.'

I pretended to glower. 'You may mock, dear child,' I said, 'but the fairies, the *sidhe*, are everywhere, all around, including inside us. Just because you can't see them doesn't mean they're not there.'

She huffed. She'd been taught that the minds and outer bodies of all the tribes came from the ancient Manu who lived before the Icetime, while our senses, our instincts, came from the animals, our totem ancestors. We, the Albin and the Eronn, belong to the Otar group of tribes, sharing an ancestral totem – Otrec, the Great Mother, and her characteristic compassion, strength and humility. So far, so real. But there's another part, the *sidhe*, the 'fairy' within us, linking us to a world we cannot see – a mirror world beyond nature. But some have *seen*, the shamans and the holy ones – and almost certainly, Osian himself. Its described as a world as real as music or moonlight. Of all this – spirits and the spirit world – she was healthily sceptical, just like her father was – or so he had told me – when he set out on his great quest, before his whole world changed.

'Well then, Caryn. What *would* you like to hear?'

'I want to hear about *that*,' she said abruptly, jabbing a finger at the jar on the mantlepiece. I was right. She did ask! So, it *was* to be tonight. I felt a pounding in my chest and looked away.

'Oh, that,' I responded lamely, my voice quivering. I waved my hand as if at some bothersome cobweb. 'Why do you ask about that, of all things?'

'I overheard you and him talking about it, when he produced it – the night before he left.' Her voice tailed off. I saw a tear glinting on her cheek.

My eyes welled. I gazed at the grey vessel he'd given to me on that night, along with his journal. In the jar, he said, was a relic from his journeys, a legacy of the curse that had afflicted the tribes, the fallout of which still plagued his line and, for Caryn's sake, still had to be exorcised, got rid of once and for all. Hence the most recent journey he was about to undertake, hopefully the last, but of which he would give no details.

The jar itself, made of some kind of grey metallic stone, was unbreakable and couldn't be opened. As long as the relic was here, sealed inside the jar, with us in the cabin, it couldn't be used against us. 'Keep it near the fire,' he'd said, 'where it can be seen.' *Seen* by whom? I'd wondered. Spirits? Sorcerers? Strangers? The village cat? The presence of such a thing, and by our fireside, always made me feel uncomfortable – particularly after I'd read his journal and figured out what, to my horror, might be in there. I wished to the Great God Yahl he'd taken the cursed thing with him.

I remembered the harrier visiting us in the small hours – perched on the balcony, waking me with its raucous squawking. I'd heard Osian go outside. He was talking to it! Then it flew off. When we rose in the morning, his backpack, his *papose,* was already packed; his staff and sword had been laid with it against the door, together with the long oars, ready for the paddle out to the *scud*, then the sail across the Broken Sea.

Then the giant Brach had come, knocking on the door and cheerfully demanding a hot breakfast. Bran had brought a huge basket of berries from the woods around his cave. And I saw he too was ready to go, weapons strapped to the back of his long *papose*, and that, as always, they would go together; his great friend and valued compatriot, sworn in blood to Osian's safety.

It had been the Moon of the Bright Leaves, so the winds would be warm, southerly and in his favour. Yamis would go with him as far as the *scud*, help set the sails, see him off and then return with our coracle.

There had been tears that morning. Caryn embraced them both and asked when he'd be back. 'Inside twelve moons,' he'd said. 'I'll bring gifts – and Eronn cloth.' Then they were gone. Fifty moons later and nothing.

'What did you overhear, Caryn, about the jar?' I prompted tentatively.

'Something about a curse, over there, across the Broken Sea,' she said, raising her arm in the direction he'd gone. Her eyes shone an azure blue now, deepened with the darker hues of her coming of age. I gazed away, wondering about her *almadh*, her destiny – what, in time, those eyes might see.

Outside the window the flakes, bigger than before, dropped past the glass like stones, frosting our root garden, settling on the pines, forcing the shivering birds and animals into their hollows and hides.

When I looked back, she was staring at me with a burning intensity. 'Well, aren't you going to tell me about it?' she said, tapping her foot.

I put away the story stick. It wouldn't be a story but true events – what really happened, though so much of that could be a fairy story – so hard to believe; some of it even harder to tell. Unlocking a drawer from the fireside cabinet, I gingerly took out a package wrapped in tricolour Eronn tribal cloth.

'What's that?' she asked, as I unfolded the cloth, revealing the two yellowed, weathered loose-leaf folios inside.

'Your father's journal,' I replied.

'A journal? I didn't know about that.'

'Well, Caryn dear, there's a lot *you* don't know,' I retorted, unable to resist a tease.

'Can I see it?' she said.

'Yes, but you can't read it.'

'Why not, Guardian *dear*?' she demanded.

'Because it's in *Askrit*! And you know how much you like that.'

This, finally, evoked a sort of smile.

'It's okay to have a look,' I said, handing it to her, 'but handle it carefully. The papers are delicate.' I drew breath at the irony of this remark. It was me that needed to take care here.

She took it, rolled it around like I'd seen her doing with the jar, turned a couple of pages and mouthed a few words, but quickly got stuck. 'Impossible. Can't even read his writing. Will you read it to me – in our language?' she said, passing it back. 'Please.'

'There's a lot for one night. And some of it is…well, difficult.'

I suppose I'd known this day would come. There were sections I could leave out, I told myself, use difficulties with the *Askrit* as an excuse to myself. After all, what possible good could come from her knowing everything? It wasn't the "fairy" stuff that was the problem. It was the stuff about her mother – the mother she'd never known

– that worried me most, for it revealed who Caryn really was. Knowing that would not be good. She might act upon it and go looking. And then what? I didn't like to think.

Outside, the wind howled and smashed against the cabin, backing a puff of wood smoke down the chimney into the room – another wild night, just like the one that led to Osian finding the *Solon*, when everything changed.

'Fetch your blanket, Caryn. It's getting colder,' I said.

She went to her room, came back with her woven Eronn stole, sat back on her feather-filled fleece and returned her gaze to the fire. Waiting. I contemplated how she'd grown; was almost fully fledged, almost the age her father was when he'd first left home and, despite my reservations, old enough to be told everything.

When Osian handed over his chronicle, he gave me strict instructions. 'Read this when I'm gone, Drion, and if I don't return, read it to her. You'll be familiar with much of it, but not all, and in the telling you'll have to judge what to leave out. As for the jar, that is something you – none of us – can open. Neither can it be destroyed. Only when the covenant that binds our line to it is finally resolved can it be buried, and…Yahl willing…along with it, the curse. When that happens, and only then, will we – our family – be free.'

On the thirteenth moon after his departure, fearing the worst, I read the whole journal, all two volumes of it. I was shocked by some of the revelations, the stuff I didn't know. I knew we were in exile here to keep Caryn safe, well away from others, all the *others,* and that Osian's journeys were tied to his desperate need to resolve the legacy of the *Solon*, the Shining Stone – the mysterious object to which he was inextricably bound. But, only from having read the journal did I know just why.

'What's keeping you?' she asked, twisting a strand of her glorious mane around her finger. It shimmered in the firelight, red, green, and blue.

'Well,' I said, opening the volume. *'If all—'*

'No "If alls",' she interrupted. The corner of her mouth turned

17

down. 'Don't be throwing in any bug-eyed bogles or donkeys that thought they were cabbages.'

'Not even one bogle?'

At this she laughed, finally. I laughed too, but my throat ached.

There's a fine line between real and unreal. Perhaps it was better, for the moment anyway, for her to think that much of what I was going to translate for her came from Osian's imagination, that it was a *story*, only loosely based upon what he experienced, what actually happened – was *still* happening. Her father was, after all, one of a long line of tale tellers. So, though I'd put down the story stick, I still began my telling in the way of the old *Sagi*, story tellers to the tribes.

'*If all were told…*'

1

THE SENTINEL

"THE PATH THAT THE GREAT ONE FOLLOWS BECOMES
THE GUIDE TO THE WORLD." AEHMIR

The Sentinel loomed out of the snow mist like a wraith from its grave. It was just a rock, with little to justify the skull mark that Grandfather Annan had given it on his sketch map. Danger from what, I wondered. Snowflakes?

I hadn't seen a single soul for well over a moon, let alone the fearsome bogles he'd warned me about. 'The Skraeling will rob you, the Skarag will tear the skin from your back,' he'd said. 'But I've taught you how to fight, and you know how to hide well enough.'

But snow? Here in a rock desert? It was the Moon of the Ripening Fruit. Winter proper was surely four, if not five, whole moons away. The flakes were getting larger and falling more thickly, the cold gnawing at my bones. I hadn't seen the sun for a whole moon and the night-black cloudbank now gathering in the eastern sky meant one thing – a big storm was coming.

It had taken me over thirty days to cross the White Mountains on the trail of my missing kin, another sunless five across the Karst, and it would at least be one more, I reckoned, before I'd reach the river crossing for Erainn. Hopefully there, along the pilgrim way, I'd pick up their trail. Meantime, I needed to find shelter from the approaching storm. In strong winds, in a landscape this open, I feared for my little goatskin bender.

The Sentinel's bent-over tip, like the proboscis of some giant insect, pointed down towards a huddle of jagged stones. Approaching them, I came to a yawning crevasse: a Karst sinkhole, but far bigger and wider than any I'd seen before. Its sides were packed with boulder scree running down to where a fast stream tumbled among the rocks. On the nearside was a pebble beach – a good place to set up camp, and there might even be fish in the falls and pools.

I wondered about Grandfather's danger mark and his warnings about predators, robber ghosts, flying lizards and the like. Bogle bosh! I decided I'd take my chances.

I clambered over the lip and yelped as I slid down the scree, stones flying around me. At the bottom, I picked myself up and stood for a moment on the pebble beach. Previous travellers had made a fire-circle by the water, a neat ring of rocks. The stones were blackened from use, but the spent coals in the centre were green – many moons old. I jammed my alder poles between two large boulders and stretched the goatskin over to make a roof. Then, using streamside flotsam, I made a pyramid inside the fire-circle, sparked it alight with my flint and was soon warming beside the flames, congratulating myself on my choice of campsite. It occurred to me that if my kin and their Aguan guides had spent any nights in the Karst, it might well have been here.

'Look for a god stone,' Grandfather had explained. 'Everything – as it moves, now and then, here and there – makes stops. Even the sun, wind and moon. So, a wanderer must also stop, make a prayer there to Yahl to win a blessing and place a god stone.'

Perhaps my father had done this right here. I looked about for the signature god stone of our tribe – a thin rock placed upright with a forked twig and single pebble at its base. But there were none to be seen.

Collecting water from an eddy at the side of the stream, I looked at my firelit reflection on the surface – the white skin, pale blonde mane and long nose of the Albin with the blue eyes of the Eronn, the tribe of my mother. I was every inch fully fledged, a hunter–warrior taking his place in the wider world, confident in my skin. But I was here alone in a lonely place; and seeing my face in the water, together with the absence of the stone that might have connected me to others of my kind, I felt suddenly homesick.

My thoughts were interrupted by flickers of movement in the stream. Fish!

I threw off my robe and fur collar, stowed them together with my sword, small bow and quiver inside the bender, took a deep breath and dived into the chilly waters – right into a shoal of darters. I swooped towards the largest, the water tugging against my limbs. Suddenly I was in the grip of a strong current. It was pulling me down. What felt like walls closed round me – I was hurtling through a tunnel. I tried to turn, kicking backwards and scraping at the rock walls with my fingers. But it was useless: the vortex sucked me along as if I were a dried-up twist of grass.

Water seeped into my lungs, forcing the oxygen from my body. Something thudded into me. I was tossed onto my back, and I glimpsed a dull red light above. I lunged towards it with all my might, my very last breath – and shot upwards.

My head broke the surface. I gulped in welcome breaths and coughed out water, my vision blurry and my head ringing. As I began to breathe normally, I looked about me. I'd emerged into an underground rock pool, in the centre of a gigantic cavern. Pale jagged rocks jutted all around, some thrusting up from the floor, others hanging from the roof like the teeth of a huge beast. They flickered red, as though tipped with blood. The air was heavy and sour-smelling, sulphurous. I shook water from my ears, and they picked up a wave of cackling and humming – and something else, repetitive – like chanting.

My heart began to pummel. Someone – something – else was here!

I paddled soundlessly to the side. There was a rock shelf just below the surface of the water. I heaved myself on to it and peered out over the edge of the pool.

Some way away from me, over by the wall of the cavern, was a fire

– the source of the red light. Beside it was a pyramid of – were they bones? A stream of dark red liquid, flecked with black foam, trickled from the pyramid's base. On a rock pedestal above, three huge bird-like creatures stretched their necks and nodded at the wall beyond the fire.

I caught my breath as realisation dawned. Skarag, exactly as Grandfather had described them – the size of wild pigs, covered in dark scales with huge yellow talons and long black beaks. Winged snakes – not bogles.

The sight of them, the realness of them, was revolting to the eye. But worse was the smell that came from them, sickening to my stomach, a stink of ordure and rotting flesh that made me retch. One of them whipped its head in my direction. I ducked my head below the pool edge and hand over mouth, crouched on the shelf and waited, shivering with cold and fear. But nothing happened, no attack or burst of flame from its horrid throat. Gradually, I inched upwards and peeped over the edge again. But the Skarag was looking the other way – at a large hollow in the cavern wall.

Two figures in dark robes lurked there. One was on his knees, yellowed arms held above his head, palms together in prayer pose, shaking so much he looked like he might fall over. The other stood, waving a smoking bowl. They chanted and bowed at an object draped in a dark cloth which sat at the edge of the hollow on a platform that looked to me like a temple altar.

I stretched higher out of the pool to get a better view.

And froze.

A bulbous, spider-like beast with a myriad of slit eyes, gaping mouths and writhing tentacles was slithering from the hole towards the altar, humming and snapping. One of its tentacles whipped out and pulled the cloth off the object. I glimpsed something crescent in shape that glimmered bright silver-gold like a small sun. There was a flash, like lightning, but weak and short-lived, before the tentacle engulfed it and drew it into its foul gullet. Then I heard a cry – a desperate high-pitched keening like someone trying to hold on in the final throes of life.

Impossible though it seemed, this was a cry for help. The object, whatever it was, was calling to me – trying to draw me out of the water, urging me to intervene. My eyes filled with tears; I felt a tugging on my chest. A fellow creature was in distress. Without thinking, I began to crawl out of the water – then caught myself. What was I doing? I had no sword or bow. Nothing to take on any of these creatures. What would I be rescuing anyway? I could no longer even make out what it was! I paused, half in, half out of the water and stared at the awful scene playing out before me, unable to look away, yet unable to act.

The keening stopped, replaced by a trumpeting sound that rattled and vibrated around the cavern. There followed a silence so complete that all I could hear was the drip-drip of water falling from a stalactite into a puddle on the rock floor. The beast was quiet, its horrid jelly-like form quivering on the spot.

Suddenly, it broke the silence with another trumpeting roar, and then with a massive squelching sound it disgorged something that flew into the air, landed with a dull thud, bounced a few times and slid across the cavern floor towards the two robed figures, coming to a stop at their feet. They threw up their arms and shrieked an unearthly invocation while the beast scuttled back into its cave, tentacles trailing, until it was no longer in sight.

One of the figures picked up the object and examined it, rolling it over and over in its claw-like hands. It was the crescent-shaped object, no longer shining, but coated black with a strange slime. The other brandished a red-hot, three-pronged iron shaped like a claw, and pressed it to the object. Thick smoke poured upwards. The smell was horrific, like burning putrid flesh. The Skarag set up a fearsome screeching, so shrill I had to cover my ears.

The figures turned away, but before they left, one stooped to pick up a flaming brand from the fire, then rushed towards the cave where the monster had retreated and threw the brand in. There was a howl of pain and fury, followed by a loud crack that echoed and rolled like thunder around the cavern walls, the vibrations so severe I felt the ground shifting under my feet; the rock shelf I was crouching on began to crumble. I fell backwards into the water, rocks cascading and splashing all around me. The bird-lizards shrieked, dropped from their pillar and flew towards me, barbed talons raking the air.

I dived deep; my only thought was to get away. But I was back in the vortex, being hurled downwards, the breath knocked from my lungs, a stabbing pain between my ears. I'd escaped those dreadful creatures only, it seemed, to drown like a rat. My chest burned. Lights exploded behind my eyes. My body stiffened.

Then the most extraordinary thing, a shadow, seemed to wrap around me and, claiming my body, lifted me up.

I was being taken.

2

THE NIGHT CREVASSE

Astonishingly, I was alive, in a pool floating freely, feet and hands tingling. The air was fresh and crisp. Above, steep rock walls stretched up to a snow-flecked night sky. I could see my little fire and my bender. I was back in the crevasse, none the worse for my experience. Or had it just been a bad dream? A night horse from a strange land.

A shoal of fish darted past. I kicked towards them, grabbed the tailender and swam to the shallows. There, I muttered a prayer for its soul and took its life. Hauling myself out of the water, I ducked under the flap of my shelter and picked up my robe.

Something was wrong. My weapons. They'd gone!

I scanned the shadows inside the bender. Nothing. I checked outside, beside the fire, my heart beating wildly. No, I knew I'd left them inside. The snow around the tent was frosted but devoid of prints except my own. My bright weapons, Grandfather's parting gifts, all gone.

I sniffed the air. No scents. My staff and *papose* were where I'd left them. Frantically, I checked inside the backpack, pulling everything out. All present and intact – including the little book of spiritual writings that Grandfather had pressed upon me. I rubbed a hand across my forehead. What was going on? That dreadful dream and now this. What was it about this place?

I put the stuff back, leaving out only my wool blanket. But, I realised, something *was* missing from it: Grandfather's sketch – the little guide from home to here and to the pilgrim ways through Erainn to Arkesh.

Without it I might as well be wandering blindfold.

No doubt about it. In the short time I'd been fishing – or dreaming – my campsite had been visited, and I'd been robbed. Now I had nothing to hunt with, and was in unfamiliar terrain, without any kind of guide. I was so angry I kicked at the ground.

But who on Yahl's earth could it have been? I thought of another of Grandfather's bogles – Skraelings, legendary robbers from the ice lands obsessed with shiny things, robbers that left no scent and no tracks. Maybe they really did exist and had been here. Or…were still here. Or close, at least. What if they came back?

My heart pounded wildly as I looked around. But there was nothing to be seen. I took a low, deep breath. I was just being foolish – scaring myself. There would be another, more sensible explanation. Then I thought of those sinister dark-robed figures from the cave. Perhaps *they'd* been here, before me somehow, taken my weapons, and gone? Of course, that would mean that my ordeal under the Sentinel was real – no dream, after all. I'd been unconscious, lost all sense of time, had a full day passed without me even knowing it?

Whatever the truth, there was nothing I could do about it. I needed to eat, I had fish, and the little fire glowed – just as brightly, in fact, as when I'd left to go fishing. As for weapons, I could improvise a sling. I was the best sling caster among my friends at home. It'd have to be that. And the staff, and my little knife.

Later, turning my catch over the flame, I thought about my mission; how I would go forward and what – after this unfortunate beginning – might lie ahead. But the fire kept drawing me back to the terrible vision in the cavern; that thing crying out from the tentacles of the beast; how I'd wanted to save it, but couldn't.

The eating gave me cheer. I gave thanks as I'd been taught to the god of little fish and fashioned a sling from a deer skin purse and a piece of sinew. Then I pondered what I knew about my destination. My mother, Mara, had talked often of her childhood home – the beauty of Erainn, the most celebrated territory in Greater Manau; its colourful settlements of conical houses, fields rich with river silt and splendid hunting forests; the Isle of Arkesh lying to its eastern rim; the great shrine of Yahl, revered by all the tribes, where grew the great ash tree that, according to legend, came from the seed of the legendary *Mundi*, the cosmic tree that connected this world to those above and below.

Mara's tribe, the Eronn, most numerous of the four Otar tribes of Manau, were, it was said, especially favoured by Yahl, the Creator. Eronn priestesses guarded the shrine and kept the sacred flame alive, while Marcher Lords from an ancient line ruled the territory and policed the pilgrim routes to Arkesh. But the line of the Lords, I understood, had come to a tragic end. There had been war, the routes had crumbled and now there were no more Marcher Lords. Somehow this had not deterred my mother and father from embarking on their pilgrimage to Arkesh – if that is indeed why they'd gone. Whatever the reason, they hadn't come back.

Grandfather had, in his time, made not one but two journeys into Erainn – the first at eighteen winters, around the age I was now; and the second much later, around the time of the Marsh Wars between the Eronn and neighbouring tribes, when he would have been in his fortieth winter or so. From that second journey had come the stories about his friends in Erainn, their escapades and the marvels he'd seen – like the skull-shaped sea ships, the giant *scuds* of the Aguan and the extraordinary rock villages of the Brach, the Bear tribe of Clachoile, the Stone Forest.

From those parts had come not just his stories. One day, he'd had a surprise visitor from the holy lands, an Eronn trader, who brought with him his beautiful daughter. She stayed on, becoming mate to

Grandfather's firstborn, and thus the first of the Eronn tribe to settle in Alba. The name in her was Mara, in him Faron; my mother and father. I was their second offspring and, following a terrible tragedy that will live with me forever, the only one surviving.

I knew of Grandfather's first journey only from something Mara had once let slip – and had just as quickly glossed over. When I asked her about it, she frowned, and told me not to ask again. So, I knew not to press her – or ask him about it.

My sling complete, I found a few good round stones and tucked them with my pikestaff and clasp knife inside my blanket, so they'd be next to me in the night. Then I laid a large stone over the fire to keep the coals warm and took a last wary look at the Sentinel, snow spiralling wildly around its dark tip. I wondered again about Grandfather's danger mark – as it turned out, this place had deserved it.

When at last I crawled under my blanket to sleep, my thoughts turned back to the keening of the object in the tentacles of the beast, how it had called out to me.

'Pah! Bogles! It can't have done!' I exclaimed aloud. Then I snapped down the flap on my bender and abandoned myself to the night.

3

REYN

The beast raged, ripping trees and boulders from their roots, hurling them into the air as it lumbered and slithered towards me, maw agape, dripping black foam. Dark birds screeched in my face, clawing at my eyes. But they weren't birds, more like...

I woke with a shudder to find my blanket tangled around my legs and my skin clammy. I opened the flap and looked out. All was still, but the shadows in the crevasse seemed watchful in the grey daylight. Flotsam was strewn everywhere; branches and twigs lay like corpses on top of drifted snow. Somehow, the storm had not broken my night, but it had certainly entered my dreams.

Rising, I shook snow and debris from the bender, loosed the skin and wrapped it around the poles. Then, tying the roll underneath my *papose*, I heaved it onto my shoulders and scrambled back up the scree wall.

At the top, giant snowdrifts smothered the ground; the trail was visible only as a gap between tall rocks. There were tracks – birds and ground huggers. I recognised rabbits, badgers, and perhaps a weasel, but nothing bigger. I was alone – or thought so.

But as I walked away from the Sentinel, I felt an icy darkness prickling the nape of my neck, as if something or someone was hiding in the snow or behind a rock, checking my every move, biding their time before an assault. I fingered my sling, felt the pebbles in my pocket and resisted the temptation to look back.

Pah! My mind was playing tricks. I put my head down and set off at a steady march through the rocks, before more snow set in. But the feeling of being watched stayed with me.

Then, turning a corner, I heard a sound like a rock falling. I stopped and looked around but saw only drifting snowflakes. I listened hard. All I could hear was my own breathing, loud inside my fur collar. I walked on, but a few steps later I heard another sound – like the crack of a stick on a stone. I whipped round and glimpsed movement – a shadow, slipping behind a rock.

'Who's there?' I called, grasping my knife under my robe. 'I'm armed.'

No reply. I waited, poised, heart thumping, until I couldn't bear it any longer, then turned and broke into a run. After a league or so I stopped and leaned against a rock to catch my breath. Looking back, I saw nothing. 'Bogles, wogles, nonsense,' I muttered. 'Probably just ice cracking the stones.'

Suddenly a shrill whistle sounded from up ahead where a cross-trail joined my path. I dived behind a rock, knife in one hand, sling in the other. Then I heard the click-clack-scrape of a stick hitting stone, coming towards me. Then it stopped – right beside my hiding place!

'Who goes?' a voice growled. 'Come out. I knows yer there.'

I edged around the rock, staff held out, ready to strike.

Before me was a smiling long-nosed figure in an embroidered red cloak, leaning on a tall pikestaff, a fox's head carved at its top. Rhuad – Red Fox tribe, from the Wester Lands, and friendly to the tribes of Alba. Not something monstrous, after all.

'Only me,' he said, tipping his staff to his forehead – the sign of peace.

I returned the gesture, staring at the Rhuad's remarkable staff.

On it was carved an array of faces – foxes, wolves, bears, eagles – and around its base curled a creature with a whiskered chin and a flattish face that was strange to me. The stranger's appearance was just as remarkable. The braided tail of his long red mane rolled over his left shoulder like a tasselled scarf, and silver hairs grew thickly on his chin and over his eyes. He was in his middle years, a fine specimen, almost regal. At home, I had heard that the Rhuad were cunning, like the fox that was their totem, but also jokers, trickster figures, though ultimately truth-tongued, powerful in war, and reliable in peace – if you didn't mind their pranks and curious humour. From his lopsided smile, this one looked to me every inch a trickster.

'Hmmm,' he said, eyeing me up and down. 'Haven't seen one of yer lot for many a whiles. Otar, aren't yeh? From Alba? Curious lot yeh are. Eats mosl'y fishes and live in hovels on sticks over lakes water, like 'em Barod, the Beaver folk with their floating mudpies?' he said, laughing aloud. He spoke in fluent Ironese, the dialect of the Eronn, and, though I spoke Albinese, I understood him easily because our language is so similar. His twang was very strange though, like someone chewing gravel.

He was either joking or simply ignorant of the ways of the Albin and our friends, the Barod, who make their houses over the mountain rivers and streams that feed the lakes we live over. The stilts that support Albin holts are only ever half over water. Always half on land. For we don't just fish we also hunt small game in the hills behind our homes, sharing our hunting grounds with the wild pasturing meadows of the Barod's goats.

'Yes, sir…' I replied, on the verge of correcting his misconception, but before I could, he said, 'Where be yeh headin' then, young fisher one? Yeh haven't lost yer way, have yeh? No water round here, none that's safe anyways.'

'Erainn, sir. Pilgrimage,' I replied, wondering what he meant about the water not being safe, but not wanting to show disrespect – or ignorance.

He raised his eyebrows, frowned and with a sudden change of

tone said, 'If I was yeh, young Albin, I'd plant that little stick of yers there in the ground, go around it half-way and go right backs the way yeh've come.'

'What do you mean?'

'Erainn's not what it was. 'Tis a dangerous place. Specially for you Otar tribes, Eronn Otar, Albin Otar – doesn't matter. Yer great mother – Otrec, isn't it? – can't protect yeh there. Anyways, pilgrimages through Erainn are finished…fer good, more likely.'

'Why so? You mean the weather? Is the trail blocked?' I gestured at the ground. I'd been told it didn't snow in the holy lands. That it was never cold. That the rain fell only at night, and that even then it was warm and gentle, like the Eronn themselves.

'That's a factor fer sure. But this is somethin' far worse.'

Here we go, I thought, sensing more bogle stuff coming my way. I nodded politely and made to move off. But I had no map. I should get directions at least – then maybe go the opposite way this character suggested. After I'd shaken him off my tail.

'Whatever it is, I can look after myself,' I said.

'And how would that be, young 'un?' he guffawed. 'Yeh looks unarmed for a start – unless,' – he smirked, glancing at my staff – 'yeh count thon twig as a weapon?'

'My sword and bow were taken,' I said. 'At the Sentinel. In the night.' I felt my face reddening. I wasn't making such a good job of things so far; but it was still cruel to be mocked.

'The Sentinel, yeh say?' muttered the Rhuad, his tone again grave.

'Yes. I took shelter in the crevasse.'

'By thon bad water?'

So that's what he meant. I thought of the deadly tumult in the tunnel underwater and the horrid creature that dwelt in the cavern the burn ran through. Unsafe certainly.

'I had no choice – the storm,' I said, wary of being mocked for revealing what I'd seen – or thought I'd seen.

'Indeed. The helm. Bad, that one. Worst I can remember.'

'Helm, sir?'

'Hell wind – storm. One of 'em that comes from beyond Kalmat; from hell itself. Never had anything like them before. Now they're all the time.'

'What d'you mean?'

'Well, stranger, there's been no spring, no summer hereabouts for over twenty moons. Karst, Erainn, Clachoile – even Rhegad, my home. Snow, floods and always this grey sky.' He waved a hand vaguely upwards. 'Anyways, thon Sentinel place might give cover from the wind and snows, but it's a crossway for foul water and all other kinds of devils. Robbed, were yeh? Any scents?' He patted his long nose.

'No, sir.'

'Skraeling, then,' he said assuredly.

I didn't wish to get into a discussion about bogles, so I asked: 'Will I be able to get new weapons in Erainn?' Eronn artisans were renowned for their hollow swords, beautifully smithed with intricate silver and mother-of-pearl inlays. My own sword was a perfect specimen; it had been a gift to Grandfather from his Eronn friend, Gwion the ferry keeper, who I was to meet and hopefully help me on my way. The sword had been passed down to me, and was now gone, stolen, lost to me.

The Rhuad shrugged and tapped his staff against a rock.

'I have cowries,' I said.

'Well, good luck with that,' he eventually replied with a snort. '*Them* in charge there now won't sell weapons to such as yeh. First off, *they* don't trade in seashells. Second off, *them* don't let the Eronn or any of the free tribes in their territory anywheres near weapons – not alive anyways.'

'*Them? They?* Who do you mean?'

'Morok, of course,' said the Fox, rolling his eyes.

'What? Who...eh...Mirrock, did you say?'

'Has not word crossed the White Mountains?'

'Word about what?' I said sharply, itching to get going. If only this Rhuad would stop speaking in riddles!

'About him who told the Eronn he could restore the old order of the Marcher Lairds,' said he, shaking his long mane and tapping his stick against a stone. 'Still can't believe it,' he muttered, seemingly talking to himself. 'As if a fakester could change the weather o' the holy lands. Hah. The Eronn were always foolish like that. "The chosen tribe", indeed. Hah!'

'I still don't understand you, sir. Someone called Morrick, did you say?'

'Calls himself Kahl. He's a skryer – a future teller. Said he could show the Eronn how to survive the storms, and that he would build flood defences. So, the Eronn allowed him to bring in an army of "workers". Them's yer Morok.' He spat. 'But they turned out to be nothing but gangs of cut-throats from beyond Manau, who couldn't even build a wall, never mind a flood levee.'

I felt a sudden surge of concern for my parents. They'd have no problem with winter storms, for Alba was arctic half the year. Even Mara had got used to the cold and the winds. And they were seasoned hunter–warriors. But they were no longer young.

'No-one told me about any of this – or these Morok,' I said, a tremble in my voice. 'When did all this come about?'

'Can't really say, young 'un,' the Rhuad replied. 'Kahl's been around fer a while, but this army of his appeared out of a sea storm about fifteen moons past, sudden-like. On waves of ships, strangely shaped, like 'em ancient Manu skulls that turns up time to time. No warning. Like they'd been jes' waiting in the fogs and swells close offshore. When they landed, they used the old pilgrim ways to get across Erainn quickly and stopped everyone else using 'em, threatening any pilgrims with slavery – or death. And before we knew it, they'd overrun the place.'

My heart pounded. Fifteen moons ago? My parents would have been on the pilgrim paths around that time. Had they encountered this Kahl, or his rapidly advancing army? 'What about Arkesh?' I pressed, thinking about their destination.

'I'm told the Sacred Wood of Arkesh is stone dead, the holy flame out and the priestesses gone. Nothing there now.'

I could hardly believe it. Such destruction in so little time. How could it be possible? And my kin caught up in it. Who – *what* – were these creatures? By what right…? Suddenly, I found myself remembering the robed figures in the cavern. 'These Moroks,' I said, 'what do they look like?'

'They're all shapes and sizes jes' like the rest of us. But think of them as being more like the lowliest of ground huggers, polecats, weasels, but on two legs and no tails, and, sorry to say, with a look like one of yer Otar tribes, yer Albin and Eronn. Mostly they're wearing mail – metal vests and helmets. A savage lot they are. Come across as stupid, but the fact of the matter is some of 'em, like their captains – of a different tribe altogether called Ferok – are cunning, and all of 'em is cruel and bloodthirsty.'

'Do they wear long dark robes? Have thin faces and yellowish skin?'

'Ah. Those sound like Krol. The type of Ferok – Kahl's own priests. Yeh've seen some?'

I nodded. 'At the Sentinel.' So that's what they were. I'd heard of Ferok from Grandfather's stories, a legendary tribe banished for sorcery from Manau long, long ago.

'Yeh didn't? Well, well. Them being this far south is unusual,' he said, waving his staff. 'Ferok and Morok don't much come this side of the river. There's none in our parts, the Wester Lands. Well, not as yet. Some says this Kahl will stop at nothing 'til all of Manau, all of the territories, including yer own Alba, are in the claws of his cut-throats. They reckons Erainn is jes' a steppin' stone on the way to total conquest. Then…' he added with a sigh, 'Yahl save us all.' He leaned back against a rock and for a moment seemed to be in a faraway place, his eyes seeing something I could not. 'The chiefs don't believe it though,' he muttered, fingering the carvings on his staff. 'Someone has to convince them.'

If all this was true, I pondered, my experience in the cavern had been no dream. A very real night horse, and one that was getting worse by the second. But I told myself, it was possible this Rhuad was exaggerating. In Alba, folk who had never ventured beyond their territory – which was most of them – saw all outsider tribes as "devils". Even the Aguan, the sea gypsies on whom all Albin depended for trade goods were feared as cut-throats. In our village, only Grandfather ever invited them into his home.

For one tribe to control, or even *want* to control, the vast fastnesses of Greater Manau and all the tribes was unimaginable. To what possible end? 'This Morok leader, this…Kahl, you called him. Did he do what he said he would?'

'By Yahl, no,' came the reply. 'Some flood works were built, to be sure, with the Beaver tribes as labour, but then Kahl's Morok army made the country bare of grain and game. They starved out the smaller tribes, even the gentle Barod, the Beaver folks, afore turning them – and then the Eronn theyselves – to slavin' in return fer food.'

The gentlest tribe in Manau forced into slavery? Surely not. 'The Eronn are still there, though? Not all enslaved?'

'Well.' He leaned back against the rock. 'There's not many there now. Some have taken to hiding in the Carron marshes, living off sour fishes, horsetail roots and marsh snails. Others have headed northwest beyond the mountains. The outlying tribes, the Brach and Sideag, the Bear and Wolf tribes, haven't forgotten the Marsh Wars; they have jes' left the Eronn to fend fer theyselves. As fer the Aguan, well, Morok are using Aguan wagons and ships – so no sympathy there.'

Of course – the skull-shaped ships he'd mentioned. I thought they'd sounded familiar from Grandfather's tales. But the idea of Aguan like the ones that had gone with my kin helping these Morok! My stomach lurched. All the more need to press on quickly, to find out what was true – and what was not. 'I must get into Erainn,' I said, shifting my feet. 'Can you direct me towards the river crossing?'

The Rhuad stepped backwards to let me past, but he shook his head. 'I'd not be in too much of a hurry, young 'un,' he said. 'The river's a mighty dangerous torrent these days, even for a swimming tribe such as yers. Oft' times even Gwion's boat does not run. And after last night's storm, I'd be surprised if it's in one piece.'

Grandfather had said his old friend Gwion would ferry me across, would help guide me to the whereabouts of my kin. The ferry keeper had great insight – and meeting travellers all the time, would be a major repository of news from across Manau. Grandfather had talked often of him. He was blind, but, it was said, the river Erainn ran through his veins – he lived by it, breathing it in night and day. His ferry port had been marked on the sketch map as a place of welcome. But I'd not only lost the map but also the precious sword Gwion had given Grandfather that had then bequeathed to me. I'd have to admit it's terrible loss, but then maybe Gwion would know how or where I could find it.

'Why's it so important to yeh, Albin?' The Rhuad squinted at me.

'My father and mother crossed the mountains some moons ago with some Aguan traders. Pilgrims on their way to Arkesh. I don't suppose you've heard anything. The name in her is Mara, the name in him is Faron. She is Eronn, and he Albin.'

The Rhuad raised his shaggy eyebrows. 'Eronn and Albin, the blue and the brown eyed, together? That explains yer unusual blue eyes for an Albin, I suppose. But then yer both Otar,' he added. 'But the answer is no, I'm afraid. However, if yer determined to go on, I'll show the way to the crossing. But hurrying won't help yeh. Take things slowly. Yeh'll need to be on yer watch all the time – particularly as yer not armed.'

He was right. I needed to be calm, extra cautious, if what I was hearing was right. I tried to relax my shoulders. 'Thank you.'

'I can walk along with yeh a bit, even. What's the name in yeh, young Albin?'

'Osian. "O-see-in." You can say it as Osin, or Oshan, as some prefer.' That was the way Mara had always said it. Oshan was the Aguan word for the great Lake of Rising and Falling Water that lay east of Erainn – the edge of the continent of Greater Manau. 'Oshan,' I remembered her saying, 'is the sound the waters make as they swell and dip.' Indeed, she had always said that my own personality was like the waves, sometimes calm, sometimes wild. When I fought in play with others, I was relentless, but also forgiving.

'Oshan it is, then. The name in me is Reyn, by the way. Reyn of Ureyn.'

'Like rain?' I smiled.

'Ah, yes, I suppose. Oshan and rain – works together,' the Rhuad replied, rolling his shoulders. 'Walk on, then, shall we? About half a league before my turning.'

He stumped away; his pikestaff held high, long nose thrust forward. I followed, admiring his proud bearing: the flowing braid, the elegant cloak, the red longbow and gleaming long sword casually slung over his shoulder.

We picked our way in silence through soft fresh snow. The country was wide open now; the ground merged with the grey sky, and storm debris littered the land. As we rounded a bend in the trail between rocks a loud screech cracked open the snowy silence. Above, a winged shape plummeted towards us out of the flinty sky, followed by another – both approaching fast.

'Quick. Get down!' the Rhuad growled, swinging his staff like a weapon.

I dropped flat into the snow. Something swished past my head. I felt the brush of air, smelt carrion on the breeze. Then I heard an agonising shriek and saw an explosion of blood and bone, followed by a shower of scales. One of the shapes had crashed to the ground just ahead of us. Lifting itself up, it lurched into a clump of boulders, trailing a broken wing. The other halted mid-flight, wheeled about and flapped off into the grey. I realised what they were – bird-lizards like the ones in the cavern. Skarag!

'Damned things,' exclaimed the Rhuad. He leaned down, picked up his pikestaff and examined it with a grimace – its delicate carvings now flecked with greeny-black slime and scales. Wiping it in the snow, he said, 'Shame I didn't kill it. But it'll not live long out here.'

I got to my feet and began wiping a bloody mixture of sludge and scales from my face. Had it not been for the quick reactions of the stranger...

'The life in me gives thanks,' I said, bowing and touching my forehead. 'Those are Skarag, aren't they?'

'Yes. Always been a few around the Karst, since the old times. The Sentinel is their home. But now they venture beyond – at the Moroks' bidding – mostly just spying.'

Truly not bogles then, but no less horrible. Grandfather had been right about them.

'In these parts, always be sure there is cover at hand – boulders, water, trees, anything,' said the Rhuad. 'Trees is safest. Skarag can't fly so easily between the branches, or scent round trunks. And if yer mad enough to go into the open river lands, my caution would be, when yeh puts up your bender,' he jerked his chin towards the poles at the base of my *papose*, 'choose the tightest of thickets.'

'I'll heed what you say. But tell me, why would they try to attack you and me – passers-by?'

'Yeh may as well ask why the grass used to grow green, young Oshan,' he replied. ''Tis their nature, that's all. Yeh, me, we aren't food – if that's what yer thinking.'

Eventually we came to a fork in the trail. The Rhuad pointed his staff at the left track and said, 'Yer way – the river – is thon direction. I'm for the other – to the Red Mountains for the gathering of the Red Fox and Red Wolf clans. First Kwakwakam since the Marsh Wars. It'll be a right spectacle most likely – sky-high totem poles, headdresses and shaman dancing.' He fingered his chin for a moment. 'Listen young 'un. Instead of going to yer doom in Erainn, yeh could join me. My father's High Chief of all the Rhuad clans. He'd make yeh welcome. And yeh'd be company for me.'

I glanced the way we'd come. 'I'm grateful for your offer, Reyn, and your guidance, but my way is in the footsteps of my kin.'

'As yeh like, young Albin,' said the Rhuad, turning towards his trail. 'But watch fer the mark of the Morok.'

'How will I know it?'

'Three black talons on red. They puts it on banners, uniforms, robes and flags on buildings. They even burn it onto the skin of their slaves.'

The branding iron in the cavern – a spur of three curved fingers – a claw.

'I've already seen it.'

'I'm sure yeh have. But beware, not all Morok wear it,' continued the Rhuad. 'Indeed, those that don't are the most dangerous. So, watch yer back – especially,' – he jabbed his staff skywards – 'now yeh've been seen. As fer the way forwards, best find yerself an *Akari*.'

'An *Akari*?'

I knew the term from home. A shaman. 'Likes yon Wildcat, Tiroc Og. He's a tracker. He'll know how to avoid the patrols. He's linked to the rebels – the forest bandits,' said the Rhuad, walking away.

'Where would I find this *Akari*, this…Tiroc?' I shouted after him.

'Yeh won't find him.'

'What do you mean?'

'He'll find you. That's *if…*' came back the response, the rest muffled.

'If…?'

'If yer not already dead,' he said, pausing and turning round. 'One last piece of advice – whoever yeh meet, trust no one. Why, not even such as me.' Then he was gone, disappearing round a bend.

My mouth fell open. What on earth did *that* mean?

I walked on through snow that was slippery and slushy underfoot. I realised I was trembling, but not from the cold. The path before me – my journey – a lot less sure than before. Indeed, I barely knew what to make of it all – the cavern, the Skarag, and now these dire warnings. But all I could do was carry on down the trail and see where fate would take me.

4

THE LOG MARTEN

The evening before I left home, Grandfather had said, 'I know my son and your mother are alive. I feel it in my bones.' On that night there'd been a quarter moon – a thin crescent with a halo on the broken edge. He pointed to it. 'Ah. Like to me, a dying moon. But if it takes a hundred moons more, I'll live 'til my son and his dam cross my threshold again.'

Hands on my shoulders, he'd said, 'Osian, you're grown now, an able hunter and a fine warrior in the making. Take my blessing. Go to Erainn. Take the trail to Arkesh. Bring them back. Then I can join the ancestors in peace. It is the word of your grandfather. The word of Annan.'

Grandfather Annan had been the first Albin in our line to have undertaken the long trek across the White Mountains through the stone desert to Erainn. Twice, even. But it was as though that first journey had never happened. Why *had* he never spoken of it? For what unfinished business had he set out once more to tread the pilgrim paths?

I navigated the dense snow and picked my way along a creek that ran through a forest of birch and tall pine. Here I saw tracks of rabbit and water rat and some bigger prints that were hard to make out. A dipper fluttered down to a stone in the creek where it peered at me, chattered loudly and then darted under a waterfall. In my lake and burn-washed homeland, dippers were friends to hunters, showing us where the fishing was good. They brought luck.

A wind sighed through the trees, sending showers of pine needles skittering off my robe and slicing into the snow. In time, there came a new sound, distant at first, but getting louder – the roar of a river. The Erainn, at last! Cross it, and I would be in Erainn itself, the holy land, home of the Eronn tribe, my mother's family, my ancestors. My pace quickened. Soon I would reach the ferry point, and Gwion. I tried to put the Rhuad's words out of my mind. Surely the ferry would still be running. The Gwion my grandfather described to me would know how to deal with a storm. Surely?

Gradually, though, the river sounds faded. The forest of pines seemed endless. Something wasn't right. Had I strayed from the path? In the gathering darkness, the forest seemed to take a breath, and I felt a tingling in the back of my neck.

I spun round and stared into the shadows. But there was nothing to see except another dark snow cloud looming above the treetops. I cursed my imagination; my earlier encounters – and what the Rhuad had told me – had left me twitchy.

There came a sharp snap – a branch, breaking. I darted behind a tree, hand flying to my knife. I glimpsed a movement high in the canopy, a dangling creeper, and above it a fleeting shadow – too large to be a squirrel or a bird. Holding my breath, I waited, but it had gone.

Someone – something – was following me, I was sure. I was a hunter, used to stalking game. Yet here it felt like *I* was being stalked. I loaded my sling in readiness against an attack, fingers tightening over the pebble in the pouch, and walked on.

By evening, nothing had appeared. The wind had risen. Snow was falling hard, hissing against the pines, drifting across the path and partially covering the creek. Darkness was creeping in, the forest black above the white of snow. It was becoming hard to see the trail.

I decided to stop where I was and ploughed through a drift to the side of the path, pulling snow over my tracks. In the lee of a bush, I found an area of flat ground, mostly clear of snow, and began to unload my poles. Then I caught something on the breeze – a whiff of wood smoke and the smell of cooking fish.

It was impossible to resist. Snatching up my poles, I shoved my way forwards through the thicket, following the scent. Eventually, I came to a clearing with a log cabin in the middle. I hovered for a while behind a tree and eyed the building for clues as to who might be inside. A red light glowed through a small round window, and a thin column of smoke rose from the roof. Hewn logs topped with snow lay in piles everywhere. No Morok mark or flag in sight. The place did not feel threatening.

Gingerly, soundlessly, I crept up to the window and peeped over the frame. Someone was busying about inside, a roundish male figure in a fur cloak setting a table. His head was bare, with a sleek brown mane edged with grey. Not Eronn, but, thankfully, not at all like the Krol in the cavern. Perhaps I could buy food from him, even hire some shelter. I had cowries, and moonsilver. Whoever it was looked alone.

Had it not been for what had happened in the cavern and the Rhuad's warning, I wouldn't have hesitated for a moment, for there are keenly observed hospitality codes among hunter tribes. As it was, I was nervous. But I was cold and hungry too, and the cabin looked warm and inviting, the inside lit with a welcoming orange glow. I would take the chance.

I knocked lightly on the cabin door. No response. I rapped again, much louder. I heard the padding of feet behind the door. I saw a shadow pass across a crack in the woodwork. I was being looked at from within, being checked out – friend or foe. After a pause, I heard a bar being removed from the door and a grunt from within. Male, in rough Ironese, 'It's unlocked,' he said.

I pushed open the door and entered a rustic log cabin, its walls neatly lined with woven twigs and branches. A fire roared in a tall stone hearth, filling the space with warmth. The occupant was hunched over a rough knotted table, a figure in his middle years, from a tribe unfamiliar to me. He was thin, had rounded ears, sharp eyes with large pupils like a night cat and a straggling brown beard with wisps of greyish white. Strapped to his waist belt over a brown fur tunic was a small axe. A forester.

'Shut the door, stranger, yer letting in the storm,' he said gruffly, glancing up from a platter of steaming pies. Then, looking me up and down he added, in a gentler tone, 'Bolt it. Use that bar. Take a seat by the fire whiles I finishes my eating.'

I didn't need to be asked twice. I jammed the door shut, placed the bar bolt across it, laid my staff and *papose* against the frame, walked over to the hearth and dropped heavily onto a three-legged stool. Then, warming my hands by the fire, I looked around. On the other side of the fireplace was a rocking chair and a tiny wooden table laid neatly with a pipe, an elegantly carved stick propped against a teapot (a *Sagi* or tale teller's stick by the look of it), a stack of old books, a pair of *tai* cups and saucers, a jug and two bowls.

Two?

The smell of cooked fish and warm pastry made my stomach growl, and the thought dropped out of my head. 'I don't mean to disturb you, sir.' I gestured towards the table. 'It being your...supper and that. But I haven't eaten today, and I wondered if I could... If I could perhaps buy...one of those pies? I have cowries.' Then, remembering what the Rhuad had said about using cowries, I added, 'And a little moonsilver.'

Looking down his nose, the forester said, 'Well, normal like I sell logs, not pies. But, as yeh aren't looking like one of those Morok, I suppose I could be letting yeh have some.' After a pause and a few more mouthfuls, he said, 'Maybe if yeh pays me for a bit of a tale, and maybe if yeh can solves a puzzle or two.'

I'd been right about the stick, then – he was a *Sagi*, a storyteller. 'A tale, yes. I can do that. But a puzzle? What kind of a puzzle, sir?'

'Well, try this. What kind of a place might yeh be thinking yer in?'

'I'm in a wood that grows needles,' I responded, falling automatically into the riddle speak of my childhood.

'And that would make me which tribe, stranger?'

I scratched my chin, staring at the other's whiskers, and said, 'Tribe of Stoat…a needle-wood Stoat?'

In response he frowned, tutted and threw back a mouthful of pie from a rapidly diminishing pile on a wooden plate. Unable to tear my eyes away from it, I grasped for inspiration. At home there was a particularly shy clan of Wildcat in the remoter part of the Albin Great Woods – was he one of those tribes, like the Beaver and Bear, the Barod and the Brach, that mirrored a little of their animal totem within their physical traits? Wildcat noses were flat, more so than the Otar tribes, with wispy chin beards and their digits furry and claw-like. They were natural trackers and hunters, but not usually foresters. And their manes were yellow. But I hadn't anything else to suggest. 'Woodcat?' I ventured. The heat of the fire was strong, and I pulled back my hood and shook loose my mane.

'Not been called one of them before. Good answer though, I suppose. Some says we are like cats, indeed,' he replied, eyes still on his plate, stuffing back another mouthful. 'It's true I lives in the woods, but I don't have cat's eyes or wear one of 'em fur robes their dams fashion up for them.

'I'm Marten tribe, by the way,' he said.

'An admirable tribe, most admirable,' said I, though for all I knew a Marten could well be a snake in needle grass.

'Come and eat, young 'un. We can riddle a bit later,' the forester said, waving me forward.

I joined him at the table, and he pushed the platter of pies over. 'Thank you, sir,' I said, tearing into the first fish pie, sending flakes of pastry fluttering to the tabletop. It was wonderful!

'Bless the weather!' said he. 'Looks like yeh've not eaten fer some time!'

'Not since yesterday, sir.'

'Yesterday? Ah well. There's some passing here don't see a square meal fer a whole moon or more; they come knocking on my door regular like, looking fer food or shelter.'

Of course – other visitors like me, wayfarers, pilgrims – hence the tea table set for more than one, for I could only see one of everything else: one robe, one pair of boots, one settle bed and a single nightcap hanging on a bed post. He could, of course, have been expecting someone – but, in this snow? I was still intrigued. It was in my head that it was *me* he was expecting – that maybe it was him that had been watching me on the trail. But it would be disrespectful to ask.

'Where be yeh heading, young stranger?' he queried.

'Erainn, to Arkesh, sir. I'm searching for my kin – my mother and father.'

'That so, that so?' He looked away, at the window.

'I don't suppose,' I pressed, 'you've heard of any pilgrims from Alba heading for Erainn, about twenty moons past, with three Aguan in one of their wagons…a *vardon*?'

'Aguan wagons indeed. No. Not seen any.' He shrugged. 'Not this way, anyways.' He was still staring at the window. Why was he avoiding my gaze?

'Is something wrong, sir?'

'What? No. No, young 'un. Just that the storm's worse. Getting up fer what it was like last night,' he said, returning his gaze to the table.

The roar of the wind was indeed getting louder. Suddenly a great crash rattled the roof and sent smoke pouring down the chimney across the room. We both sprang to our feet, the Marten exclaiming, 'What in Yahl's name?'

In the haze, time seemed to slow, and shadows flickered and danced. I shivered, my heart suddenly racing. My inner world was turning over. I saw figures in the dim smoke – familiar – my parents, like ghosts. Something was happening, somewhere – as if a fixed point, a certainty, had been removed. I felt an inexplicable urge to leave, to go back out. Coughing and spluttering in the fumes, I said, 'I should get on.'

'Hold on there,' he replied. 'Yeh won't want to go back out in that. There's always a tail to the helm – or two. Take yer seat, stranger. Yeh'd be welcome to bunk up in my log store fer the night. It'll be calm by morning, no doubt.' He peered out through the only bit of windowpane uncovered by snow. 'Maybe jes' a tree falling,' he said, 'weak from the helm. The afterstorms usually bring them down.'

I sat down as the smoke cleared and began to calm. As he said, it was probably just a tree. I had to stop getting spooked like this.

'What's the name yeh have in yeh then, young Albin?' asked the Marten.

'Osian.'

'Well, young Osian, come sit by the fire. I'll tell yeh a story to while the evening away. Maybes in the morning, instead of payin' for the tale, yeh could help cut some hazel wands.' Walking back to the fireside, he took up the story stick I'd seen earlier and sat back in the rocking chair.

I nodded, pleased to be inside, and followed him to my place on the stool.

The stick's carvings were small and intricate, the totems winding among a myriad of spirals and whorls. At home, the tellers did tricks with fire to highlight their stories. I'd always suspected they kept special powders in their wands – that maybe there were inner chambers full of the stuff and they were fired with hidden levers.

Glancing at the *tai* cups, set on the table, I asked, 'How often do you see other visitors, sir?'

'Well, as yeh ask, I had two last night – but not the kind I'd welcome.'

'What do you mean, sir?'

'It was the strangest thing,' he replied. 'Very late it was, and the helm was building. They came batterin' on the door – wanted directions to the river ferry. Morok priests, they were, devilish fellows, but looked sickening to die.'

I felt a chill. Morok priests. Krol. Maybe the ones I'd seen?

'One of them was clutching something curved to his chest – like his life depended on it. It was all covered with sticky black stuff. Some of it was on him, even coming out of his nose and ears. Horrible, it was,' he said with a shudder. 'They had 'em curved swords, but they looked too weak to use 'em. Anyways, me, I had my trusty axe in my mitts. I was taking no chances.'

I gulped. The crescent-shaped object! The Krol in the cavern. They must have headed this way too – perhaps they'd even passed in the dark where I was sleeping in the crevasse.

'So, what did you do?'

'Sent them on their way. I weren't letting them kind in here, and not with that thing they had, whatever it was, leaking slime everywhere,' he said. 'Made me quiver all over, I tell yeh.'

'Don't the hospitality codes of the tribes apply here?' The tradition that wayfarers are offered shelter during storms.

Goodness, no. Only those of the free tribes can sit at my table – an' from them at times we gets the odd traveller, like yeh perhaps,' he replied firmly. 'Anyways, doubt we'll ever see 'em two alive again – not the way they were, and out in that storm. They'll not be missed, I tell yeh.' He rose, placed a log on the fire, and stood with his back to it. 'Anyways, enough of all that. Now what kind of a story would yeh like to hear, young Albin? I know some good ones from Clachoile, the Stone Forest. *The Lost Brach and the Raven* is a good one. Bit sad, though. Or there's *The Ghost Wolf and the Beaver Queen*, which is a bit scary. Shall I tell yeh one of these?' Still speaking, he leaned over, picked up the story stick and rolled it around in his hands, stopping at one of the tiny carved faces – a grey wolf, totem of the Sideag, the powerful Wolf tribe of Clachoile.

At home, of course, such stories were a common way of passing an evening. We'd sit with friends around a winter fire at the home of a tale teller; or sometimes a travelling mendicant would stop and tell a story in return for food and a place for the night. Some tellers were better than others. Grandfather told a good tale but couldn't compete with the true *Sagis* for their ability to weave magic with words and tricks, and sometimes with music from a hand harp.

I was tempted to say yes to anything, then I stopped and thought for a moment. Right now, especially after what the Rhuad had said, I needed not a tall story but as much information as I could glean about what I was heading into. What could I ask that would be useful to my quest?

The Marten sat in patient silence, rolling the story stick and examining the different faces in turn – wolves, badgers, bears, otters, horses, deer, wildcats – a pantheon of wild creatures expertly carved and glimmering red in the firelight. 'Well?' he asked, after a while.

There was one thing I needed to know, so I said, 'The pilgrim ways used to be open to all – the rights of those who take the pilgrimages upheld by the Marcher Lords. I know about the Marsh Wars, how the ways were closed but were reopened afterwards. Now I've just learned that the Morok have blocked them off again. But I've never understood what happened to the Marcher Lords and why no-one else protects the rights of the pilgrims now. Do *you* know? Could you tell me of that?'

He visibly froze. 'Yeh'll not be wanting that, young Osian.'

'Oh, why is that? Because it's not a story?'

'No, no. There is a story there alright. But us *Sagis* don't much like to tell it. 'Tis too recent, too real. 'Tis always best to tell of the old days – from before all our times – or of the ancestors. And there's something else about all that.' He nervously rolled the story stick in his hands.

'What is *that*, sir?' Now I was all the more intrigued.

'There's a curse in it, and it's bad luck to tell stories about curses,' he answered, placing his forefingers against his forehead, a sign meant to keep away evil.

I sighed. More bogles. But after all, what could I expect from a *Sagi*?

'Aye, a curse. Yeh said yer mother was Eronn tribe. Surely, she told yeh about what happened to the Marcher Lords?'

No. It was odd that she hadn't, now I thought about it. But then I'd never asked.

The Marten seemed discomfited, trading rapid glances between me and his hearth. I decided to persist. 'When was this...er...curse?'

'If yeh really must know, about sixty or maybe seventy winters back. All happened before my own time so I only haves the tale.'

But, I realised, any such events would have been in Grandfather's time – and he'd never mentioned anything about a curse in the holy lands. It was probably just bogle stuff, but bogle or not, if nothing else,

I'd be able to stay longer in shelter and by this lovely fire.

'I would like to hear this tale, sir. What is the name in it?' I asked, formally inviting a telling – and its name, for the names of tales, like names themselves, are considered sacred, not given or told lightly. Passed on from others through the generations, they must be afforded due respect. As the Marten was clearly a tale teller, he'd be more likely to agree to tell it in greatest detail in a tale form. I was sure I'd be able to separate out truth from fairy story. Or so I thought!

'The name in the tale, young Albin, is *The Fall*,' replied the forester in a sombre voice, already slipping into the timbre of story speak. 'It's a frightening story to be sure, a *chilling* tale. I'm just warning yeh.'

Now that I'd asked for and received the tale's name, the teller had no choice but to begin. I'd already fought off a few yawns and knew I might have difficulty staying awake. Nodding off during a tale was not considered rude, but little did I realise the power of this storyteller, or the true significance of what he was telling me. That revelation only came to me long after my encounter with the Marten. At the time, I thought hearing it from him, and at this point in my journey, was pure chance. I would come much later to realise it wasn't.

'As yeh like then, young 'un. I'll tell it. And I'll tell it all.'

I sat back and waited. Almost immediately I had to suppress a yawn and my head began to droop. I shook myself and moved a little away from the fire to stir my weary limbs.

And so, the Log Marten cradled the story stick on his knee, and commenced his telling, his voice in the fashion of the storyteller – rhythmic and hypnotic.

'If all were told…'

5

THE FALL OF THE HOUSE OF ERAINN

"FOR ALL THINGS BORN IN TRUTH MUST DIE.
AND OUT OF DEATH IN TRUTH COMES LIFE." AEHMIR

The wind banged hard against the side of the cabin. Suddenly I was wide awake.

'*...Uron, he of a long line of Marcher Lairds that watched over Erainn and the pilgrim ways, had one heir, Erin, whom he loved more than anything. Many a suitor came to the castle of Erintor from afar, trying to win her sky-blue eyes and inherit the legendary treasures of her line.*

'*All manner of Otar and other tribes vied for Erin. But to keep the rulings of Erainn within his blood kin, and ensure that his daughter stayed close, Uron decided to match her to his own cousin, he who had the Helmison holdings by the great Weir downriver from Erintor. He was of the Otar, but half Eronn and half of another tribe, with a mane black as night – a solitary fellow, twice Erin in his years.*

'*What her father didn't know was that Erin had already taken up with a young adventurer of her own age – a roving outlander who was not of the Eronn, who'd taken up with a group of outlaws encamped in the deep pinewoods that lie between Erintor and the far mountains that stretch beyond Erainn into the northern icy wastelands. This outlander* had encountered Erin whilst hunting near the castle and the pair had taken to meeting secretly in a hidden ghyll in the woods. But Uron found out and, in his fury, locked her in the tower, to stay there until her bridal day.'

It was, as I'd feared, beginning to sound indeed like a tall tale, a fairy story which surely would be no help to me in my quest. But the Marten, quite the *Sagi*, was very much the stylish storyteller. In the glowing coals of the fire, I could almost imagine myself as the young adventurer rescuing the lovely Erin from her captivity, escaping with her into the woods, lying side by side in dappled sunlight, by a streamside glade...

'On the great day, the heads of all the tribes and clans came from across Manau to view the spectacle and partake of the Laird's splendid bridal fare. Erin was subdued but garlanded in flowers of field and forest, lovelier than ever and duly hand-fasted to her cousin–uncle.

'Now, an old legend of Erintor holds that it's ill luck for bread to be broken or wine to be tasted on festive days until the last rays of the setting sun have slipped off the castle walls. Yet at dawn on the very day of her bridal, Erin was seen partaking of a courage glass – a full stoup of blood-red wine. It was ill omened. But the wedding rituals went ahead.

'Afterwards, the bride and groom prepared to commence the final ceremony of the day, without which any wedding in the Marcher line could not be concluded – the Crossing of the Water and the Riding of the Bounds. The party had to cross the castle moat then go through the pasture lands to join a bridge that passed over the sacred river that gives the holy lands its name, Erainn, the Green Land. From there they would tour the in-bye woods and villages around Erintor, there to receive the blessings of the spirits of stone, stream and wood, and the honours of the ordinary folk of Erainn.

'And so, the party duly assembled in the courtyard to conclude the nuptials.'

Here, the Marten paused to pick up a large pinecone from the fireside log basket. Tapping it with the talking stick, he placed it in the flames. It exploded alight, then died back to a rainbow of tiny swimming tongues of fire that swirled into a pageant of life-like shapes.

To my astonishment, a vision formed in the fire – Erin, high on a white steed, turning towards me, her glorious three-coloured mane flowing over her shoulders, her shining eyes filling with tears and a look of such unutterable sadness that I too felt my eyes welling. Then, as her horse began to follow that of the groom, she drooped her head and turned away. The husband, a giant among the Otar, taller than any pure-bred Eronn, seemingly oblivious to – or uncaring of – her grief. He rode ahead, proud upon a jet-black heavy-footed stallion. To their rear rode a guard of nine Eronn knights, their swords and armour glittering in the afternoon sun.

The Marten then placed a gnarled elder log over the coals, quenching the vision, and continued.

'But as the party reached the portcullis, a black cloud filled the sky and flashes of lightning struck the keep. The horses reared, bringing the bridal train to a sudden halt. Before them, on the moat bridge, barring their way, was Uron's fool, he of the Wind Hare. "Don't cross the water," the fool screamed. "This wicked match will bring death upon this house, destruction to Erainn."'

Suddenly, the room went dark. The elder log was like a shadow covering the sun. And I started, open eyed, as out of the smoke another vision rose.

'There was confusion and screaming. The horses bucked and bolted; the men muttered and cursed. And over all could be heard the words of the doomsayer:

"Cross the water and all is lost. Forever lost."

'Whereupon, Uron the Marcher Laird rushed to the front of the train, caught the groom's tossing steed, and yelled, "Go forward, I command yeh. Ride the bounds as yeh must and return afore sunset. Leave now." Then, putting a sword to his fool's throat, he hissed, "False prophet. Go from Erintor and never return. Stay and I'll kill yeh on this very spot."

'He of the Wind Hare pushed away the sword, then turned away,

53

distraught with grief for he loved Erin as if she were his own child, while the bridal train, much unsettled, carried on, crossing the moat then through the pasture lands towards the river, the villages and the pinewoods. But almost as soon as the train passed over the bridge that crosses the sacred water, a white hart with dazzling eyes leapt out of the forest into their path. It pawed the ground three times then sprang into the thicket, inviting chase. And, following the halloos of the groom, chase they did, charging after it into the green fastnesses.

'And so, the afternoon passed quietly in the great castle of Erintor until the light began to fade. Uron, though briefly angered by the intervention of his fool, was not much disconcerted and remained well pleased with the match. With Erin wed to his cousin, Erainn and the riches from the pilgrim ways would remain within his control and that of his own line.

'But by the time the sun began to set upon the castle walls, the bridal train had not returned. The great banqueting table, decked with a wondrous array of food and wine, lay untouched, glimmering in the light of a thousand candles. The guests were restless and the Laird became troubled. He sent out rider after rider to bring in the bridal party. One by one each messenger returned alone. Then returned the last, covered in blood and in such distress, he couldn't say what had happened, what he'd found, even under mortal threat. For he'd been struck dumb.

'Darkness fell; such a darkness never seen before. When then a crescent moon, jagged edged and ominously blood-red like a broken battle shield, broke through the blackness and rose high above the castle walls, the guests, servants and even the castle guards fled in terror. Only two stayed – an old retainer too long in winters to leave, and the gate porter, who was stone blind.

'But Uron had not given up hope. He took his place at the head of the feasting table, muttering over and over, "They will return. They must return."

'Finally, at midnight, on the third stroke of the castle clock, a procession of hooves was heard crossing the moat bridge. The old blind porter counted out ten riders slowly passing his gate and rang his bell for each.

'Uron stood and rejoiced as Erin and the nine knights entered the hall and sat down at their appointed places but remained hooded. Then, when at his command one after another took off their hoods, he saw to his horror that their faces were covered with gaping wounds and disfigurements, unspeakable to behold. The lovely Erin's beautiful face was hardly recognisable.

'Upon them all lay the ghostly pallor of death.

'Uron leaped to his feet in dismay, and screamed to his retainer, "D'ye see them? D'ye see them? They're all wounded to the death, dead, dead I tell ye! What have I done? What have I done?" The other, who saw nothing, tried to calm him, but he was beyond comforting. Finally, a huge gust of wind tore through the keep, extinguishing the great fire, the candles – and the ghostly mirage of the bridal train.'

The elder log dropped out of the fire, pouring dark smoke across the floor. I flinched, nearly falling out of my seat. The air in the room had turned icy, a bitter chill folding into every corner, the ghosts of the dead bridal party seeming to hang among the shadows. I shivered and pulled my blanket tight over my shoulders. The Marten leaned down and replaced the log. It crackled, and the fire flickered lamely back into life. But the vision had gone.

'Uron,' he continued, his voice quieter in the low light, 'rocked back and forth, repeating aloud the words of the doomsayer. "All is lost. Forever lost." Endlessly he chanted it, again and again through the rest of the night. These were the last words he ever spoke. For the old retainer, who'd huddled elsewhere in mortal fear, returned at sunrise to find the Laird still there, but in body only. His soul had been taken. The Laird was stone dead.

'Later, the forest folk reported hearing sounds of battle coming from a deep ghyll. When they dared to venture in, they found torn-up ground, slashed trees and the burn running red with blood. But no weapons, bodies or even dead horses; just a set of footprints in the mud leading away from the skirmish in one direction and a lone set of bloodied hoof marks in the other.

''Tis said that Erin's lovelorn swain had tried to rescue his sweetheart, *and ambushed the party with his outlaw friends, the skirmish turning into deadly battle. Nobody knows, but whatever the truth, nothing more was ever heard of Erin or any of the others. And in the moons following, the castle of Erintor went to rack and ruin, its life sucked away.*

'The great line of the Marcher Lairds of Erainn was no more.'

6

THE AFTERSTORM

With a deep sigh, the Log Marten lifted the stick to his forehead, muttered an invocation to the *sidhe* so that the story would not bequeath bad luck upon the listener, placed it back on the table and took up his pipe. The tale was at an end.

The cabin and the air around my face felt gripped in a frozen embrace; this chilling story from the past had sent an icicle through my heart, shallowing my breathing. Worse, I had a creeping sensation that somehow, I, a stranger to this land, had some kind of connection with the tale and its characters. My brain swam with the vision of Erin in the fire. It had seemed that when she stared straight at me, she was pleading for my help. And I wondered even then whether this dire tale, and the events it detailed, would have consequences for my quest. It was not the first time within the space of a day and a night in this land, that it felt my help was being sought – and I was unable to oblige. As if I could – and catching myself in the act of almost believing in bogles – I shook my head and stood up, stretching my hands out towards the remnants of the fire for warmth. For I was shivering.

The afterstorm which rocked the cabin had abated, and all was icy still. Through the little window I saw that the snow had stopped falling; the frost already hardening. I knew from Albin winters that the way forward would not be easy. There would be deep snow on the trail and treacherous ice where the open ground was wind-blown bare.

I glanced over at the Marten who sat, pipe on his knees, gazing trance-like at the greying embers, his eyes glistening. As I stood there my mind returned to the tale, running again and again over its details, trying to figure out why I'd been affected so deeply. It had been a powerful tale, powerfully told. But surely there was nothing more to it than that?

We remained in silence, unmoving. The Marten made no effort to stoke the fire. I pulled my blanket tighter and opened my mouth to speak, when suddenly the wind roared up again, throwing debris clattering against the outside of the cabin. We both jumped, and the Marten's head jerked up. He stood up, muttering something that was drowned out by another noise from the woods, this time a low rumble like falling rocks. His eyes darted to the window, fright in them. Then, as if just noticing my presence, he selected some kindling sticks, threw them on the embers, leaned down and blew on them. The fire spluttered at first, then came back to life. The room began to warm and fill again with light and life.

I held out my hands to the flames, feeling at last it was appropriate to speak. 'What you have told me, sir. There are things I don't understand,' I said.

'Yer not alone in that, young 'un. What are yer worries, then?'

'You said these were real events. Surely all this did not really happen. It's a just a tale, a terrible tale.'

'All true, as I live and breathe. I told yeh it would make fer uncomfortable listening.'

'If there was nothing found in the woods, how could anyone be sure they'd all really died?' I queried.

''Tis a good question. And one I've often asked meself. Well, probably Okwa wolves and wild mastiffs would have dragged off the carcasses – even the horses. The ravens would have taken their share, and Skraeling of course would have picked off any weapons, jewellery, armour and such.'

'Hmm. The "doomsayer", the Wind Hare, what of him who was banished?'

'Oh, him? Aehmir. Went to the far mountains, became a holy one. Still alive somewhere, I hears. Wind Hares are long lived,' he replied, filling his pipe and blowing smoke rings towards the hearth.

'Aehmir? I have a book of sayings by a sage with the name in him of Aehmir – here, in my pack. He was a friend of my grandfather's. Not,' I said, feeling a little guilty, 'that I've studied it fully – yet.'

'Is that so? Here we say "Ehmer" not "Ay-meer". But it could well be the same one. Wind Hares are few and far between. And he became a sage all right.'

'"Ehmer",' I repeated to get the sound right. I would be sure to look at the book properly the next chance I had. 'There's something else bothering me,' I said. 'In the story, the porter only counted back the sound of ten returning horses. What of the other, the eleventh? Who was that? Did they escape the battle and live to tell the tale? And whose were the footprints? One of the outlaws?'

'Aye. Well, the hoof prints found leavin' the ghyll were from a very big horse – possibly the steed o' the groom himself. Helmison. Perhaps he of the Weir did indeed draw more breath. But certainly, neither he nor his horse were ever seen again.'

'What of the footprints leading the other way? Someone else lived – survived to tell the tale? One of the outlaws perhaps?'

'The forest folk say a kind of ghost, male and young in face with a white mane and a sword, was spotted in the area afterwards, wandering distressed at night within the woods; but it can't have been a real ghost 'cos where it had been seen fires had been lit and once a scrap of bloody rag was found beside one. But who it was – or whether there is even a connection – no-one really knows. And after twelve moons, the "ghost" was never seen again.'

'Could it have been Erin's swain?'

'That's the thinking. His company were 'omeless stragglers from various tribes, but the swain was supposedly Otar, and white maned like the *sidhe*, and some says that's what he was; an Otar fairy that had enchanted young Erin and taken her spirit into the mirror world. Though if that were true, he wouldn't have been doing the twelve moons mourning. All part of the mystery.'

Mystery indeed. I thought it odd though that I'd never heard any of this incredible story before, from Grandfather or my mother or the Aguan tale tellers, for the fall of the Marcher Lords will have been a great thing in its time. As for this thing of its telling bringing bad luck to the listener seemed like pure bogle wash to me.

'There's another curious thing, young 'un, yeh should know,' the Log Marten suddenly added, with a long draw on his pipe. 'Uron had a twin who, as first out of the womb, was really the rightful heir. But after the old Laird died there was a disagreement about the succession, and it came to a duel. Imagine that! Between twins.'

'What happened?'

'As they took up fighting positions,' he continued, 'the elder, stricken with shame, threw his sword to the ground and left Erintor, never to return. Even after the news of the tragic bridal and the death of Uron had spread across the territories, he never reclaimed his Marcher rights. Some say he be alive today – and in Erainn, but with another name, his whereabouts known only to hisself. He mus' be well hidden is all I can say, for he'll be easy spotted, him with the eyes of Otrec, the great mother, deep sky-blue like the lovely Erin herself. And those yeh cannot disguise!'

'So, because of all this, the pilgrim ways fell into disuse, and Erainn became cursed with the Long Winter?' I queried.

'Cursed all right, but not jus' wi' bad weather. Some elder Eronn tried to keep up the old rulings, but without the power and wealth of the old Lairds they had, by their reckonings, to take tolls, taxing trade goods and the use of the ways, with tollbooths and checking places, to cover the costs o' policing. But the other tribes took against this mightily, for free movement across the holy lands is a right as old as the hills yeh've crossed to get here. In the end, it came to war 'atween the tribes. The Marsh Wars they wuz called. Terrible, they were – thousands died. In the end, old Gwion, the blind ferry keeper, the Wildcat, Lir Og, together with one of the holy ones, managed a peace by making friends with Amon, Great Chief of the Brach. And there was another,' he added, with a look of curiosity at me, 'an outlander – of such kind as yerself.'

This gave me a jolt. The outlander. Of course. Grandfather! He'd certainly talked about the wars, the part in the peace process played by his friends, Gwion, Lir Og and Aehmir. But he always downplayed his own role in the affair. He was, he'd said, a mere bystander.

'The wars were over, but the curse had bitten deep. For now,' continued the Marten, 'we have the helms and the river floods – the Long Winter. And if that wasn't bad enough…along came *them*.' He shook his head, muttering, 'Curse 'em – and all that came with 'em.'

'You mean the Morok?' Though I hardly needed to ask.

He nodded, staring into the dying coals.

Clearly, without the power and strength of a ruling house, Erainn and the riches of the pilgrimage routes had become easy prey to a predatory force, particularly after the tribes had exhausted themselves with war. I thought about Erin in the fire, the way her haunting eyes had entered my soul – a vision from another time, another place. I sighed deeply. Past lives.

I was on the verge of asking if there was somewhere I could sleep, when there came from outside a crash so thunderous the boards and rafters of the little cabin shook and rattled violently, bringing us both to our feet. The door slammed against the bar, crockery clattered down from the shelves, and cutlery flew off the table. There followed another crash, then another, echoing through the woods.

The Marten darted to the door, unbarred and opened it and peered out into the dark. 'Yahl's name! The crossing!'

I glimpsed over his head a tower of red smoke rising high above the trees. Something was on fire! A crossing?

The Marten stared for a second, turned round, his face twisting in fury, then grabbed a robe and a knapsack from the door pegs and strapped an axe to his waist. 'Listen, young Albin,' he barked, 'I have to go…help if can…warn the others.'

Others?

'What can I do?' I asked, watching him rummage in a boot box.

'There's nothing yeh can do, young 'un,' he replied. 'Best stay out o' it. There's furs here and food.' He pulled on high boots and ran a finger down the edge of the axe. 'Help yerself. Yeh'll be safe tonight if yeh bolt the door after me. Don't answer if anyone calls. When yeh leave, tie up the door from the outside.'

'Can't I go with you?' I asked, 'Is it…are your friends…in trouble? I can help…if you lend me arms.'

The Marten stood erect and glanced at me, mouth open, horror in his eyes. 'Yeh can't come where I'm going,' he said. 'And don't yeh even think about heading out there tonight. Yeh'd not find the river trail in snows this deep. Leave in the morn. But wherever yeh go, stay clear of Morok…and…and whatever yeh do, don't try to cross the water.'

But I *had* to cross the water. Otherwise, what was the point? I had to get into Erainn proper. 'What d'you mean?'

He looked at me as if I was an idiot. 'Have yeh learned nothing, stranger? Morok are all over the place there. *Don't cross the water.*' That phrase again!

What was I supposed to reply? I had to get over the river regardless.

I must have looked wounded, for he spoke to me in a gentler tone. 'Look, if yeh're insisting on heading for Arkesh, avoid Erainn proper. Keep to the trail on this side of the river. Above all stay clear of the Weir – where the rivers meet.'

'You'll be back later?' I pressed.

'Can't say, young 'un. Can't say,' he replied. Then, with a farewell nod, he darted into the night, leaving me gaping and speechless in the doorway. Whatever was going on, it was obviously important enough to make him abandon his warm cabin to the deep cold – leaving it in the hands of a complete stranger.

Watching him disappear into the snows, I thought about his strange manner and that terrible story. And why did he stiffen like that, suddenly look away, when I asked about my kin? What hadn't he told me?

Bolting the door as instructed, I loaded up the fire and lay down on the Marten's furs with Aehmir's book. The page that opened automatically could have been written about the story I'd just heard. It said: 'Desire and wrath, born of passion, are the sum of destruction, the enemy of spirit.'

The little sayings and wisdoms somehow failed to soothe me on this occasion. It took ages to find rest, and my night was troubled, the darkness filling my sleep with strange dreams – a pair of shining blue eyes; pale knights, cruelly disfigured; a ruined castle where a table lay spread with rotting food; a white deer with glittering eyes standing in a burned-out wood; a hooded figure gazing down from a high rock, a bloody sword by his side; and an army of reptilian forms slithering along a snowy trail, coming ever closer.

7

THE DISCOVERY

I woke with a jolt. My clothes were damp. I'd sweated in the night and was now shivering in the cold morning air. The Marten's fire was out. A line of snow lay at the doorway where it had drifted in across the threshold through cracks in the timber. The outside had come inside. But all was quiet. The storm was over – but the aftershock of the Marten's story still swam round my head, churning my stomach.

I shook myself to clear away the darkness in my head, hauled on my robe and fur collar, found a brush and swept the snow at the doorway to one side. But when I double checked the fire to see if it was safely out, I noticed the story stick had gone. It had been there, I was sure, when I lay down for sleep. Now I wasn't so certain. In fact, after what I'd seen and heard since my arrival across the Karst, I'd not been so certain about anything, what was real and what was unreal.

Anyway, I needed to be gone. Collecting the last of the Marten's pies in a small cloth bag and filling my water horn from a jug, I placed three cowries on the table, took up my staff and left the cabin, securing the door latch as instructed, using a piece of frayed cord hanging from the frame.

Great billows of snow lay everywhere, obscuring the trail. The forest around me was a sea of dazzling white. Which way to go? I turned blindly on the spot. With no sun to give the direction, I couldn't tell. Then I remembered what Grandfather used to say: 'If you find yourself lost, close your eyes and breathe slowly. Think with the inbreath, feed your senses.'

Duly, I inhaled and exhaled, shuddering as the icy air seared my lungs. My nostrils began to itch, and I caught a trace of something familiar – the sweet aroma of water wood. River willows. Then came another scent – the musty smell of wet burned wood – faint, distant. Of course, the conflagration in the night! The Marten had muttered something about the river crossing. This, then, was my direction.

I pushed my way through the waist-high drifts to the edge of the clearing. There, under the thick clustered pines, the trail opened out between the trees. The day was calm, the snow mostly crisp underfoot, and the walking was easier. My mood lightened.

Dark clouds threatened above, but morning drew on without further snowfall. I saw the tracks of ground huggers, but little sign of any two-footed traveller, nothing to show which direction the Marten had taken. No birdsong or other noise broke the snowy silence, until suddenly I heard the sound of a conch, three distinct notes echoing faintly across the snowy wastes.

I stopped and waited for more. Conch horns were used in Alba by hedge priests, shamans and trackers and blown endlessly at tribal ceremonies – births, bridals, seasonal festivals or feast days. They made a sound like the sacred letter 'Q' as if it was being breathed through trees, or through sand rising on a windy beach – 'Q'ooosssh…'. Travelling backwards and forwards across the land, their haunting echoes were usually received with gladness, for they signified a happy event or a successful hunt. But back in Alba, three solitary spread-out notes like these meant something bad – an avalanche; or a sighting of Okwa or sabre-toothed cougars creeping down out of the mountains, hungry and looking for food, sheep, poultry. Or worse.

This was a warning call. I was sure of it. But about what, I wondered; and in this remote place who was calling who, and why?

Trudging on, I tried to dispel my fears with comforting memories of home, of earlier happier times – me sitting by the hearth; Grandfather smoking his pipe on his rocking chair; the smell of my aunt's cooking wafting from the kitchen.

Home though hadn't been much of a haven in recent moons. After my parents left, and no word had come, Grandfather had taken to disappearing for days into the hills, returning with a haunted look, but saying nothing. My aunt said he'd done this a lot when Grandmother passed away, but even before then and confided her belief that his solitary walks had something to do with a very disturbing memory that reared up from time to time. She was convinced it originated in some tragic or horrific event that had occurred during his first journey into Erainn – the one he never spoke of.

There were no more conch calls. And the dark cloud that had promised a new storm passed on.

When morning turned to noonday, I heard the reedy cries of dunlin up ahead, and then, close by, the light chatter of willow warblers. Water birds. The river!

Pulse racing, I clambered up a trailside boulder and there in the middle distance it lay – a blue–green colossus; a slithering, roaring, pouring, winding wonder. The river Erainn, mightiest in all Manau, the Sacred River, bequeathed, it is said, by the gods to their chosen tribe – the Eronn – to fertilise their fields in return for watching over the holy shrine of Arkesh at its eastern end. Here, where it flew over rocks and tree stumps, the water reared high. Where it twisted around bends, detritus spun and churned between the banks.

I sat on the boulder breathing in the welcoming energy of this wild world of water. Even the sky, though still clouded, seemed lighter, with more birds than I'd seen since leaving home soaring and wheeling through it. My spirits soared with them. This, I felt, must be a new beginning – the kind of day that changed everything.

My shoulders had begun to relax and my mind to wander upon gentle thoughts, when I heard tramping feet approaching – and in large numbers. My reverie cut short, I slid down the back of the boulder and tucked myself into a drift at its base. Then, what sounded like an entire army came thundering past, so close I could smell the sweat of unwashed bodies; could hear the rattle of weapons and the jangling of armour. I caught a glimpse of a forest of forked spear tops passing by. Momentarily, I feared they might see my tracks or smell my presence and wondered how I'd be able to get away. But, if they saw or sensed anything, they didn't react.

I waited till they were well away, huddling deep into my snow hole and packing the edges around me to keep warm. When I eventually dared to come out and rejoin the trail, it had been stamped into slush. Troopers – Morok, I assumed. I wondered if there were more up ahead – if the conch call was a warning of their presence. But no more calls came.

The trail now ran close to the river, just under a levee with the water spilling over its top in places. Up ahead were a huddle of buildings straddling the barrier, the first signs of occupation I'd seen since my journey began, with the solitary exception of the Marten's cabin. A trickle of dark smoke rose up from their midst. As I approached, a pair of oystercatchers raced past at eye level, bleating alarms.

My chest lurched as I came to the little cluster of buildings and saw what had befallen them. The first was the burned-out ruin of a water tower, its uprights charred and teetering, its stone sides smashed and blackened, its circular shape barely discernible. Just beyond lay the smoking remains of two conical buildings and a broken-up jetty, the struts poking out of the swirling waters. On the bank, bits and pieces of a boat workshop, broken tools and pots, paddle ends, and rusted boat irons lay strewn about, along with crushed domestic items – baskets, buckets, fire pans and bits of furniture. A heavy-looking door, the bottom section scorched by flame, lay across the edge of the trail. Its upper half was splintered, and above the gashes a crossbolt was impaled in the wood. The bolt was jet-black and barbed.

This was the river crossing – the ferry point – or what remained of it. It had been attacked and burned to the ground! It was this that had sent the Log Marten into the frozen night. This was the cause of the explosion we'd heard; the red smoke I'd seen through his doorway.

The burned-out buildings were still smoking. A charred smell hung heavy in the air. But there was no ferryboat, and no signs of life. No Gwion the ferry keeper!

Grandfather's friend. Gone?

I slumped to the ground. This was a setback worse than any obstacle the Rhuad had suggested. Clenching my fists, I fought back tears of rage; the one place I might have found friendship and news evaporated in smoke. And no apparent means of getting across the swollen river and onwards to the pilgrim ways – other than swimming, a certain death sentence in these racing frozen waters.

The nightmare at the Sentinel was continuing. Nothing was as it should be. With Gwion gone, what chance was there of me being able to track and find my parents – never mind enter Erainn proper.

For some time, I knelt there in the snow, oblivious to the cold, unsure what to do next, where to go, angrily swiping away tears that came in waves. After a while a small bird on a nearby tree broke into bright song, and I looked up. It hopped on to a stone beside me, cast a wary eye my way, puffed out its radiant breast and chirruped. A robin, the midwinter song-king.

'Ah little songbird,' I said, 'no doubt in the past you'll have feasted upon the crumbs from Gwion's table. Where will you go now?'

As if by answer, it launched into a full-throated song, and I found myself thinking of Grandfather's story about how this little bird had come to have a red breast – how a Manu prophet-king dying upon a cross had been brought water by a wounded robin. The creature had put compassion for another before concern for itself. By way of reward, the gods bequeathed its descendants with a golden voice and a red breast – the sacred blood of the king. Citing this story, Grandfather had said, 'Self-pity is not the way of the warrior. Life, all life, is a test. Never bewail your fate. Learn from it, go forward. Keep your pity for others.' And here was this little bird cheering me, rather than bemoaning its own fate – the desperate search for food in this sunless winter.

As it twittered, its song was answered by others, and I understood that, desolate though things might look, I was very much alive; and

I was not alone. Gwion might not be dead. I just had to find him. So, leaving some pie for the bird, with a determined tread, I strode onward.

The afternoon wore on. I looked for alternative crossing points, but the riverbank was thickly forested with tangles of blackthorn, alder and willow, all stacked high with snow. Eventually, however, I came across a gap in an alder thicket. I shoved my way through and clambered up onto the levee. The river was in deep flood, the far bank shrouded in grey mist with no type of crossing place anywhere in view. To make matters worse, a squall was blowing up, and thunder was rumbling in the heavens.

Turning to go, my eye was drawn to a silvery glimmering below the water's choppy surface, something shining, just out of reach. I peered closer. It had the shape of a quarter moon, crescent like the object in the cavern in the clutches of the beast. I glanced at the sky, hoping to see a moonrise, most likely source of the reflection, but no. The sky remained filled with clouds and was darkening. Then, oddly, when I lowered my eyes, the silvery image was gone. It had merely been a trick of the light. Silver eels, maybe.

But as I turned away, I glimpsed a dark shape snaking towards me under the swell. It came to a stop on the water's edge at the bottom of the levee before me, snagged on a half-submerged branch. I clambered down and bent over, curious to see what it was. At that moment a great flash of lightning struck the ground in front of me. A massive shock tore through me, sending me lurching backwards. It was if the world was erupting around me. A green-white light exploded before my eyes. A surge of energy, a tremendous feeling of power and pain, coursed through my body. Gasping, head reeling, I hauled myself to my feet and tried to back away from the spot. But I couldn't. My legs had turned to stone. I couldn't even turn around.

I'd been struck by lightning – yet I was alive!

I tried again to pull away and found I could move, but only in one direction – towards the dark shape, now bobbing before me in the water and, it seemed, urging me to pick it up! I edged forwards and tried to cradle it with the crook of my staff. Suddenly, lightning struck again.

I felt taken up, lifted off the ground by a green-white flash, sheathed, enfolded in energy. I glowed with light – the light of a thousand suns. Then I fell back down. There came a deep darkness. How long it lasted I don't know.

Next thing I knew I was standing on the riverbank, infused with warmth, clutching a small crescent-shaped shell-like object, hardly the length of my forearm, against my chest with the dizzying thought that I'd been standing in that spot for thousands upon thousands of winters and had just woken from a deep sleep. I gazed around me. Everything else was as it had been – the swollen river, the mist-covered far bank and the slope of the river levee at my feet. I stared in disbelief at the object in my arms. Only then I did I feel the cold returning. Bitter cold.

I shook and rolled my shoulders, relieved to discover that I could again move freely. The darker clouds had lifted, and the lightning storm was over. Time to go.

Slowly, head swimming, I scrambled up and over the levee and dived in among the alders. Huddling into the bushes for warmth, I examined what it was that I'd rescued – that I'd been *forced* to rescue – and in such an extraordinary way. From nowhere, it came to me that this was the very object from the cavern that I thought had cried out to me. It too was crescent shaped, but then it shone like sungold. Could it be? I stared open-mouthed, disbelieving. I lifted it to my nose and sniffed. The smell was sour, but there were other scents, faint, coming through – one woody like a forest in spring, the aroma of risen sap, of new leaf; the other of salt water, but fragrant, ethereal. If it was the same object, then the beast's webbing must have hardened, for the surface was cold to the touch, but smooth just like a pebble worn-washed by water. Indeed, it looked very much like a stone, a crescent shaped stone. And it looked heavy, yet it had no weight at all. And, of course, it had floated!

I shook it, expecting it to be hollow, but it didn't rattle. I held it up to the light and rolled it over. There was no opening of any kind; no seam or place where the webbing had joined. But there were indentations in the membrane – three long thin marks joined at one end. I traced them with a finger without thinking, and recoiled in shock – it was the brand put there by the Krol – the mark of the Morok I'd been told of. 'Ugh,' I exclaimed, and made to sling it into the thicket.

But, to my shock, it wouldn't leave my grip.

I tried again – and then again. But to no effect. Worse, every time I attempted to cast it aside, I felt my body turning cold, my limbs stiffening. But if I brought it close, my muscles loosed, and I felt a strange, comforting warmth. And if I held it against my body, I felt invigorated, full of energy and purpose, the strangest feeling – that I was more *alive* than I'd ever been before. I did not need the mark of the Morok upon it to know that this *was* the very object I'd seen in the cavern. It had called out to me, and now here it was. It had come to me in the end, and I knew now that I had to do what I had failed to do before – answer the call. Rescue it. Keep it with me till I found out who or what it should be with.

As I crouched there, dumbfounded and breathing hard, I felt again the prickling sensation I'd experienced before, in the wood. I was being watched – still?

I whipped around and listened hard. But, as before, there was nothing to see or hear – only my instincts screaming at me that someone was there, looking at me. I thrust the strange object inside my robe and, leaving the thicket, stumbled back onto the trail. Once there, I stuffed it into my *papose*, checked around again and, seeing no-one, went on my way.

8

THE WEIR

Hardly was I back on the trail when I heard a fearsome screech from above. I looked up to see a shadow plunging out of the sky, wings beating furiously, and coming straight towards me. Clutching my *papose* to my chest I launched myself into the thicket. The wings thrashed close, louder even than the roar of the river. I pressed into the woody slush. Branches and brambles tore at my mane and scratched my face as I hugged the ground and rolled onto my back readying my pikestaff to strike up at it. Any moment now...

But whatever it was flapped past with one last shriek and was gone.

I waited, sniffed the air and clambered out of the scrub. I saw nothing – only a solitary oystercatcher retreating into the distance. It was hardly that.

Was it Skarag? After me? Or a warning? But what could I do, other than keep going and be wary?

After a while I came across a giant crack willow laden with icicles and, beyond it, a flat rock among a pile of rocks, a little off the trail and hidden from it. Clearing some snow, I sat down, ate more of the

Marten's pie and lay back, my *papose* between me and a boulder. The many strange things that had happened to me weighed heavily on my mind and body, and my eyelids began to droop.

I drifted off and strange dreams began to pour in. A pack of giant Okwa, dreadful timber wolves, were at my heels, fangs dripping blood, wasting everything in their path. Fire arrows peppered the ground. Flames surrounded me; smoke choked me and stung my eyes. My ears rang with high-pitched whistling. I ran, but my legs were like water. The wolves were gaining. I carried something monstrous on my back that dragged me down. Finally, I tripped, and the wolves were upon me, teeth and claws stretching towards me, tearing at my back. There was a loud crack, and a bright green flash. Lightning.

I woke suddenly to see the huge willow falling in slow motion towards me, icicles flying off it, floating through the air like cotton grass. I grabbed my *papose* and twisted away, then watched in breathless horror as the tree crashed with a great explosion across the rock; splinters of wood and ice scattering everywhere. Overburdened, the aged tree had given up. Where I'd been lying seconds earlier was now a morass of broken branches and stone shards, the rock itself cracked in two. Under one side lay my precious staff – snapped into pieces. That was bad news, but I told myself that I'd been lucky. A narrow escape.

Feeling a sudden nervous need to check my other possessions, I rummaged through my *papose* and counted out my tooth-twig, the cloth bag of pies, fishing hooks, flints, sling, knife, spare robe and fur collar, under-things and the little book of Aehmir's writings. There, too, was the crescent-shaped stone I'd found, snuggled like a baby hedgehog under its blanket. And as I gazed at it, again I felt something emanating from within, an invisible force penetrating my body, warming and empowering; and I knew that it was this that had saved me from being crushed by the tree. The flash of lightning that woke me, the sense of time shifting. *This* was the source.

In future though, I'd still take better care where I put my head. Now I'd need a new staff and resolved that when I found shelter for the night I'd carve a new one. There was river alder everywhere here.

Perfect. Maybe my strange find, the stone, I chuckled to myself, would empower a new staff too.

Back on the trail, the day was waning. Along the riverside, the pine and birch forests of the Karst's higher ground made way for stark lines of alder and willow. The trail, slushy with snow, was wetter underfoot with reeds and marsh grasses in winter dress – though, by my reckoning, it should still have been autumn.

I passed a set of rapids and came to a tiny deep channel running out sideways from the river, then circling around to rejoin further downstream. The channel banks were edged with layered stone that had broken in places – the race for a watermill. Further on, what had been the mill itself was now just a pile of rubble and rusted wheel struts.

It wasn't the only ruin hereabouts. The mist across the water had cleared enough to reveal a structure towering over the far bank – a tumbledown castle, wrecked and open to the mists, with dank vegetation crawling out of every nook and cranny. Nearby sat a cramped huddle of crumbled conical buildings surrounded by gardens and fields that had seen no recent harvest. Scattered along the waterline were piles of whitened bones. The sacred water that had once powered the mill wheel to keep the castle and its community alive was now just a watery abyss, every swirl and wave a carrier of death.

Only then did I realise where I was – the Weir at Helmison. It had been marked, I remembered, on Grandfather's map. The castle ruin must surely be Helmison itself, which I now knew as the former home of the Lord of the Weir, Erin's groom in the Log Marten's eerie tale. It looked as though it had been derelict for long years – river mist swirling through its broken battlements like ghosts.

The Weir. The Marten had warned me to stay away from this place.

I stood for a moment staring across the water, wondering what possible danger this sad collection of lifeless structures could hold.

Suddenly, hurtling through the torrent in front of me, I caught sight of a shadowy figure clutching desperately onto a branch. 'Hold on!' I yelled, stumbling down to the water's edge.

The figure responded, shuddering as if trying to leap out of the water in a desperate grasp at freedom. Suddenly, it separated from the branch, sailed directly towards me and flew out of the water. I jumped back as it crashed into the bank beside me. But on impact it collapsed to nothing. Just an empty robe, puffed up by the current.

It had looked so real. I bent over and picked it up, but immediately dropped it with a loud 'euch,' for it stank. Worse, it bore the brand of the Morok. In fact, it looked like one of the robes worn by the Krol in the cavern; and I began to wonder if this was how the strange stone in my *papose* might have ended up in the river. Lost, like its carrier, in the storm. Light, just like a robe, it had floated away and been taken downriver by the swell. The Marten said the Krol had looked ill – that they'd had death on their faces. Had they drowned in the end? Disgusted by the stench of the robe yet annoyed with myself for feeling no compassion for the lost soul of its owner, I shoved it into the torrent with my toe, then turned away. When I glanced back, it was gone.

Ahead lay another set of rapids, in the middle of which rose up three rocky fingers that divided and narrowed the torrent, creating two tunnels of frenzied foam and flotsam. I caught a glimpse of something trapped in the nearest tunnel, caught between the rock faces, eerily suspended in the air above the spout. It looked very much like the spine of an Aguan *vardon*.

I strained my eyes to catch more detail but immediately recoiled – impaled with crossbolts to the frame of the wagon was a pair of long, thin skeletons. Strips of greyish blue cloth hung from their rib cages – the unmistakable remnants of once deep-blue Aguan cloaks. Above their ghostly skulls, scratched on the paintwork, three talons. Morok!

My stomach heaved; my legs began to give way. Mother? Father? Was this the *vardon* that had brought them across the mountains; were these poor dead souls its drivers? I had told myself all this time that they lived, but I was surely wrong. There could be no hope.

I slumped to the ground, a low moan coming from deep in my gut. Why? Why had they made this journey when they must have known the pilgrim ways were unsafe – known only too well that they might never return?

But wasn't that what I, too, was now doing? Following blindly and recklessly in their footsteps?

Childhood images flashed before me – mother nursing me when I was unwell, comforting me when my friend died in a fishing accident; father showing me how to forge tools, guiding me patiently even when I dropped the hammer. And now I might never see them again, might never have the chance to say goodbye!

Maybe this was what the Marten's warning had been about. Perhaps he'd known all along what had happened to the Aguan *vardon* – and to my parents. Here, in this dreadful place, the home of Erin's groom. The source, the root of the curse he'd talked of.

If my kin were dead, there was nothing left to do but go home.

As my breathing gradually slowed, so did my thoughts. *Was* this the same *vardon*? Each wagon carried its own unique mark, denoting the clan of its Aguan drivers. Closing my eyes, I tried to visualise it trundling on wooden wheels into the yard all those moons ago. The mark was always emblazoned at the wagon base, where the central spine met the wheel axis.

I remembered it – a deep blue sea dragon with fiery red eyes.

I hurried to the bankside and peered across the choppy waves at the grim wreck. The paint mark was nearly gone, but it wasn't blue; more of a ruddy yellow. The faded shape looked like a starfish. My shoulders dropped and I let out a great hiss of breath that I hadn't even known I was holding. There were, after all, many *vardon*, many Aguan traders, traversing the Manau territories. Or there used to be. This was just one of many.

Not my kin's.

'Thank Yahl,' I muttered, but felt shame for expressing relief. If it turned out that something like this had happened to my kin, I knew I'd want vengeance; I'd seek out the Morok leader and kill him and as many Morok as I could, if it was the last thing I ever did. But, for the moment, there was still hope. Yet, I wondered, too, about the Aguan traders who had taken my parents. For hadn't the Rhuad said that the Aguan now worked *with* the Morok? What might that mean for my parents' fate? And if the Aguan were in league with the Morok, why had these two been murdered so cruelly and their remains left on display in such a horrible way?

I strode onwards, pulsing red blood empowering my every step, aware of the strength of the mysterious crescent-shaped stone surging through me at moments of crisis, urging me forward, enforcing my resolution. As far as I knew, my parents lived. Whatever had happened to them, there was no reason to think – yet – that they were dead.

I was going to find them and bring them home.

Whatever it took.

9

THE WILDCAT

Night was coming in, so I looked around for somewhere to erect my bender. To one side of the trail lay a thick alder scrub and behind it a clutch of ice-capped boulders. I picked my way through the brush and came to a clearing with a rock outcrop looming over the far side – the highest rock I'd seen since the Karst. Under its lee looked a good place to camp.

At the edge of the clearing, overcome by sudden caution, I hesitated. And wisely so, it appeared, for I became aware of sounds – heavy breathing and rhythmic muttering. Someone was nearby and talking. I peered into the gathering dusk and made out the back of a single thickset hooded figure standing atop the outcrop. I waited for a moment but didn't sense a threat. A fellow traveller? But who was he talking to?

'Hello. Can I approach?' I called up. No response. I moved forward about thirty paces, clasping my knife in my hand, till I was just below the rock. 'Good evening, sir,' I said. 'A wayfarer. I walk in the peace of Yahl.'

Still nothing.

The figure on the rock was wide in the shoulder, clearly male, wearing a long greenish cloak and leaning on a pikestaff, the hand furred, clawed like a cat's, and – I could see even from down below – that it was shaking. A pair of small cat skulls hung from the staff, knocking gently together with the vibrations. A green stone glinted on a rope at his left wrist. A curved long green *papose*, yellow longbow and a quiver of arrows lay against a nearby rock edge.

At the base of the outcrop, poking out from some bushes, I made out the nose of a little yellow boat, the horn of the prow bearing the insignia of cat's eyes – the totem of the Wildcat tribe. Looking closer, I saw that the boat was a coracle like those we used at home, light to carry and swift on water. My heart sped up. Such a vessel could take me across the Erainn even in flood. 'Greetings, sir,' I said, with a loud cough, 'I don't wish to interrupt, but…'

The figure – who of course I assumed was of one of the Wildcat tribes – reacted by raising his staff and banging it down onto the rock, a clatter that echoed around the clearing.

'I'm looking to cross into Erainn, sir,' I shouted up, undeterred. 'I see you have a boat. Can you help me? I have cowries…and moonsilver.'

I waited, but there was no response. I began to feel a little foolish. Finally, after a while, the figure shifted, and pulled back his robe to reveal at his side a curved sword and, beside it, a yellow conch. A conch! Was this the source of the calls I'd heard earlier that day? Still, he didn't speak. He was warning me away! I decided to try again. I was about to shout up my request again when the figure tapped the hilt of his sword. The gesture, I assumed, was a simple one – 'Leave, or else.' Then it came to me that the figure hadn't been talking but praying and was shaking like an *Akari* – a shaman – just as they did at home when incanting, invoking the spirits, naming a newborn, or blessing the dead. Hence the conch, a shaman's conch, and the staff with skulls.

I sighed, ruefully eying the coracle. Then I called up, 'Forgive me for troubling you in your prayers. May Yahl go with you,' I muttered in Ironese, half-heartedly, following the convention. I edged away into the scrub and found my way back to the trail with some difficulty in the gloom.

Coming eventually to another clearing, weary and nearly blind in the darkness, I stumbled straight into a bundle of firewood neatly stacked for drying. Nearby was another, and beside that a third. Walking along the line, I counted nine in total, the last piled beside a rounded dwelling. I recognised the form of this – a *chukka* – a cellular beehive construction of layered stones, where hunters and waysiders could get refreshments, mostly hot *tai*, but also cooked food – invariably stew. At home, *chukkadars* were often Beaver elders no longer able to do the hard labouring of their tribe. *Chukkas* were their homes, and callers-in would share gossip and stories while slaking their appetites.

Creeping up, I stopped to listen for sounds from within. 'My crossbow is armed,' I said aloud, clutching my knife. 'My friends are right behind.' When there was no answer, I tore aside the rug that hung across the entrance and ducked in. There was no-one there, but a fire smouldered and, beside it, a cooking pot with wooden bowls and spoons set to one side. One bowl had been used – someone had recently been here, cooked a meal and gone out. Perhaps they would soon return. A little away from the fire was a small pile of kindling and some logs that looked from the wet moss on them that they'd just been fetched in.

I crouched and waited, eyes on the opening, casting famished glances at the pot. It smelt delectable. Drifts of steam wafted up where the heart of the fire still warmed the pot. Snow was now beginning to fall outside, drifting up to the doorway. On I waited, but no *chukkadar* nor anyone else came. Looking longingly at the pot and the fading fire, I decided it would be a shame and a waste not to use this travellers' shelter and avail myself of its provisions. Not at the very least trying the food would be the greatest shame and waste of all.

Thus, I justified using the *chukka* to my advantage, and decided to leave behind some cowries in exchange. If this was a Morok haunt, my mind – and my desperation – would not have it. And it did not feel like it. So, jumping up and snatching wood from a pile near the entrance, I fed the fire till the flames leapt high and the little round room was full of warmth and light. Outside, a night wind sighed through the river rushes and crack willows, rattling them like beasts in a cage. The snow at the threshold was now piled high, and it really did seem as if no-one was coming, so I pulled the door flap down, secured it with stones and turned my attention eagerly to the pot. I lifted the lid and, inhaling deeply, savoured the aroma within – a trailside stew of fish, dry herbs and *gadera*, the wild forest turnip. I ate my fill, leaving a small amount in the pot as a token offering to the spirits of the place. Sated, I looked for the best place to rest my weary limbs and – now less troubled – soul. The flat stones that served as seats around the fire were bare of the usual welcoming deerskins, but there was a pile of aged and musty fleeces against one wall – an inviting bed for any weary traveller.

A gnarled yew staff lay to one side of the threshold. Fixing it against the opening so that it would fall over if anyone came in, I helped myself to the last of the stew, guiltily scraping the dregs into a bowl. Afterwards, I wrapped a fleece around me, and with my knife and sling on my lap, the *papose* at my head, I leaned back on the fur pile and dozed to the sound of the wind whipping snow against the *chukka* walls.

I slept the sleep of the dead and woke to daylight filtering through cracks in the beehive ceiling. Collecting my things, I checked that the fire was safe, placed three cowries on a stone and went to the door flap.

I stopped. Something was different. Everything looked the same but for two small details: a flint lying on the rug by the door, with a little pyramid of powdered stone beside it. And on the inside wall a claw mark with five talons. Not the sign of the Morok but maybe polecat or wildcat. If it was there the night before, why hadn't I seen it?

Chest thumping, I looked closer. The rough yew staff I'd put at the entrance was still in place, but tiny scrape marks on the soft ground showed that the stones had been shifted. The door flap had definitely been moved and, from the look of it, delicately put back. I sniffed the air. But there were no new scents, just the musty smell of the *chukka* and spent fire ash.

Skraeling? Surely not. Frenziedly, I opened my *papose* and checked its contents. But everything was there; even the crescent-shaped stone, right at the bottom, still wrapped in the blanket. My knife and sling were on the floor, where they'd slipped off my lap in the night. I tore open the flap and looked for tracks in the snow. Nothing. Far too deep. I hadn't been robbed. Nevertheless someone had definitely been here while I slept, seen me, and left.

I looked again at the mark. The five-part claw. Of course – Catamount. Wildcat tribe! That figure on the rock with the cat skulls on his pikestaff, the *Akari*. Something about a Wildcat shaman chimed in my memory, but so much had happened to me in recent days that, at first, I couldn't drag it out. Then I remembered what the Rhuad had said about a Wildcat tracker with the name Og – alike a name Grandfather had often mentioned, of a friend in Erainn. That he could help me. What was it the Rhuad had said when I asked how I'd find him? 'He'll find yeh…'

Well, if it was indeed him, *I'd* found him – and probably this was his lair, not a *chukka* at all. But, as this *Akari* wasn't willing to engage with me at the rock, or here at the *chukka*, there was nothing I could do about it. So, leaving the shelter, I resealed the door flap behind the drifted snow as best as I could and made my way back to the trail, but feeling heavy in my heart, weighed down with fresh mystery and uncertainty. The flashes of confidence my strange find appeared to have given me was, I felt, still there, buried somewhere, but my nerves were frayed.

The snow underfoot had turned to a thick, icy slush that sucked at my boots. Hard going. But soon a new landscape opened up before me of wide snowy marshland dotted with clumps of reed forest poking out from the snowdrifts. This, I remembered from the lost map, must surely be the Carron marshes. The Rhuad had said that there might still be Eronn hiding out here from the Morok. I felt my pulse quicken at the thought.

Gradually the slush on the trail mixed with greeny marsh mud and seeped into my boots, making my feet feel like stones. Tedious wet *hora* rolled by, with no sign of any living thing, not even water birds. Around noonday I paused on some raised ground to dry off a little and rest my aching legs.

That was when I heard the first scream.

10

THE RAID

S parks of ice shot down my spine. There came another scream and a thunderous crash, an explosion – just like the one I'd heard at the Marten's cabin. Then a strange chanting drifted across the marshes, punctuated by raucous shouts:

'Death to the river dogs. Death to 'em all!'

The language was unknown to me, yet…somehow, I understood it.

Without thinking, I sprinted towards the sounds, slipping and stumbling across marsh mud and tussocks, and came to a reed-fringed ridge overlooking a low-lying creek where thick brown smoke poured from the reed mass on the opposite bank. Below, in the creek, two figures were struggling to beach a yellow coracle against the steep side of the far bank. One was tall, male, stout, of middle years, with yellow braided hair peeping out from a green hooded robe. The other, much smaller, also male, wore a light blue robe with its hood down, revealing a tricoloured Eronn mane. Their efforts were being hampered by tongues of flame dropping around them – reed seed heads on fire.

The coracle was marked with the cat's eyes – like the one I'd seen before in the clearing. A staff poked out from the side of the boat – two cat skulls dangling from it. The tall one in the green robe – it was the Wildcat *Akari!*

'Quick, Hiron,' I heard him bark in Ironese, 'take yer paddle. Get the boat back up the creek when I'm gone. Don't let them sparks burn the skin.' Then he jumped from the boat into the water, scrambled up the bank and crawled into the fiery reeds.

A great plume of smoke jumped the creek, engulfing everything. I dropped to my knees to get below the reeking fumes and whipped my kerchief to my face. Then, peering through the reed stalks before me, I glimpsed the source of the fire – a conical building twisting in flame on the far side of the water. Around it, other fires and figures in dark mail staggered and wove between them, waving curved swords. Two had crossbows strapped to their backs; another carried a barbed spear. One was swinging a club in mad circles. A prostrate form lay silhouetted against the blaze. A She-Eronn was kneeling alongside it, keening and tearing her mane.

The sight of her made my heart rise. It could almost have been my mother! My fists tightened; blood rushed to my head. I loosened the drawstring of my pebble pouch, armed my sling, wrapped it round my wrist and scrambled down the slope towards the creek.

As I neared the water, another billow of smoke engulfed me. I fell back against the bank, clutching my kerchief over my nose and mouth. Through streaming eyes, I saw the Eronn on the boat clasping a bow in one hand and an overhanging branch in the other, readying himself to jump from the coracle. But the Wildcat suddenly reappeared out of the maelstrom, yellow hair flying. Scrambling down the bank he screamed at the Eronn, 'Don't let go,' and slid into the water. 'Pass me my sword, bow and quiver. Quick now,' he yelled. 'Don't try to follow. If I don't return, make sure yeh get those weapons to the others.'

Another flurry of smoke surged around us. Through it I heard chanting – 'Morok, Morok, Morok.'

I shouted aloud in Ironese, 'I'm coming to help.'

But I heard no response. Smoke now obscured everything except the water just below me. I plunged in and, holding the *papose* above my head, waded to the other side. But when I reached the far bank no one was there. The coracle was coming loose, banging against the side of the bank, about to drift away.

Thunder rolled in the sky above and a lightning flash strobed the scene in glowing yellow. As I reached for the boat, another flash struck the vessel, heaving it out of the water. Heat raged up my arms and filled my head with greenish-white light. I fell back into the water. Then the light was gone. I lay for a moment in the creek, staring up at the smoky sky, my eyes brimming with stars.

I stood up. Incredibly, I seemed to be unharmed. A deep peace had come over me. Indeed, I felt almost empowered, invigorated – and left with a most curious sensation. For during the second I'd touched the boat and the lightning had flashed, I seemed to be in another place, a space filled with colour and bright light pulsing slowly, like a heartbeat that had slowed down, and everything I saw around me was crystal clear. In that brief moment I was apart from the space I was in, standing outside it looking in, but also part of it. It was as if I'd seen inside the world – a vision of its inner workings. The sensation was like the one when I'd been hit by lightning at the river – just after I'd touched the object in the water that was now in my *papose*. Only this time I seemed to have taken something out if it. Some new physical force. For my muscles and bloodstream coursed with strength, with power.

It began to rain, heavy like a waterfall. I knew what I had to do.

Taking hold of the coracle, I untangled the mooring cord and tied it to a hanging branch. That was when I noticed the virtual armoury of small bows, crossbows and quivers, swords, knives and spears lying at the bottom of the boat. I needed weapons and – remarkably – there they were! Moving quickly, I tucked one of the swords into my belt, threw a small bow and quiver over my shoulder, used a branch to pull myself out of the water onto the steep creek bank and scrambled up the slope. At the top, the smoke was thick and, with the rain pouring down, I could see nothing at all.

Neckerchief over my nose and mouth, I dived towards the conflagration and immediately crashed straight into something moving.

I was sent flying to the ground and, looking up, saw a Morok trooper looming out of the smoke, astonishment in his face. With a roar, he lifted a curved blade and began to bring it down. I tried to move but he was too near and too quick – I was a sitting target. Suddenly, the air around flashed white and green. I felt a surge of electricity pouring through my body. Another lightning strike!

The Morok's blade froze in the air, inches from my face.

As at the river, the world around me seemed to stop. Yet I found that I could move, in slow dreamlike motion, and I could clearly see – the smoke parted on either side of me. I stepped into the gap until I was sidelong my assailant. Then came another flash and the world was back. I lifted the small bow from the boat, swung it hard into the Morok's head and kicked his sword upwards. He dropped to the ground, blood splattering everywhere, mouth open in wordless surprise. His own sword had pierced his neck.

He shook for a moment, then went still.

I stood staring at my victim, killed with a force I hadn't known I possessed.

Grandfather had talked about "hunter's eye", a kind of trance that took over when a kill was nigh. But he'd said nothing about flashes of light and time standing still. I felt a rush of blood to the head, a quickening of my breath. I'd only ever killed game before. For food. This was different – and it had been so easy. First blood! Grandfather had talked too about the power that was transferred from killed to killer during the act of dealing death. "Red rage", he'd called it. But he'd also warned, 'Never let it overwhelm right action. Kill because you have to – not because you want to. Bloodlust is not right action.'

Had this been right action? Surely it had.

A scream came from ahead. I raced towards the sound but in the smoke again collided with someone, this time the young Eronn, crouched over, coughing, trying to catch his breath. I was leaning down to help when a Morok trooper emerged from the gloom swinging a mace. 'Look out,' I screamed, hurling my stolen sword through the air like a spear. It crashed into the chest of the on-comer with a sound like a butcher slicing meat. The force of it sent the trooper flying to the ground, crumpling into the dirt at the Eronn's knees.

The latter lurched backwards, darting terrified glances between the dead Morok and me. 'What...who...?'

For a moment, I stood staring at the corpse, again astonished at what I'd done. This time, though, there had been no green flash. No suspension of time. Whatever power had possessed me, it had been all my own. More screams. I ran into the smoke, shouting back: 'I am friend, brother Eronn. Follow me, stay close.' But when I looked over my shoulder, he wasn't in sight.

The smoke was impenetrable. My eyes streamed. I wiped at them desperately, sensing enemies nearby but unable to see a thing. Digging one foot into the ground, I whirled around and around, sword held out, ready to strike. The gloom closed in, so thick that I had absolutely no idea where the threat was; I could barely tell right from left.

The rain beat down in an unceasing roar. My sword arm began to tremble. Still, I could see nothing. I couldn't even tell where the screams were coming from.

Once, hunting small deer in the mountains with Grandfather, we'd become separated in thick fog and I found myself encircled by timber wolves – a hideous pack of Okwa, growling and creeping closer. All I could do was jab my spear at their ghostly shapes and cry out. Suddenly, Grandfather's voice had boomed out of the mist: 'Feel for raised ground, run, find a tree. Get high. Get above the mist. Show no fear. Make noise, scream at them. A warrior's scream.'

Now his words rang in my ears. I let out the loudest roar I could and ran blindly to one side until I found some raised ground – a mass of reed roots and dead wood. There I clawed my way to the top. It was just enough to get above the smoke. Now, finally, I could see – two helmet tops belonging to a pair of Morok, twisting and turning in the gloom, their ghostly forms backlit by fire, both swinging their swords wildly. I readied my sling. One of them, a She-Morok with a lanky greyish matted mane, saw me, dropped her sword, screamed at her companion and began to arm a crossbow.

I spun my sling. The stone found its mark. She dropped to the ground with a screech. The other made a dash towards me swinging a barbed mace. I spun again. My target flew backwards with the force of the stone, club thudding to the ground, blood pouring from his head.

As I started to reload, a great force thumped me to the earth. My face was pressed into the dirt, the breath driven from my body. I managed to wriggle free, shove the weight off and stumble to my feet. Beneath me was a huge Morok, stone dead, bloody sword clenched in his mitt, a smoking spear embedded in his spine. Above it stood the young Eronn, staring at its shaft, his face ghostly pale.

My *papose* had come loose and lay nearby. I grabbed it and threw it over my shoulder as another cloud of black smoke enveloped us, sparks landing on our robes. Frantically brushing them away, I covered my mouth and nose with my fur collar. 'Where's your Wildcat friend?' I spluttered.

He mumbled between coughs, 'Don't know, sir. Haven't seen 'im.'

'Come, we'll find him. Put this over your mouth and nose and stay low,' I urged, stuffing my neckerchief into his palm. Then, crouching under the smoke, we ran towards the red light in the fog.

Ahead, silhouetted against the blaze, I made out as I ran some moving figures; towering above them was the Wildcat, green stone flashing at his wrist, wielding a sword with one mitt and longbow with the other, hood tossed back, braids whirling in the air, dealing blows around him in a fearful frenzy. As we neared, I saw one Morok fall and another running away, dropping his weapons. I saw him stumble, a knife in his back. A third was on his knees, hands in the air for mercy, but still the Wildcat's sword fell. None of them were a match for this Wildcat shaman, this warrior *Akari* in his fighting fury.

Seeing us running towards him, me in front, the Wildcat turned, armed his longbow with lightning speed and pulled back the string.

'No, Tiroc Og,' screamed the young Eronn, diving in front of me. 'It's me – Hiron. With a friend.' That name. Then I knew, this was Tiroc Og, the tracker, the one the Rhuad said would find me, that he could help me. Cautiously, he lowered his bow.

Suddenly, a Morok trooper emerged from the reeds at his back, crossbow raised. 'Behind you,' I yelled, and released a slingshot. The stone whizzed inches past the Wildcat's ear and struck the Morok's crossbow, sending the shot wide. With a defiant roar, the Wildcat whirled round and fired an arrow. His assailant screamed, tumbled sideways and dropped out of sight, the Wildcat tearing after him.

Looking around for other raiders, I saw the young Eronn tearing towards the burning spars of the conical building. I followed, and what I saw brought rage rising to my throat. For the She-Eronn whose screams had brought me here was now lying deadly still, laid across her mate. Tears rose to my eyes as I saw the young Eronn cradling her head in his lap and bowing over, sobbing bitterly.

I turned slowly in a circle, bow armed and raised ready for any other Morok in sight, vengeance coursing through me. A light wind had appeared, and the smoke began to drift away, exposing in horrible reality an Eronn homestead that was now just a pile of smouldering wreckage. The reed fire was dying away, leaving trails of smoke and a blackened waste.

In that mournful peace, in the clearing smoke and the quiet of death between the creeks, I sank to my heels, exhausted, shaken, overcome by the immensity of what had taken place – and my part in it.

What had happened here? An Eronn home and its householders had been destroyed by a group of crazed drunken predators. For what? How had things in the Erainn, the great holy lands of all the tribes, come to such a pass? And what about me? Charging headlong into extreme danger, turning from an untested warrior into a voracious killer, dealing death in such frenzy that all thoughts of anything else – my own safety, my quest, my kin – had been overtaken. Grandfather had trained me how to fight, but not like this.

I'd acted like a thing possessed! I hadn't imagined the lightning flashes and slowing of time. It was as if some force had been acting through me, rendering me ruthless, merciless against all threats to me, and others.

Contemplating the changes, I suddenly became nauseous and

rolled over onto my side. There were voices in my head, a crowd of them, a babble, not making any sense, screaming for my help. Shrieking voices that reached such a crescendo that I raised my hands to my ears. 'Stop. Stop!' I yelled, shutting my eyes, desperate for rest, for relief.

Relief came quickly. The voices died away. Then came another voice, at first distant, then closer, then crystal clear – and now coming from within me, calming, reassuring. I lifted my head and opened my eyes to see the Wildcat crouching over me, patting my shoulder. I felt as if he was lifting something from me. Then he stood and walked away.

I lay there for a moment, breathing deeply, then I sat up and looked around. The Wildcat was nearby, standing beside the young grieving Eronn, still hunched over the dead Eronn couple. He rested a furred hand upon the youngster's head and talked gently to him, as he had to me. I could hear every word clearly, as if he was standing right beside me. Another change – but not just my hearing, all my senses felt sharper than they'd ever been.

'There's little yeh can do fer yer parents now, Hiron,' I heard him say. 'There's nothing left fer yeh in this place. Yeh're with us now. Collect what weapons yeh can. Wait for me by the boat. Those small trees over there. We can make use of them to make a bier. Go there and select the straightest rods and commence to cut them. I'll join yeh after I've seen yer friend over there.'

The young Eronn trudged away towards some alder bushes, shoulders slumped. As I watched, a wave of something like pain, or loss, swept through me. Eyes welling, I rose to my feet and gazed at the Wildcat now walking towards me, seeing the keen tracker's eyes of the one called Tiroc Og.

'Now,' he said with a gentle smile, 'the wandering Albin.'

'Yes, sir…' I stuttered.

'Yer disturbing me a bit timelier on this occasion, methinks.'

I nodded, remembering my intrusion at the rocks and my annoying persistence.

'Yer first kill?' he asked, gesturing at the Morok corpses.

I nodded again, rising to my feet. I seemed to have run out of words.

'Yeh handle yerself well,' he said, 'and with our weapons.' He pointed his sword at the bow I'd taken from the boat. 'What happened to yer own, young stranger?'

'I have this,' I spoke at last, holding up the sling. 'The...the rest disappeared...were stolen, sir. Back up the trail. At the Sentinel Rock, in the Karst.'

He gave a tiny nod, almost, I thought, as if he already knew. 'Jes' a moment,' he said, and he lifted his yellow conch from his waist belt, put it to his lips and blew three long notes. The response was immediate, if distant. I recognised the calls as the same exchange that I'd heard before. Clearly, from almost the first moment I'd joined the riverside trail, my presence had been observed and was being reported. My instincts were right. I *was* being watched! I hadn't seen them, but they'd seen me. It was all happening just as the Rhuad had said. I'd already been found by the tracker – well before I found him. Then I remembered rescuing the strange object from the river – and gulped. Had they seen this too?

'Are you thinking I'm a spy – come to steal your weapons?' I said clumsily, a little lost for words. I held out the armaments from the boat with both hands. 'I meant only to use them to help you in your fight.' My cheeks flamed, for of course this was not the whole truth.

'Can't say about that, Albin.' He laughed as he tied the conch back onto his waist belt. 'But yeh're certainly good at finding and killing Morok with them.' Resting on his sword, he added, 'Yeh know they'll murder yeh just for being in these parts.'

'So I hear.'

'And they'll take the rest of yer goods,' he said, pointing to my shoulder. I turned and saw my blanket hanging half-out of the top of my *papose*, the curved edge of a dark crescent just visible. I moved to cover it; my hands suddenly clumsy. I felt his eyes boring into me as I fumbled over my shoulder.

'What's the name in yeh, young warrior?' he asked.

'The name in me is Osian, of Faron, from Alba, across the White Mountains.'

'And yeh are here, Osian of Faron, because…?'

'I was hoping to cross the river, but the ferry and the ferry keeper—'

'Gwion, the ferry keeper. Yes, we too have sought him. As indeed have these devils,' he growled and gestured at a Morok corpse.

'What happened at the ferry point?' I queried.

'This same troop destroyed it, probably,' he said, clenching his fist. 'And they did this,' – he glanced around at the devastation – 'thinkin' Gwion was here, hiding. They think he has something they wants badly. Anyways, I have to press yeh…yer reason, if yeh please, fer being here in these troubled times?'

I saw no harm and briefly explained my mission – stressing my need to get across the river. 'The boat you have in the creek, sir? Would you be willing to hire it?'

'Yahl, no, young 'un' he replied, with a shake of his head. 'It's needed fer us to get round the marsh creeks. Anyways, them Morok patrols the river on both sides. They'd fill thon thing with holes like woodpeckers drilling trees well befores it got to midstream – and yeh with it.'

'Then I must find another way,' I said.

He sniffed the air and, with a grunt, turned away, leaving me standing there nonplussed.

I stood for a second, no doubt open-mouthed. Surely, he owed me some better explanation, I thought, never mind that I'd saved the life in him. But it looked like none was forthcoming. In a burst of frustration, I dropped the borrowed sword, bow and quiver to the ground and turned for the creek. But I'd not gone far when a shout came from behind.

'Albin. Wait there. We're not finished.'

I swung round to see him striding towards me with Hiron in tow. Unhooking an Eronn short sword from his belt as he neared, he proffered it with a tiny bow of his head. 'Please to take this,' he said. I drew breath when I saw what it was – the very duplicate of my own lost sword, except that it was slightly curved and the hilt bore the face of a cat, not an otter, its feline features glistening eerily in the dying glow of the flames.

'This was gifted to my father by Gwion,' he said. 'Take. Take this from Tiroc Og, son of Lir Og.'

'Lir Og! He was my grandfather's friend. And you are his son?'

'The same.'

Although I should probably have been surprised, I really wasn't for I was already beginning to learn how little of this encounter was mere chance, a whim of the fates. As for the sword, I remembered Grandfather mentioning that mine was one of two such gifted by Gwion to his friends. And Lir Og was Grandfather's closest friend in his Erainn venture.

'How can I take the sword of Tiroc Og?' I asked formally.

He remained impassive, holding out the sword. 'I owe yeh, Albin. Yeh have my life unless yeh takes this to help keep yer own. Accept it, Osian of Faron, use it well.'

The code among the tribes required that if you saved someone's life, as I had his, their life was, in effect, "yours" until the debt was evened out. This could be by a return gesture, or the gift of something very precious; to a warrior there was nothing more precious than the weapon that bore the totem of their ancestor. Gifted, it had the effect of binding fates together, for good or ill – even beyond the grave. Like the exchange of names, this was part of the universal belief in *almadh*, destiny; the observance of pacts forged in previous lives and revisited in future ones. So perhaps, then, this was one such rebinding of fates; an echo of something that had happened between Tiroc Og's father and my grandfather.

Holding out both hands, I replied in formal tones. 'It is the sword of he of Lir Og that is being offered me. I accept in honour of the bond between the fathers. Lir Og is, I hope, in good health.'

'Sadly, no. Just as the sun sinks into the earth at day's end, the father to me went to the *sidhe* many winters ago, but unlike the sun, he did not rise again. The sun in him was glorious – a life spared the coming of the pestilence that is the Morok.'

'I am saddened to hear this – as will be my grandfather,' I said. I had hoped to encounter Lir Og, as like Gwion, someone Grandfather had said might help me in my quest. But at least here I was in the company of his son – and he, surely, could help me.

We stood together in silence. I fully expected him to ask about Grandfather. But either he'd decided to keep his own counsel or was lost in his memories. Eventually I said, 'I must now make forward my journey, Tiroc Og of Lir Og.' Again, I waited for a response – an offer of help to cross the river would be of far more value to me than any sword.

Finally, he released a deep breath and said, 'My heart has ears, Osian of Faron. But yeh must follow yer own path. I cannot help yeh right *now*. Hiron and I have duties here, things that we must do. As for yeh, meanwhile, it would be wise to follow the river on this side till yeh meet the raised way. It stands above the quick marsh. Look for a circle of trees beside a lake. There is shelter there – yeh'll find sanctuary in that place.'

'No Morok there?'

Glancing over my shoulder, he shook his head. 'I can't say that. They're everywhere now. If yeh see any, use yer hunter instincts, when to hide, when to fly. When there's no other choice, fight like the warrior yeh are now. That's all I can I say. For the present, anyways. Yahl preserve yeh.'

For the present? What did he mean? Did he intend to meet me again? Then, as I readied to leave, Hiron, who'd been standing quietly nearby with head bowed, seemed to rouse himself. He laid a hand on my arm. 'I must thank yeh, sir stranger,' he said, stifling a sob. 'I hope to see yeh again.'

There was no life debt owed here. Hiron had saved my life by acting as he did, just as I'd saved his minutes before. 'And I, too, Hiron. Meantime, Yahl go with you,' I replied.

The tragic loss of his kin brought to mind the dangers that my own must have encountered – perhaps might still be meeting. I just had to hope that there were others around them to help them in their time of need. 'I wish both of your lives well,' I said, turning away.

I left to the sound of raised voices coming from behind me. It sounded like the young Eronn was pleading. What was being said,

I could not tell. But the subject was clear enough – me.

Wading across the creek I passed the coracle with a regretful look. Surely it could be used to cross the river by night, when the Morok patrols could not possibly see anything? If I were a thief, I could have just taken it there and then. But I was no thief.

I heard the conch, echoing out across the marshes – three notes, loud and clear. It was Tiroc Og the Wildcat, signalling to others – maybe that I was on my way again. And at this, a curious idea – a revelation perhaps – came to me. I wasn't being watched! I was being watched *out* for.

Once I was back on the other side of the creek and on the trail, I heard it again, coming from further up the marsh. I looked back and smiled. The Wildcat's call had been answered.

Someone knew I was coming.

11

ROMI

Afternoon set in, bitterly cold, sunless and heavy clouded. In places, the Erainn's swollen waters spilled over the river trail, yet the ground felt hard. Like my purpose, I thought, renewed, firm. I had weapons again, even if they weren't my own, and a place along the trail to seek out, a sanctuary. Maybe even company.

I strode forward through wintry willow and alder scrub overtopping rushes and reeds bulbous with seed heads. The death and fury of the morning, and the prickling feeling at the easy taking of life, began gradually to dim. I'd repaired the rent in my *papose*. The crescent stone lay deep in Mara's woven blanket like a thing asleep, a small animal hibernating away from the river land's wintry bane.

It seemed somehow right that it was there – even though I didn't know what it was. If the Wildcat knew something, he wasn't telling. I remembered his expression when he saw it poking out of my *papose*. Curiosity, yes. But also, a flash of concern, almost fear, in those cat-like eyes. Did *he* know what lay within that dark shell? And seeing his concern, why did I not feel more worried about it – and the fact of me carrying it, unable to separate myself from it.

I reflected on this and the changes that had come over me – the furious fighting spirit, the enhanced senses, and the appearance in me of fighting skills that I'd barely trained in. I'd automatically assigned these to some freak effect of the lightning strikes, but the more I thought about it, the more I wondered if the changes had, in fact, something to do with my strange acquisition – the crescent-shaped object now in my *papose*. Was *this* the real source of the changes, not some random storm event? The odd sensations I'd experienced when I first rescued it, the stopping of time, the sensation of being in another world, first happened when I rescued it from the water. If the "stone" was indeed sorcerous, were its powers being used to aid and assist me, as the one who carried it?

I stopped by the side of the trail, sat on a boulder and took the stone out of my *papose*. There I examined it for the second time, rolling it around in my hands and looking for a sign, any clue as to what might lie within the smooth dark shell. Even with the Morok mark on it, and the memory of it in the cavern, it felt benevolent to me. I felt comfortable in its presence. More, with it in my possession, I had the oddest sensation of all – I felt complete in myself, almost as if finding this strange object was the purpose to my life! And I wondered if I'd somehow been meant to come across it; it was part of what Grandfather would have called my destiny, my *almadh*. Its fate and mine were somehow linked – at least until I could find out who it really belonged to, and how I could return it to them.

Gently placing it back in my *papose*, covering it with my blanket and strapping the *papose* over my shoulders, fastening the straps at the front tighter than usual, I rose and, carefully checking around me, I rejoined the trail.

As I walked, contemplating my new situation, I knew I hadn't the remotest idea what the "stone" was, other than something within an outer shell that I'd seen being created at the command of Morok priests, then branded by them before being lost to them. So how was I to think of it? How was I to put a name to something that I didn't understand?

After a while, an answer of sorts came to me. When I'd first briefly spotted it in the cavern, it shone with the brilliance of the sun, yet with a silvery hue, as if an alchemist had forged together the best sungold with the brightest moonsilver. It was a luminous moonsilver-like glow that had later drawn me to the water when I rescued it. And, of course, it had the shape of a crescent moon. In simple *Askrit*, the word for both sun and sunshine is *sol* and the word for moon and moonshine is *lon*. Combined, these form the word *sol-lon*, or *solon,* which has its own meaning: shining. So even if sheathed in some kind of shell-like material, that allows no light in or out, what lies inside is something that shines. Add *solon* to *skim*, the *Askrit* for stone, and it becomes *solon skim*, the shining stone.

And thus, I named it, but in the shortened *Askrit* form, *Solon*, the shining.

As for finding out what it was, or might be, I had one possibility – the Wildcat. He'd seen it and reacted. He knew something; of that, I was sure.

I resolved then that, should we meet again, I'd show it to him – ask outright. Surely, the son of Grandfather's friend – if indeed that's who he was – could be trusted with the secret of it? But, as I thought this, the warning of the Rhuad rang between my ears like a calling bell – 'Trust no one.' Perhaps it would be best not to ask. Better to wait to see what, if anything, developed.

Since I'd rejoined the trail, the far side of the river had been obscured by fog. But now, this had almost completely lifted. Gaps in the riverside thickets already revealed a huddle of buildings on rising ground across the water – the beginnings of a hill settlement of some kind. Was it Iteron? Grandfather's map had shown the holy city as lying just downriver from the source of the Erainn, in the midst of the fertile river lands. Iteron was fabled through Manau, and no doubt beyond, for its great beauty – its conical red roofs, drum-like tors, needle temple pinnacles and its famous *Solar*, a spiralling sky-high sun tower that was both shrine to Yahl the Creator and a meeting place for the elders and priests of the city.

But my excitement at the prospect of coming to Iteron quickly turned to horror and more disappointment. For when I climbed up the levee, the buildings appeared to be just roofless ruins, stretching beyond them nothing but dark, shapeless piles of stone.

I surveyed the scene, looking out for the *Solar*. The only tall structure visible was a spiral staircase that rose out of a rubble mound. The steps looked broken, the final one hanging at an odd angle in empty space. From it dangled a battered blood-red flag, in its centre a dark circle and a three-claw insignia.

Morok!

As I watched, a column of dark figures suddenly marched into view from the back of one of the ruins. Dangerously exposed atop the levee, I dived down into a clump of bulrushes, lay on my stomach and pulled aside the stems to see what was going on. The figures, dressed like the raiders back in the marsh in dark chainmail were of many differing shapes and sizes – fat, thin, tall and short, and heavily armed. I saw barbed spears and crossbows, double headed aber-axes, curved swords and maces strapped across backs or belted at waists.

The column came to a halt behind a male figure in a blue and brown robe like a jay's feathers, a patch over one eye, taller, thinner than all the others. His arm was raised and on a hawker's glove an eagle fluttered its wings. Suddenly, alarmingly, the bird turned in my direction, stabbed a claw straight at the spot and squawked loudly. My stomach lurched.

The hawker started, shot a glance in my direction and screamed a command at the column. In seconds they were running down the slope of the hill towards the river and the far levee, brandishing spears and arming crossbows.

No doubt. The eagle's eyes had caught me. I'd been seen!

In an instant the sky was black with crossbolts, plummeting like hail, but falling just short of me – the first wave splashing into the river, the second wave thumping into the mud just below where I hid. One even bounced upwards through the rushes at my face, making me flinch. I crawled backwards, intending to make a dash back over the levee and head for the pinewoods behind, but I saw the hawker release the bird and gesture at someone or something just downriver from where I was hiding. Morok – on my side of the water?

Heart racing, I jumped to my feet, but still within the bulrushes. Which way should I go? As I wavered, I heard yelling from nearby and, along with it, the rattle of armour and the tramp of feet. Above me a great shape began to circle, pinpointing my position.

There was nothing else for it. Clutching my weapons in one hand, my *papose* tight to my back, I leapt out of the bulrushes and dived headlong into the freezing floodwaters. We Albin Otar are very strong swimmers, even encumbered with packs, clothing and weaponry, but no match for a raging current. I was tossed downstream like a cut log. Unable to control my direction, I could feel the weight of my robes, boots, *papose* and weapons dragging me under. But if I could just hang on, the racing flood might pull me beyond the reach of my pursuers.

After a while, gasping breath between mouthfuls of water, the current eased. I was able to lunge towards a nearside bank and grab an overhanging branch. Bracing my feet against the bankside I gained a hold, slung my weapons onshore and hauled myself out. There I crouched in the scrub shivering violently, wet robes stiff with the cold and listened for any sounds of pursuit.

I had to find shelter – somewhere to dry off, somewhere better to hide. Desperately, I looked around. Above my head were the needle encrusted branches of a clump of pines. Everywhere else was thick with impenetrable thorny undergrowth. From far off I heard a horn – or was it a conch? I thought of the Wildcat. But if it was him, I had no means of calling out to him without revealing my new position.

In the event it wasn't long before the ground vibrated with the thumping of feet and the rattle of weaponry. I crawled deep into a mass of thorny bushes, sliding between the lowest boughs, the dark shadow of the eagle passing over, hunting me down. Blackthorn barbs tore at my face and hands, and blood from the scratches blurred my vision. Shadowy figures were soon in the bushes, slashing with axes, cutting a path through the thicket towards me. The scrub around me was so dense and thorny I could crawl no further; my arms and legs were shaking, the wet clothing and furs against my skin already frosting white, my fingers and toes becoming numb.

A bolt shot through the bushes past me, then another, the second closer than the first. 'Yahl save me,' I muttered and, raising my sword, steeled myself for the onslaught.

Suddenly, a thin dark shape plummeted down towards me. I rolled on to my side and slashed wildly upwards, only contacting branches, bringing a shower of needle thorns raining down on me. Then the thing came to an abrupt halt just above my nose. To my astonishment, it was a rope!

I heard a voice, gruff but female, calling down in Ironese, 'Catch the riggin', stranger. Grab and hold tight. It'll bring yeh to me.'

I hesitated, but not for long. Another bolt shot through the bush, the barbs grazing the side of my face. I grabbed the rope and found myself being dragged at speed out of the bushes and high up into a tree. When it stopped, I found myself beside a branch thick with frozen snow.

'Wrap the rope round yer middle, tie it tight, 'n' pull. Quickly now,' said the voice. I still couldn't see the speaker, whoever she was. A bolt thudded into the branch, sending snowy splinters into my legs.

I moved quickly, fumbling the rope with the numb fingers of my free hand, and managed to knot it around my waist. 'Done,' I said through chattering teeth. There was a whoosh of air, and I was falling – no, I was flying – the breath knocked out of me, the wind whistling past my face, a forest of red-bark pines whirling dizzyingly round my head. Now I was swinging in wide looped arcs, going higher and higher, faster and faster, now forwards, now sideways from one treetop to another. Then, before I knew it, I was dumped on to a wide branch high in the canopy, the wood below me swimming, drifts of dislodged snow spiralling everywhere around. I looked down, and my stomach heaved.

'Don't try to turn. Close yer eyes,' whispered the voice – now right over my shoulder. 'Get yer sea legs first. Take big breaths, slowly till yer stops spinning. I'm going to untie yeh.'

I breathed deeply until the dizziness abated. When I finally opened my eyes, the trail was some distance away – as was the thorn thicket where I'd sheltered. I could just make out a melee of Morok troopers poking their spears into the bushes, whistling and yelling.

'Don't worry. They can't sees yeh up here,' said the voice. 'Yeh can look round now.'

Sat astride the branch was a stout female of an unfamiliar tribe, draped in a blue–green cloak, the sea-going garb of the Aguan. Her nose was flat and high between pointed ears nestled in a jungle of red hair in pigtails, each weighted with seashells. Gold earrings peeked out over rosy but lightly scarred cheeks, and she wore necklaces of thick rope that disappeared into the depths of the tree. At her waist hung a curved Aguan cutlass. Despite the scars, she was beautiful, a creature in her middle years, with twinkling eyes and tanned skin. On her face was a roguish grin.

I glanced below and my head began to spin again. 'I can't stay on this,' I said.

She chuckled and attached the rope at my middle to a loop round the branch. 'Here. This'll allow yeh to crawl along behind me. And I'll catch yeh if yeh fall.' Then, grabbing the Wildcat's bow and sword from me, she elegantly tiptoed along the branch to where it met the trunk of the tree. 'Close yer eyes again and let your limbs take yeh. I'll do the rest. Quickly now.'

I allowed myself to be guided towards the trunk, where I could feel the branch was wider, and opened my eyes. She'd gone, but a bundle of interwoven ropes hung in her place.

'What?' I hissed.

'Shh! I'm up here. Grab the riggin' and climb.'

Anxious to be somewhere more solid, I duly clambered up towards an ice-encrusted ball of twigs resembling a hanging giant hornet's nest. She was inside, her smiling face visible through a hole in the bottom of the twig ball. From this dangled another thickly knotted rope. 'Untie yerself first,' she urged, 'or yeh'll end up dangling in mid-air, perfect target fer those varmints.' Obediently, I loosened the knot around my waist, grabbed the hanging rope and felt her hoisting me up into the ball.

Wide-eyed, I stared at my surroundings. The nest was a perfect sphere made out of interwoven twigs lined with moss and bark. From its curved sides hung various items of boat craft including the jawbone of a giant fish, a rusted anchor, some wooden floats and a ship's wheel. There was a slit window high on one side below which dangled a hammock draped with furs. On a low shelf on the floor was a stone flag on which sat an ornately smithed metal fire-ring. Charcoals glowed inside it. A frame suspended from the ceiling supported various cooking utensils, clothing and a lit candle in a glass ball. On the roof to one side was a smoke hole. A fire in a tree made the place so warm that steam was already pouring off my soaked robes and making me sweat. It all seemed highly improbable – but no more so than the colourful character in ringlets sitting on the bed, toying with a thin clay pipe and eyeing me with a toothy smile.

'Take a bench,' she said, pointing to a log on the floor behind me. 'Yer quite safe up here in me crow's nest.' She placed the Wildcat's weapons on the floor, dipped a handful of tree moss into a bowl and handed it over. 'It's not sphaggy or sea-green but it will clean yer scratches up wonderfully.'

'I've been rescued,' I said, receiving it and wiping my face and hands, a little taken aback by how much blood came away on the moss. My limbs were stiff and weary. 'My life – it is now yours.'

'Doesn't know about that. Yeh'll be a hunter. Us seafarers don't follow that daft code. If we did, we'd be owin' each other's lives to ourselves all over the place,' she replied, chuckling. 'Anyways, them pirates must want yeh alive, else those bolts they're usin' would be purple-tipped – deadly nightshade. And they'd have found their mark by now. Anyways, Romi's the name in me. Tarsin tribe.'

'Tarsin – Flying Fox, yes. I've heard of them. But the first time I've met one of your—' A piercing whistle from below cut me short.

'By the god of the seas, one of them bloomin' varmints right under us,' she whispered, crouching over the opening. 'Here, take a look.'

Sliding off the bench, I could just make out between gaps in the branches a wiry figure far below standing in a snowdrift. He looked like the Morok hawker I'd seen across the river – tall and long in face, with a patch on one eye.

I heard a fluttering of wings nearby. The eagle, again. I froze.

'Relax,' urged the She-Tarsin. 'The varmints can't see us here unless yeh moves or shakes me crow's nest. Keeps very still.'

The hawker was aiming a crossbow upwards, wavering it about, looking for a target. The eagle passed by again, wings flapping in hunting mode, making rapid changes in direction. Then it was gone.

'Don't worry. They're just guessing, they can't see into the tree – too many branches,' my companion whispered, casually shifting her attention towards the bowl of her pipe, examining it closely. 'Blocked again,' she muttered, 'should keelhaul the bloomin' thing.'

While she fussed with her pipe, I waited for what seemed like an age. The hawker below remained as he was, still looking up. The fire had gone down, and I was beginning to shake uncontrollably with the cold, my vision blurring. I began to slump, teetering towards the hole.

'Watch out, matey,' she snapped, grabbing my shoulder and pulling me upright. 'Ahoy, that was close. Look, the varmint's off at last.'

I glimpsed the hawker dropping his weapon and moving away. But abruptly he whipped round and aimed his bow directly at the nest. Suddenly, a shrill scream sounded from nearby. He cursed, lowered his bow and loped away in the direction of the sound, barking orders. One by one, others appeared from the bushes, gathered in a line behind him, then tramped towards the trail upriver. Before long, they were out of sight and hearing.

The She-Tarsin stood, the ropes around her waist dangling, spat through the hole, tapped the contents of her pipe bowl down it, and with a hiss of breath said, 'They're gone. Devils, all. I'd put 'em to the plank, I would. Feed 'em to the sharkies. But look at yeh. Yer shiverin' to yer death. Take yer robes off. Put this fur round. I'll dry yer things over them coals. I'll not look,' she added with a laugh.

While I changed, she blew on the fire embers, refuelled them, added liquid to a pot and settled it over the coals as they sparked back to life. 'Yeh'll have *tai*?'

'Thank you, yes,' I said, huddling close to the coals in her bearskin robe, feeling myself begin to thaw. Steam rose in clouds from my robes, now festooned like hammocks over the frame above the fire. I sat silently sipping the drink while my saviour puffed away on her pipe.

After a while, she turned my robes over, pronounced they were drying well, and said, 'Yer probably wonderin' what them below is up to?'

'Hunting me?' For that was how it had seemed.

'They's the guards of the souther curfew, beatin' the outer bounds, lookin' fer unwary victims, though they's not normally so persistent like.'

'What d'you mean?' I pulled my hands back from the fire.

'Well, they're usually more careless like. Not so pitched. There's been lots of runaways in recent moons.'

'Runaways?'

'Escaped prisoners. Off them wagons going to Rakhaus, up in the Kaliyag, the Firehills,' she said, 'where they become slaves, making weapons fer the Morok. Rakhaus is huge, I'm told. Bigger than Iteron ever was, better fortified they say than any man-o'-war. There's no escape from it, I understand, not even...' She paused, sadness in her voice. '...for old buccaneers.'

My kin. Could they be in this Rakhaus place? 'What kind of prisoners? What tribe?' I asked.

'All kinds. Eronn, Wildcat, Beaver, other tribes in their thousands. Forced to work and half-starved to boot,' she replied, tears forming in her eyes. 'Kami, me twin brother, was taken there when the Aguan ship he was masterin' ran aground during a helm.' Wiping her cheek, she took down a *baco* pouch from a shelf, pulled out a fresh tangle of smoke weed and began refilling her pipe.

'There are Aguan there too?' I pressed.

'Well, no, not as such,' she said, sparking a twig from the fire coals for her pipe, then blowing a thin trail of smoke up through the roof vent, the smell reminding me immediately of Grandfather's evenings by the fire with friendly Aguan traders. 'Not as slaves, anyways, but its Aguan ships and wagons they use to take the slaves to Rakhaus. Damn

106

'em, collaborators that they've become, traitors. I'd keelhaul 'em all, every last one, and feed 'em to the deep along with 'em Morok pirates.' At this, she coughed violently. A plume of smoke tumbled out of her mouth and nose, filling the nest. Many in Alba didn't like Aguan – well, any incomers, really – and couldn't understand why my family were so friendly with them. Maybe, I thought now, there might have been wisdom in that.

'Are *all* Aguan collaborators?' I asked.

'Not all, no. But there's some kind of dirty deal between their chiefs and the Morok.'

I thought of the murdered wagon drivers hung up between the rocks in the river. The Morok had clearly thought nothing of killing them – and making a show of it. 'Are any of *my* kind there – in this Rakhaus?' I finally asked, heart now thumping in my chest.

'And what kind would that be, young sir, I wonders? No, don't tell me. Let me guess. I can see yeh have a Wildcat sword. But then mine is Aguan. So, yer certainly from one of the Otar groups o' tribes, them with the otter totem, either Albin or Eronn, I can see that.' She looked me up and down, scratched her chin then said confidently, 'Yer either Albin or Eronn. Yer certainly Albin coloured – with yer mane and skin – from the few I've met. But yer eyes, yer eyes, they're not Albin – they're blue likes the Eronn.'

'Yes, I'm half and half. Born in Alba, the father of me is Albin, the mother is Eronn.

'Ah, that's it,' she mumbled, nodding her head and busily fumbling with her ropes.

'My kin travelled this way about twenty moons ago – on a pilgrimage to Arkesh. They were with Aguan, in an Aguan *vardon*. I don't suppose you saw them by chance – or heard of their passing nearby?'

She shook her head and said sadly, 'Not a good time to be roun' these parts – wi' them Morok everywhere.'

'I knew nothing of this when I left Alba. Are there many of these Morok in Erainn, and Rakhaus?'

'Numbers unfathomable, I hears, like the waves in the sea. Anyways, young Eronn–Albin,' she said, 'not much we can do about 'em up this here old tree.'

'This then,' I waved at the walls of the nest, 'is your home?'

'Time being anyways,' she replied. 'No tradin' ships these days – except collaborators. And I wouldn't serve on one of them if yeh gave me all the treasure in the deep.' She looked into my eyes. 'Howevers, too much about me. What's the name that's in yeh, young Albin?'

I told her, and then said, 'Why did you help me…Romi? I must ask.'

She shrugged. ''Tis nothing for me,' she said. 'I'd help any of the free tribes in peril but not one of 'em bloodthirsty sea pirates.'

This made me think what the Rhuad said – how they'd appeared suddenly in Manau off ships. 'Sea pirates. Is that what they are?' I asked.

'Not all. Yeh knows there's two types o' Morok – one is Ferok, like thon varmint down below, tall and very cunning. The Ferok are them that is mostly in charge, 'cept some of them are called Krol, Morok witch-priests, 'orrible they is. Ferok 'n' them Krol are an ancient Manau tribe but,' she added with a grimace, 'were banished to the ice deserts and forbidden from enterin' the pilgrim lands by the Eronn, fer, I understands, dealin' in devilry. Now they're back here in charge of everythin', joined to the hip with the outlanders.'

'Outlanders – the pirates?'

'Yes, that's 'em others. We don't know where they hails from. They're not sailin' tribes that's fer sure and didn't come from any of the Manau territories or islands that we knows of. But the ships they come off were not yer usual Aguan two-masted or four-masted *scuds* but large ship-o'-war lookens like skulls – a type we'd never seen before in these parts, and I've certainly never sailed. They're not like the Ferok, most of, they're drudges wi' little about them, 'cept good at obeying orders. But if they don'ts, I understand, they don't survives. An' they live in fearful dread o' him they call Kahl – who's not 'un o' them, nor Ferok either, and his chief capn' – a really nasty Ferok called Krachter.'

I tried to digest all this new information – which certainly tallied with everything I'd learned from the Rhuad and the Marten. There were so many names and terms to remember: Morok, Krol, Ferok, Kahl, Krachter. But even at home – with so many different tribes and clans – I could be confused. Now I was hearing about sailing craft very different from the tiny, Barod-built, lake-land coracles and bigger curraghs on our lakes that probably wouldn't do well in open icy seas.

'That…Ferok then, the one below – and with the eagle – he's the one that gives orders. He looked the same as the one I saw across the river. How did he get across the flood?'

'There's more than just 'un. And more than 'un eagle too. But 'tis true yeh don't see 'em Ferok much this side of the river, young Oshan. So, there must be summit up for him to be here. Summit up, indeed.'

I tried to ask more questions, but the She-Tarsin raised her hand. Enough, she indicated. She seemed to be tired of talking about it. And tears were often in her eyes, upset by much of it – her imprisoned brother, those strange ships, the Morok cruelties, the invasion of the holy lands. So, we contemplated the fire in silence while she poured more *tai*, the hot liquid slipping down my throat like velvet, warming, enlivening.

'Not been tae Alba meself,' she muttered after a while, turning over the glowing coals. 'Sounds too cold fer me. I prefers warm sea waters, not hidin' behind a bunch of ice hillocks!' She started to laugh, taking me with her.

It was a relief to laugh. I'd never heard the White Mountains being called "ice hillocks" before, but from a distance – and up a tree – I supposed that they would indeed look like small icy bumps on the horizon.

Still laughing, she stood to adjust the clothes on the frame but suddenly tripped over a rope loop and disappeared from sight! I leaned over the nest hole and watched helplessly as she crashed and bounced down through the tree until her neck became caught between a pair of crossed branches. There she lay completely still.

'Romi. Are you alright?' I shouted down. No answer.

I shouted again. Nothing. I'd have to go after her! My heart pummelling, I took up a rope end, looped it round the bench and threw down the coil, meaning to try to climb down. I watched it plummet below, my stomach weaving with every bounce. The rope end landed upon her nose, at which she abruptly came to and righted herself. She was still laughing! With a glance upwards, she somersaulted onto a branch and, to my amazement, the flaps of her cloak opened up as wings which she used to launch herself into the air and then glide soundlessly between the branches, deftly moving upwards with each flap. In seconds, she was back in the nest as if nothing had happened, pulling up the redundant rope after her.

'I was just kidding, young 'un. But thankee fer the rope though,' she said, rubbing her neck. I wasn't wholly convinced.

When she'd finally settled, she began humming what sounded like a sea shanty. It was a mood change so, still full of queries, I took my chance and asked, 'Your tribe, the Tarsin. Is that one of the Erainn tribes?'

'Yes, though most off we're looked down on by the Eronn – which is odd, considerin' they have to looks *up* to see us,' she replied with a cackle. 'We're seafarers, though the old saws tell us we originally came out of the deep forests, and it wuz from masterin' the treetops that the tribe learned how to manage mizzen masts and topgallant cloths. My first memory was of flyin' between the billowin' masts o' sailin' *scuds* across the Lake of Risin' 'n' Fallin' Water.'

I could just imagine, even with her squat shape, soaring between the sails, cloak outstretched – every inch the seafarer. I smiled at the thought.

'Seen the strangest sights on my voyages,' she continued, 'tribes and even sea monsters like you wouldn't believe, young Albin. But never came across nothin' in foreign parts, I haves to say, like 'em blasted Morok.'

'I saw what they did to Iteron – and the ferry crossing,' I said.

She growled. 'Many's a good friend of mine perished defendin' it. Sticks, stones and hay pikes are no match against barbed crossbows, poison spears and aber-axes.'

'Why do they do this – these terrible things?'

'Ah! It's all about control. Control of everythin' – territory, ground huggers, sheep, cattle, borders, victuals, fishin' and farmin' produce, even wild fruit. Thon Kahl, their leader, him whose face is never seen, tells all 'em Morok what to do, and if they don't do it, they die. Simple as thon – and as cruel.'

'How was this allowed to come about?' I asked.

She shook her head. 'The loss o' the Marcher Lairds, the Marsh Wars, then the coming of the helm storms set the Eronn adrift. They needed help and sought it out but took it from strange shores. Now look at 'em – what's left, anyway. Thems that aren't killed or taken on the prison wagons have flown like the swallows from the land that was once theirs.'

'What of the other tribes?'

'Well, round here there's only no Morok in the Brach or Sideag territories – yet.'

The Brach, I knew, were the most powerful tribe in all of Manau. They were traditionally great rivals to the Eronn, and the homeland they shared with the Sideag, the Grey Wolf tribe, where both tribes kept cattle and hunted for food – Clachoile, the Stone Forest, was vast but notoriously harsh.

'Them tribes have enough to worry about with the long winter and everythin' and, of course, they don't much likes the Eronn. The Easter Lands, where the tribes of the coast, mostly Aguan as yeh may knows, are only "free" 'cos they collaborate with the Morok, supplyin' ships and fish catches to Kahl's armies, scum that they is. The Wester Lands, though, they're still controlled by the Rhuad and their allies. As fer Alba and the other Souther Lands – you'd know about that, surely?'

'No. There's no Morok in Alba.'

'Not yet, young 'un,' she said. 'Give 'em time. They'll soon be there.'

I felt chilled at the prospect. Grandfather. My aunt. The sooner I found my kin and returned home to warn and help family and friends the better.

'We'd resist.'

Romi gave me a blank look. I could imagine many at home who *wouldn't* resist – the same narrow kind that didn't like the sea gypsies or the wandering mendicants that roamed our roads in the warm seasons, begging alms in return for prayers and blessings, but could be easily bullied by outlanders bearing arms. Some might even collaborate – I shuddered at the thought.

'But there *is* resistance in these parts, this I know,' I said. I thought of the raid, the "others" the Wildcat mentioned, and that weapons cache in his boat. And those conch calls – were they messages between resisters?

'Just a few of…' She cut herself short, I was sure, before she said the word 'us'. 'And,' she added with a smile – maybe a touch of pride, 'there's them painted warriors o'er in the Terai forests – renegade Eronn, Wildcat, Brach, Sideag and other tribes, even some rebel Aguan. Small numbers though. Their cap'n's summit special, I tell yeh. Cana-Din's the name in her, with sky-blue eyes, and wonderful to behold – so long as yeh're not at the receivin' end of one of her fire arrows. For she's a deadly shot.'

Sky-blue eyes. I thought of the vision in the Marten's fire – Erin's eyes, fathomless like deep sky on a summer's day – and my heart skipped.

'Anyways,' Romi carried on, 'good luck to her, I say – so long as she keeps to killin' them that tooks my brother. The Morok hates her for it. But Cana-Din's rebel raids are small beer, small takings. Morok is evil, and as Aehmir says, "Evil is as evil does." Old Aehmir warned about the coming of a dark army. But, humph, did they listen?'

Aehmir again. That name – the doomsayer in the Marten's story, same name as the writer of my little book of sayings. I didn't pursue it – I'd already asked enough. And there was something about the friendly She-Tarsin, maybe in her manner, or just my instinct that told me to be wary of her. She'd helped me, saved me even, but I had the feeling I wasn't getting the full picture of her. Maybe though, it had something to do with the resistance, maybe her role in it, for she clearly hated the Morok.

Then something odd happened. In the midst of refilling her pipe and absently humming a tune, she suddenly reached for my *papose* and said, 'I'll dry this for yeh, young one.'

'No. Please,' I said, grabbing it just as she touched it. 'I'll sort… see what needs drying.' I pulled it towards me and began checking its contents but taking nothing out.

'As yeh like,' she said, turning back to fiddling her ropes, but casting a sideways glance at the *papose*. Only then did I notice the crescent-shaped impression at its base. The heat of the fire had tightened the damp goatskin round it. It had been the side facing her and she'd surely noticed the shape – maybe even the indents of the Morok brand. As with the Wildcat, I sensed suspicion. Did these two know something about what I was carrying?

For a fleeting second, I wondered if I'd been pulled from one trap into another more subtle one. For Romi's sudden appearance had almost been too good to be true. And her interest in drying the *papose* seemed more than that – it was as if she was reaching for the stone itself, and maybe with more than just curiosity.

As I shuffled the contents of the *papose* to ensure that what was in there was well covered, I vowed again, with a determination that seemed more than my own, that until I knew more about my curious find, the object I'd named the shining stone would remain a secret. This was to be *my* secret, hidden from all. And I no longer felt the need to question where this desire, this impulse, came from. If before it was from a force outside, now it was coming from deep inside of me.

There was a noise coming from below. Romi clambered up the ship's wheel and put her ear to the slit window. 'Shhh… Listen,' she whispered, as she jumped down and pointed to the entrance hole. 'Look.'

I expected to see Morok, but from a billowing fog issued a crowd of ground huggers, badgers, foxes and rabbits, followed by deer and then small wild ponies. They ran in blind panic, crashing into and over one another, sending snow, ice shards, frozen mud and broken branches flying into the air. Vibrations shook the tree, causing some of Romi's knick-knacks to drop off the shelves and clatter around us.

Then they were gone, the sounds fading into the distance. The ground they'd trampled was black with churned up slush and broken wood, and littered with the bodies of smaller creatures crushed underfoot.

'What's going on?' I spoke. Romi's face was turned away. I thought I saw a tear on her cheek; and I, a hunter, also felt grief at the scene – the useless waste of life.

From deep in the forest, three long conch notes rang out.

'Where is it?' Romi muttered, rummaging under a cloth bundle. 'Here somewhere. Ah, found it.' She produced a ram's horn, lifted it to her lips and blew three times. Then she strapped the horn to her waist and muttered. 'Sorry, young 'un. I needs to go.'

'What about me? I can't stay up here,' I said. Once again, as with the Log Marten, my host was about to abandon me and leave me in their lair. This time, though, I'd never get out on my own.

'Yer kit'll be dry by now. I'll set yeh down. Don't worry,' she answered, grabbing my robes from the frame. 'Dry indeed. Keeps thon fur, though. Yeh may need it in this cold.'

I nodded my thanks and, feeling hurried, dragged on my robes, grabbed my weapons and tied Romi's fur to the base of my *papose*.

'That stampede down there,' she said. 'It's an escape from Morok cages. Someone's let 'em poor critters loose.'

'What are you going to do?'

'Can't say, can't say, young 'un,' she replied, gathering rope into a coil, wrapping one end around my waist and tying it so tight I gasped. 'Now, close yer eyes.' Without warning, she pushed me out of the nest and I plummeted through the air, stomach in my mouth. In seconds, I was back on the ground, dizzy but without a scratch, unlike the ruin of animals and broken branches at my feet.

Romi landed gracefully alongside me and, unwrapping the rope from mine and then her waist, threw it over her shoulder and said, 'Wherever yeh go, stay in sight of the trail, and keeps yer eyes and ears wide open. If yeh hears Morok coming, take to wet ground, wettest yeh can find.'

The horn sounded again from upriver. Romi glanced in its direction, then pointed through the thicket. 'The trail's back over there,' she said. 'If yeh get challenged, pretend to be lost. They may let yeh go, just for the pleasure they'll take in givin' yeh false steerins so ye'll fall into a sink marsh. Take these fer your journey,' she added, handing over a scarf that had been tied into a bundle. Inside it I felt hard lumps.

I bowed my thanks. 'What is it?'

'Tree nuts. Good raw or cooked. Squirrels aren't the only ones that eats 'em,' she answered. 'Only the difference is…' she paused.

'The difference is…?'

'I remembers where I hides 'em.' And, with a cackle, she bounded away.

I watched her join the trail upriver, her motions clumsy on the ground – for I saw she was bow-legged. I waved and called out, 'I shan't forget your kindness, Romi.'

'First yeh've to keep alive,' came the reply. 'Go well. Think of ol' Romi and her twin when yeh kills yer next Morok.' And with that, she was gone.

Next Morok? How could she have possibly known that I'd already killed Morok? But then she moved so swiftly between the treetops anything was possible. And who knew what those conch calls conveyed. With a shrug I tied her bundle to my waist belt and headed for the river trail.

Coming a little later to a gap in the river levee, I noticed the water level had dropped; the swell, though the flow was no less rapid, was just as dangerous. The air seemed a little warmer, though not enough to melt the snow. I felt comforted by this, and my encounter with the jovial She-Tarsin had been cheering, apart from the obvious; though she did make me feel wary. But it was good anyway to be back alongside the sacred river Erainn, a breathing, pulsing force, meandering towards its own destiny. It was alive and, for the moment anyway, it was all the company I had.

12

AVALOR

efore me lay a forest of reeds – patchy at first, then becoming denser along both sides of the trail. The track, such as it was, veered away from the river onto higher ground. A strengthening wind made the reed sward sway like a thing alive, whipping up showers of seed heads. Thunder, distant at first, rolled nearer and more frequent. Black clouds loomed overhead, turning day into night. Lightning crackled and flashed.

I feared the coming of what might be another helm and being caught in the open. Hailstones started to fall, huge and violent, poking deep holes in the snowy path and tearing at my robes. I pulled my hood tight to shield my eyes and looked around for shelter. But there was nothing in sight.

Suddenly, I heard voices from up ahead – high-pitched squabbling. Before I could dive into the reeds two Morok troopers limped into view – one a squat bald male, dragging a huge, barbed mace; the other a female, twice as tall, her grey, bedraggled mane poking out from under a rusted helmet, her mitts clutching a long twin-headed spear. Seeing me, they stopped abruptly and glowered through the waterfall of crashing ice. I kept going, but moved to the trailside, showing that I meant to pass. At my back I felt a sudden vibration. I knew it was the stone in my *papose*. Was this a warning? But if it was, I was too near them to act upon it.

'What's yer hurry, stranger?' barked the female, wedging her spear across the path. 'Look what's here, Icik – one of 'em horrible Eronn dogs.' I thought at first that she spoke in Ironese, but if it was, it was a pidgin form – uncouth, rough.

'Scum of the earth 'em Erring dogs, Dillig, my sweet,' echoed the other, trying to lift the mace, but giving up in the attempt. He also spoke a guttural pidgin, accented like his companion. It wasn't Ironese, I realised, and it was curious how I understood them at all, never mind so well. My hunter's hearing was keener than ever, but that wouldn't explain understanding a different language form altogether. And while I might be able to understand them, I was sure I couldn't speak their dialect. So how could I explain myself?

'Armed too, dear heart,' crowed the hag, looking me up and down.

They were thin-faced, hollow-eyed, emaciated and drawn, like starving rats. Hail melted as it struck their rusting coats of chainmail, forming pools of yellow liquid at their feet. I was taller and more agile than them. I could easily knock aside the spear and bolt past this comical pair. But I thought it better to act lost, as Romi had suggested. There might be others following.

'Excuse me,' I said, attempting to move around them. I was astonished to hear words coming from my mouth that were not Ironese but were strange to me, the form guttural like theirs. Incredibly, I realised, I was speaking Morok!

'No yeh don't,' snapped the female. She jumped forward and raised her spear to my throat. 'What's the rush?' she barked. 'What be yer purpose here?'

I flinched and stepped back. She followed, jabbing my shoulder with the spear. As she moved, I noticed, part-revealed under her cloak, my sword – the one I'd lost back at the Sentinel! And there too was my small bow – strapped over her shoulder. My very own weapons with these strange creatures! What were the chances? But how was I to get them back?

She jabbed my shoulder again. 'Well?'

'Wayfaring is my business, your honour. Travelling through.'

'Wayfarin', is it? Yer honour, indeed,' she whined back, leering up into my hood. ''Ere Icik, 'ee's not an Erring dog. ''Is mane's not coloured but white – more likes 'un of 'em...'em ghosts!'

Here we go again. Ghost indeed. Just because my skin is pale.

'Ghosts don't wayfares,' the male guffawed. 'What's yer real business, dog?'

'I'm a simple pilgrim,' I said, raising my voice over the clatter of the hail. 'I mean no harm to anyone, good folks.'

'Hoot! Good folks, is it now? Pilgrims, is it?' spoke up the female. 'Very polites, it is! Not so scary fer a ghost, haw-haw.' She turned to her companion. 'Maybe's if I pokes 'im through with me spear 'ee'll disappear like a ghost, too,' she said with a cackle that turned into a bout of throat rattling wheezing.

It was my moment, while she was distracted. But they still had the advantage, where I stood. Silently, I stood my ground as the hail pelted down, watching for sudden movements.

'Where yeh from then, sir ghost? Tell us afore I sticks this in yer gizzard,' the female barked, lowering her spear to my stomach.

'Alba,' I replied. She looked blank. 'You know – beyond the Karst.'

'I knows where it is, ghost dog – that way,' she snapped, gesturing in entirely the wrong direction. 'Karst, eh? Everyone knows there's no dogs go into the Karst. 'Cos there's nothing to eat or drink there. Unless, haw-haw, yeh eats stones.'

I only needed three quick moves – first, dart sideways into the reeds; then knock them both over with two slingshots; then retrieve my weapons and get away. But not yet. The spear was pressing into my robes. Too sudden a move could be my last.

'Yer not one of 'em rebels, dog?' the male snarled.

'Do I look like a rebel?'

'Yeh's all look like rebels to me, dog,' came the reply. 'Can't tell the difference between one and the other.'

'Here, Icik, my sweet,' interrupted the female, squinting down at her companion through the volley of hail. 'Ain't we supposed to be lookin' fer one of 'em stranger Otar dogs – 'n' bring 'im to the Ferok?'

'I knows,' he snarled. 'But this 'ere one's white. Thon Ferok – he saids nothin' about 'im being like a ghost, yeh eejit.'

'Eejit, is it?' remonstrated the other. 'Eejit yerself. How dares yeh eejits me afters I got us safe through thon marsh, yeh turnip-brained excuse fer a sewer pipe.'

'Eejit is as eejit says,' he snapped back. 'Dillig the eejit!'

At this, they both whipped round, nose to nose, bristling and spitting. I took my chance and darted to the side. But I wasn't quick enough. The spear of the one called Dillig was at my throat.

'Not so fast, dog – if yeh values your gizzard. What's yer real business here?' she barked.

'Yeh. Not so fast, dog,' the other repeated.

Suddenly, without any warning of thunder, a bolt of lightning tore into the marsh alongside the pair, sending a slew of mud and shards of ice into their faces. They recoiled and scrambled backwards as a fresh torrent of hailstones cascaded onto their heads.

'Leave 'im,' gasped the male. 'The marsh beasts'll get 'im anyways. Save us a lot of trouble. Let's get out of here. I'm freezin.'

'Can't, Icik,' she replied, struggling with her weapon in the deluge. 'Thon Ferok said we had to search all 'em that passed along either side of the river path – see if they had anything they shouldn't have.'

'But didn't say what.' He shrugged, moving in close. 'But the dog mights have food. Let's search 'im anyways.'

I made my move, pulling the Wildcat's sword from behind my back, but found myself immediately thrown to the ground, sword slithering out of reach into the slush. I was on my stomach, my face pushed into the muddy snow; one of their feet was on the back of my neck, another pressing into the base of my spine. I gasped for breath as a greasy paw rummaged under my cloak. Over my shoulder I glimpsed the male pulling out Romi's bag, sticking his snout in and emerging with a face full of nuts.

'I'll be having some of that,' screeched the female, jumping off my back and flying at the other.

This was the moment. I shot to my feet and dived into the reeds. When I glanced back, I saw the comical pair scrapping on the ground, pulling hair and screeching, oblivious to the fact I'd disappeared, the nuts spilling everywhere. Loading my sling, I detoured into the marsh and circled back to take them by surprise. But then I heard two high-pitched, echoing screams followed by silence.

When I emerged from the rushes, they were motionless on the ground, half buried in slush, dark splashes of blood everywhere. I edged forward, sling at the ready. But they were dead, both with terrible wounds to the neck. My stolen sword lay nearby on the marsh edge, and my lost bow was half visible under the corpse of the female.

I pulled the bow free and collected my sword. Both were unmarked, unbloodied. The bow I tied to my *papose*, and with both swords at my waist belt I ventured forwards, puzzled by the new mysteries I had to add to my collection. How had this pair come by my weapons, and how had I been lucky enough to bump into them? It all seemed so unlikely. Not only that – how had they managed to inflict mortal injuries on one another so quickly? All, it seemed, over a bag of nuts.

Perhaps the strangest thing of all was that they'd made no effort to investigate my *papose* – almost as if they hadn't seen it. And apart from the initial warning the stone had shown no reaction to the Morok presence.

I moved on regretting only the loss of the She-Tarsin's nuts. I'd nothing else to eat, and fishing in a river flood was nigh impossible. So, it was marsh frogs or nothing. I chose nothing. Tonight, I'd just have to go hungry.

The hailstorm passed, but the river ran over its banks again, turning the ground into sodden marsh, the trail even thicker with slush. Night was coming in. I needed shelter, somewhere to dry off. Looking about, I saw a canopy of tall trees off to one side in the distance, a luminous silvery light gracing their tops. The sanctuary Tiroc Og had mentioned was near some tall trees. Perhaps my luck had not yet run out.

I left the trail and plunged across a mat of rushes, roots and rhizomes that quaked with every step but didn't give way. The reeds, though thicker than before, parted easily to let me through, then closed behind, as if claiming me for their own.

Eventually I came across a raised mud bank, odd in the middle of open marsh, but when I clambered over it, I was astonished to find a muddy beach fringed with lake-weed that opened out into a vast body of water. A lake! The silver-topped trees I'd glimpsed before were on the far side, their upper branches floating like ghosts above a pillow of thick swirling mist. But if those trees were the sanctuary, they were reachable only by boat – and heavy paddling through a morass of lake weeds. Why would the Wildcat have directed me here?

Aching and shivering, I slumped on the mud bank and looked about for a dry spot to put my bender. But every place I put my feet filled immediately with water or sticky mud. There was nothing for it but to return to the trail and continue my search.

Then, as I wearily shouldered my *papose*, I caught sight of a woodpile further up the mound and thought maybe I could use the wood as a platform to keep my shelter above the marsh. Duly I plunged into the clutching, sucking mud and began to plod towards the pile. But when I reached it, I found only the remains of a dugout from a tree, rotten and covered in marsh moss. Quite useless. Further up there were others, some half-in, half-out of the water.

Not expecting much, I trudged towards them. Indeed, the second dugout was like the first – rotten to the touch. Next to it lay a curragh, so old it had lost its colour, the skin rent with holes. Beyond that lay an upturned dugout. With a heave, I turned it over. But my heart sank when I saw that it had been purposely holed, a stake driven right through the middle. It was the type carved by the Barod boat-makers at home, wide at the base with a high prow displaying the owner's clan totem. But the totem on this one had been smashed; the tribe was unrecognisable. I carried on down the line. All holed. All made useless. I felt like crying.

Had I been deceived by the Wildcat? Wrong trees, wrong place?

I contemplated spending an uncomfortable night in a damp, holed dugout and was just about to decide which one when I noticed, a little further back in the rushes, the prow of one more dugout, right side up. Dried reeds had been laid carefully over most of it – it had been purposely hidden. I trudged over. The totem was partly intact – a bear – Brach tribe. And more hopefully, there were signs of recent use – drag tracks towards the water, and a short, curved paddle neatly placed and bound along the bottom. It had been damaged, but only at the prow, a small hole just above the waterline, maybe even accidental. I knocked on the sides – it was solid. In calm waters, this would easily float but might struggle in any waves set off by one of those winds that seemed to rush out of nowhere. But the night had fallen calm, windless; the lake a sheet of glass.

I set about making an impromptu repair. Selecting and cutting out a thick reed rhizome, just as I'd been taught, I flattened it between two stones, fashioned a plug by rolling it in my fingers, stuffed it into the hole and sealed it with mud. Very soon the dugout was watertight; temporarily, anyway. It was cheery work in the cold damp air; it warmed me nicely, and my spirits rose high. The effort in the repair justified using the dugout. It was not theft. I would return it – and hoped its loss did not inconvenience a friendly traveller.

Before long I was midstream, paddling swiftly towards the far shore in the direction of the silver-topped trees. At home, our tribe virtually lived on our lake coracles, curraghs and dugouts. Catching fish from a boat on a calm night was as pleasurable as life could get.

As I sped forwards, fish bumped and rubbed against the side, as if inviting capture. So, I'd eat tonight, after all! Waiting for the right moment, I leaned over, grabbed the nearest and hoisted it into the boat where it flapped about helplessly. Freshwater pike. Not huge, but if I could make a fire onshore, good eating.

As I took up my paddle again, cold lake mist descended around me, sinking into my bones, rendering the land invisible, masking even the silver-lit trees. I pulled my blanket over my shoulders and allowed the familiar work of paddling to warm me.

Far quicker than I'd expected came the scrape of shingle under the prow of the boat. It came to rest, tilted to one side. I'd made land! And there was light in the sky, soft and silvery, reflecting the thin layer of mist that hugged the water; through it, the shadows of tall trees.

Below my feet was a shell-like shingle, shining white in the dim light. Here and there, tiny trails of vapour rose out of the ground. There was no lying snow or slush in this place, and the air was slightly warm with a smell of sulphur – like the hot springs at home. On this night, in this magical spot, perhaps I could even find a hot pool to have a bath.

I felt a prickle at the back of my neck and whipped around to see who was watching. Then I saw it. The moon. It held me spellbound, frozen in wonder. A perfect crescent – the new moon with the old one in its arms; the heavenly body of the archer goddess, deity of the hunters, crystal bright in her waxing form, carved like a bow out of the firmament. Around it glimmered the first stars I'd seen since crossing the mountains. I stood for a moment basking in her radiance, her soft white light caressing my skin, infusing me with hope. A crescent moon was a happy hunter's moon, a good omen, a sign of success to come.

I pulled the boat into nearby reeds and walked inland, my step slow and dreamy, thin trails of mist trickling around my feet. I came to a flat grassy bank leading up to a group of tall pines encircling a small hill topped by rocks – the treetops I'd seen across the water – lit, I now realised, by moonlight. Spread-eagled across the upper branches were large nests, but flat in shape, unlike Romi's. Some had collapsed, with twigs and mosses dangling from the branches. I walked to the top of the hillock and saw I was on an island, for the ground on the far side sloped back down to the lake shore. As far as I could tell, I was alone, without even the sounds of night insects, and no other signs of life. No company, I mused forlornly, but no Morok either.

Mid-way between the mound and the water, on the side where I'd beached, was a small alder wood. Here I chose a flattish spot to place my bender. Cutting some alder poles, I placed them in a circle, tied them together at the top, draped over my goatskin and set about collecting driftwood for a fire.

Later, fire lit, supper of roast pike complete, I sat on the threshold of the bender, taking in the soft sounds and smells of the island night; marvelling again at the silver sliver in the sky, imagining it in its full form – the eyes, nose and mouth of the huntress and the split-lip hare familiar that ran with her. It seemed, at that moment, that she was smiling on me. I'd arrived, as if by magic, in a special place, a sanctuary indeed. I was warm, fed, and reunited with my weapons. Surely, I told myself, it would only be a matter of time before I found my lost kin.

After a while, white mist thickened out on the water and swirled inland, around my bender and up into the sky. The stars ceased to glimmer, and the moon was no more. The air changed. A deep chill ran through me, right down to the bones of my feet. Time to sleep. I placed a large lump of wood on the fire, wrapped myself tightly in my blanket, and tucked myself up in the bender.

I had only just laid down when I heard a mournful moaning coming from out across the water, and with it, in dread solemnity, the slow swish of oars. I was no longer alone. Morok? Here?

Throwing aside my blanket, I grabbed my sword and crept out of the bender towards a line of reeds that lay between me and the beach. Shuffling into them, I parted the stalks to see beyond. And there, a low-lying vessel slid out of the mist towards the shore. A yellow coracle with two hooded figures on board; one tall and thickset, the other much smaller with head bent and shoulders slumped. It was the young Eronn and the Wildcat from the raid! Between them, straddling the coracle, was a frame bearing a bundle of some kind.

I was on the verge of calling out when I saw that the frame was a bier carrying two shrouds. I stopped, unsure if I should reveal myself and watched on as the pair came onshore lifted the bier and began carrying it up the beach.

Of course. It then came to me. This island was a *ghat* – a spirit yard, a resting place for the dead; the "shells" on the beach were not shells at all, but the bones of the departed; and the "nests" in the trees were the elevated funerary platforms of forest tribes, whose dead were laid there to be picked clean by birds, their bones scattered by the winds.

The pair were here to perform funerary rites. And, uncomfortably, I was now an intruder to a ceremony reserved among the Manau tribes for the grieving family and their priest. I shouldn't be here at all. But then, wasn't this place the sanctuary – where the Wildcat himself had told me to go? If he was coming here, why had he not said as much?

I began to back away and brushed against the dry reed stalks causing them to rattle. I slid to the ground, but hearing no reaction from up ahead, I decided I'd just have to wait and retreat when I could. After a while I lifted my head. The Wildcat was lighting a blaze. The flames reared quickly, forming a thin tower of fire. Chanting, he threw powder into the blaze, while the young Eronn sat off to one side, his frame shaking. Their faces had been painted white; their moon-pale features lit up in red by the tongues of fire that leapt into the air every time the powder was thrown.

I heard a fluttering of wings above and saw a marsh harrier hovering then gracefully settling upon a nearby pine and folding its wings to rest.

The damp was seeping into me, but I couldn't move without revealing my presence. After what seemed forever, the Wildcat blew his conch, raised his face to the heavens and threw up his arms. At this, the bird suddenly cried out – once, twice, three times across the night air. And, from across the marshes came the voices of other night birds, crying out a great wave of sadness that swelled to a glorious crescendo, then faded to silence.

The Wildcat quenched the fire. Steam rose from the ashes and bloomed into a cocoon of silvery-white mist which divided into the shapes of two beings, both Eronn. These hovered for a second, then, with a loud "pop" they streaked across the firmament like shooting stars before fading from view.

I'd attended many a passing ritual at home, including that of my beloved grandmother, but had seen nothing like this. I'd been taught that all creatures have *taibh*, astral bodies, that finally leave their physical forms after the death ritual – but I had never really believed it. Of course, it could just be an Akari trick with the light and powders.

125

I was exhausted and my head was full of wonders. Perhaps I was seeing things.

Finally, they lifted the bier, carried it to the water and set it adrift, gazing after it as it dissolved into the mist.

It was time to reveal my presence. But before I could move, the harrier left its perch and alighted briefly on the Wildcat's shoulder before flying up and over me, its feathery talons grazing the seed heads. When I looked back to the beach, the Wildcat and his companion were already aboard the coracle and paddling away.

I stood, shivering from head to foot, suddenly aware of how cold I'd become while watching – I'd been so hypnotised by the sight. Now I felt strangely peaceful.

I returned to my little shelter on this, an Isle of the Dead, lay down and thought about what I'd seen. But in spite of my wonderment, sleep came quickly; deep and dreamless, like the sleep of the spirits themselves.

13

RENEGADES ALL

'What should I do with 'im, chief?' boomed the voice.

I started awake. A great weight sat on my chest, so heavy it made me gasp for breath. It was a huge, gnarled foot. A heavily scarred face leered over me. I was shivering with cold.

'Can't breathe,' I panted, trying to wriggle.

'Look, it talks,' growled the face.

The foot slowly lifted, but its owner remained standing over me, peering down threateningly. Gulping air, I hauled myself up. No wonder I was cold. I was in the open. My bender had been ripped apart and cast to the side – the poles, skin and my *papose* tossed carelessly nearby. A cold morning mist obscured everything except the huge face looming above me, a thick nose protruding over a jagged, broken set of teeth, each one bigger than all of mine put together. The body attached to the face was twice my size, cloaked in a patchwork of small animal furs. Over each shoulder hung a shrunken bear's head complete with grinning toothy visage. This was a Brach – the infamous Bear tribe of Clachoile. My first ever Brach encounter. And he looked far from friendly.

I felt for my weapons. Yes, they were in place from the night before

– under my blanket. Slowly, I reached down for them, trying to feel for my knife. But Broken Tooth moved swiftly, jabbing the tip of a sword into my wrist and leaning his weight on my leg, pressing me into the ground.

'Ouch,' I exclaimed with a sharp intake of breath. I could feel my knife under my hip, but I couldn't move.

'I'll cut yer wrist if yeh tries that again,' he growled, then turned to speak to someone I couldn't see. 'He'll be a spy, chief. Shall I strings him up from thon tree?'

'No, don't do that. Yeh'll scare the ghosts,' snapped a voice from nearby. A female. I wasn't able to turn my head to see her. Other shadows moved in the mist. Some were laughing.

'What then, chief?'

'You know it's bad luck to be disturbing the dead,' she said.

'No worries. I'll not let 'im squeal.'

More laughter. My leg felt like it was going to break. But I wouldn't cry out – wouldn't give them the satisfaction – not if they were going to hang me.

Who were they? They were speaking Ironese. Indeed, the voice of "chief" was accented like Mara, the polite form; schooled, the tone husky, but young. I could just make her out under the giant's armpit, her back to me, a long silvery bow draped over her shoulder. Around her others hovered, coming and going, in furs and dark green cloaks. Some had longbows strapped on their backs. One carried a twin-headed aberaxe, another a jagged mace, another a black crossbow with a beltful of purple-tipped barbed bolts.

Morok weapons!

Finally, the foot lifted. I tried to stretch my leg, still trembling from the weight.

'Take him over by the fire – he's cold,' said the female, walking away. 'The Catton can deal with him when he returns.'

'Why can't I jes' torture 'im, chief?' the giant grunted. 'He'll already have told 'em where we are. Find out what he's up to, I say.'

'He's Albin – probably harmless,' she said, firmly. 'But we can't be dealing with strays, Bran. As I said, talk to the Catton. He'll know what's best. I have to get back to the Terai for the gathering. Get the Catton to send one of his harriers to me when you reach Trisuldur.' Her voice was fading as she walked away.

'What if yeh're not there, chief?' asked the Brach, Broken Tooth, whom she'd called Bran.

'Assume the worst. Avenge me,' she called back, and laughed. She had a beautiful laugh, wild, free. It made my skin tingle. I wanted to see her face, her smile.

She headed towards the water, dark green robe swaying with her motions. A sudden breeze tipped her hood back, revealing waist-long Eronn type tresses tied together with white ribbon, but silver-grey, the colour of fire ash; not the normal red, green and blue of the Eronn tribe. Two males followed her into the lake mist, bare headed, their manes the usual tricolour.

I heard the clack-clack-swish of oars disappearing into the distance – a boat being paddled away. It was daylight – I'd slept through the dawn. But the mist was lowering again. The day was dark, greyer than the moonlit night before. No sun.

'Don't be tryin' anythin',' muttered the giant named as Bran between gritted teeth. He grabbed my arm and yanked me up. Then, kicking my weapons out of reach, he released his grip and ushered me down the beach towards a huddle of figures seated around a fire. I made no attempt to struggle or escape – it would've been pointless, given his size and the number of them. Then, almost as if for show, he grabbed my shoulder and pushed me down near the fire, so close at first my robe began to singe. But the heat was welcome; I was still shivering after my exposure to the morning chill.

The Brach disappeared. Others sat nearby, drinking from clay bowls, some laughing, some arguing, some ominously sharpening knives. The company were not all Eronn or Brach but of different tribes, some unknown to me and, despite their weaponry, clearly not Morok. All were hooded against the chill mist. No-one took much notice of me – the stranger in their midst.

I shifted away from the fire, pulled my blanket tight over my head and waited to have my fate decided. My calmness in the circumstances was odd. I still hadn't spoken a word. Surely at least they would find out who I was, before… But my instincts told me I was meant no harm. But what?

Then I remembered. My *papose* – where was it? My stomach lurching, I stumbled to my feet, muttering, 'Where…?'

But a hand was on my shoulder. 'Yers, I believes,' grunted the Brach holding out my *papose*. Nodding thanks, I clutched it to my chest, noticing it hadn't been tampered with. My muscles relaxed.

'Here, give 'im some of the soup, Bran, for Yahl's sake, and don't be tormentin' him,' said another. The speaker was an Eronn in his middle years, smiling broadly at me, eyes sparkling, seated next to a steaming metal pot hanging from a tripod over the fire. Ladling from it a bowl of thick soup, he handed it to the Brach who in turn passed it to me with a grunt.

'I am grateful,' I said, taking in the soft un-warrior like features of the Eronn, noticing that his loose tri-coloured mane, was streaked with grey. His eyes sparkled in the firelight, blue like my mother's, and around one wrist was a band with a glistening stone – like the Wildcat's but blue.

I drank slowly from the bowl, watching those around me gulp theirs down then get back to work. The Eronn smiled again at me as he rose and left the fireside. Only then did I notice that one of his sleeves was tied to his belt – he had only one arm!

The Brach called Bran came back to the fire, threw back two bowls of soup, then, pointing to the simmering pan, grunted over at me, 'There's more there, Albin, if yeh wants. Yeh've been lucky. Thon Aguan Aridh over there would 'ave slit yer throat whilst yeh slept. Least when I comes for yeh, yeh'll be able to cry out.' Then he laughed and walked away again, and I realised I was being teased. I was not to be hanged, after all. Though I still had this "Catton" – whoever that was – to worry about.

Now, left alone, it seemed there was nothing to stop me just getting up and going back to my boat. But I'd have to leave the warmth of the fire, and the prospect of more thick soup, rich with mint and rosemary, was irresistible. In any case, the weapons I'd come with were nowhere to be seen and I'd no intention of going anywhere unarmed, let alone being separated from my own weapons again. I waited, sipped soup, watched the goings on in the camp and saw the Brach striding uphill towards a huddle of dark green benders at the top of the island, carrying a bundle of some kind. Around the benders, others moved, busy with morning tasks.

The night before, this whole area had been empty; they'd landed unbeknownst to me and set up camp while I slept. My own bender lay where it had been collapsed – a short distance from theirs, separated only by a thin line of reeds. They must have known I was there the whole time yet decided to let me sleep on, not seeing me as any kind of real threat. Then, anyway.

I tried to pick out the different tribes from their manes and telltale fur cloaks. I saw Wildcat, Eronn, Wolf, Fox, Aguan and Beaver of varying sex and size. All were young except the one-armed Eronn, but some faces were scarred. A couple wore bloodstained bandages around their wrists and forearms.

The Eronn returned to the fire and started ladling more soup into bowls. Other warriors followed, accepting steaming bowls as they arrived. He smiled at them as if they were his children. The warriors eyed me casually as they sat, but no-one spoke to me, or even seemed particularly surprised at my presence. They were more interested in the fare – and the warmth of the fire.

So far, the Eronn had been the friendliest face I'd seen. 'What is the name in you, please?' I said to him, putting down my empty bowl and rubbing my wrist – still smarting from the Brach's sword point.

'The name in me is Drion, of the house of Llan,' he replied, glancing at my wrist. 'I have salve for that – if yeh can wait. Ah...' he said, suddenly turning his head towards the water.

I heard the swish of paddles and the clatter and scrape of a boat being beached. Then the sound of footpads on shingle and some lively exchanges, all in Ironese. I heard the *Askrit* word *Kaif* – chief – a number of times. One of the voices was Bran, grumbling loudly, clearly agitated by something. In spite of the hubbub, the others round the fire remained busy with their breakfast. One, though, stood a little distance away – an Aguan male, tall and thin, his hood hiding his face. I felt his eyes staring in my direction. I looked away, sensing menace.

The one called Drion stood and walked down towards the shore, then returned with Bran and another. The Brach separated from them, striding past us, back up towards the bender huddle at the top of the hill, while Drion and his new companion approached the fire.

It was none other than the Wildcat, Tiroc Og. He'd returned.

So, this was "the Catton". The one who was to decide my fate. I relaxed back, comforted by my last encounter.

'Ah. Osian of Faron, we meet again!' he said with a laugh. 'So, this is Bran's dangerous spy.'

I stood and bowed, guiltily remembering the night before. I shouldn't have been there, but it certainly didn't make me a spy. And the one named Tiroc Og had himself directed me to this place – or so I'd thought.

Before I could speak, the Brach was back, striding furiously towards us. 'Chief. What did I say? Take a look at these,' he spat out, throwing down my weapons.

The Wildcat shook his head wearily. 'Bran...'

The Brach picked up the sword Tiroc Og had given me and held it out. 'Isn't this one of yer own? And this, too – one of our short bows if I'm not mistaken.' Then, glaring at me, he demanded, 'How d'yeh come by these, Albin?'

Tiroc Og spoke. 'Actually, Bran, I gave him them – well, not all of them. But let me see thon sword – no, not that, the other one.'

Bran picked up my own recovered sword. Running his mitt down the hilt admiringly, he said, 'Eronn blade, of the old type – look at those carvings. There's their totem, Otrec, and other stuff. Who d'yeh steal this from, stranger?'

I looked helplessly at Tiroc Og. A short while ago the Brach had been threatening to string me up. It looked like he still wanted to.

'He's not Morok,' the Wildcat said firmly. 'For Yahl's sake, Bran, give him back his weapons.'

'Just my own is fine,' I said. 'And I thank you for the loan, Tiroc Og. I can now give you back your sword.' The act of giving had annulled the life debt. I didn't need to keep his weapon.

'What about that other thing,' grunted Bran, dropping my sword and pointing to my *papose*. 'In there. Look yerself.'

With an abrupt dismissive wave Tiroc Og said, 'Bran, what's in his pack is his own business; we're not thieves.' Then he added, more gently, 'Never mind all this, my old friend, yeh should eat. Yeh'll need all yer strength for later. Leave our visitor to me.'

The giant huffed, then turned away.

'Don't be minding him,' said Tiroc Og to me. 'He's suspicious of everything, everybody. But with good cause – someone has betrayed us – that's how the Morok found Hiron's kin's hideaway. Maybe even one of our own. But Bran has a good heart. And he's our best fighter – someone to have on yer side, to be sure. Now, collect the rest of yer bits and come back here.'

I picked up my own weapons, leaving the rest, and found my collapsed bender. Wrapping the skin around the poles, I tied the bundle under my *papose* and slung it over one shoulder.

Returning to the fireside, I found the Wildcat by himself, staring trance-like at the coals, muttering under his breath. It was as if he was trying to figure something out. Remembering my first encounter and the way he'd ignored me then, I waited respectfully without speaking.

'Now. Come,' he said eventually. 'Bring yer things.' He rose and strode towards the rockpile at the top of the island.

I followed him up the hill, past the huddle of benders. In a lee below the rocks at the top of the island stood a large green bender around which several figures were gathered. Some were seated on stones, sharpening swords and knives, talking and laughing as they worked. One, an Aguan, was beaming proudly as he held out a blade by its tip for the Wildcat to inspect.

'It's good, Garidh,' Tiroc Og responded, taking it by the hilt and running his mitt down the edge, 'but needs sharper still. We don't want Morok calling out when you slit their throats.' The Aguan responded with a laugh that seemed too hearty – a trifle forced.

To one side of the bender was a small tripod of tools; on the other, some iron cooking utensils. Beckoning to me, Tiroc Og ducked into the bender, sat on a log, pointed to a pile of dry ferns and said, 'Please to sit.'

I settled on the bracken which yielded softly under me. 'This island, it's a spirit yard?'

'Yes. This is Avalor. Final resting place for the dead of the tribes. We use it as one of our refuges. Morok have not been known to come here – yet.'

'Because of the deep marshes?'

'That,' Tiroc Og replied, 'more likely their fear of ghosts.'

'Was I not meant to come here? Isn't this the sanctuary you meant?'

'No! Yeh'd have found yer sanctuary – yer safety behind the boat beach – just back from it there's a group of hollow trees. We stay there sometimes. That's what I meant when I told yeh – but maybe I wasn't clear enough. I see yeh used one of them old dugouts to cross over. I thought we'd destroyed them all.'

'It was very dark. I could hardly see anything; and I was drawn to the light above the island – the moon. First open sky I'd seen since crossing the mountains.'

'Well, I'm impressed, anyways. The older dugouts were holed in case Morok ever used them to cross. Our own are hidden in a creek not far from the hollow trees, surrounded by spike traps. A hunter – such as yerself – would've seen the traps, but Morok wouldn't.'

Spike traps! I gulped; glad I hadn't gone looking in the dark. 'I have to confess,' I replied. 'I saw you arrive in the night. But...well...you were busy, I couldn't interrupt.' He didn't respond, so I continued, 'And now your friends think I'm a spy.'

'A hopeless spy yeh'd make,' he quipped. 'I saw yer tracks on the beach. The boat, of course. Smelt yer fire ash and yer supper remains. Heard the din yeh made among the reeds. And the harrier saw yeh.'

Of course – the bird on the branch. I'd heard of shamans having animal familiars. 'None of those were here last night,' I said, gesturing to the warriors outside. 'Who *are* you?'

'We have a weapons cache in the rocks,' he said, 'and have need of them. Though it was not our plan to come here this time. The death of Hiron's kin…changed that. Anyway, our plans change with every move the Morok make.' He looked away from me, out over the lake. 'Don't worry about Bran. For all his bluster, he wouldn't have hurt yeh. Bran wouldn't have hurt yeh. As for who *we* all are – we're from tribes that have lost families and friends, homes and livings to the invaders. The Aguan, though, are mostly with us for the lootin'.'

'Looting?'

'They get to keep any stolen sungold or moonsilver we recover. Aguan are good with the marshes and the mules, and they know their way around the Easter lands like none other. I'm not that keen on using them, but we depend on them – just like the Morok do up in the Norther Lands. And,' he added with a slight grin, 'they can be useful in other ways.'

'You are the resistance then?' I asked.

'I suppose, yes. But we're small in number. We only pick small targets. We attack by night, take their supplies, isolate their fortalices, obstruct their replacements, that kind of thing. As the Eronn have either been enslaved or flown wherever they can, we no longer fear reprisals; though there were some at first which made it harder for us.'

Bran was outside, arguing with someone. I thought of his threats, still a little unsure where I stood with him. Tiroc Og, perhaps sensing my concern, said, 'Understand, young Albin, we needs to be cautious who we deal with. To my friends yeh could well be sent by the Morok to worm yer way into our company and get us all killed. For after all's said and done, who would take to these ways in these times – alone – and get as far as yeh did? And still be alive!'

'What I have said is true, I've nothing to do with them,' I retorted, bristling.

'I've told them yeh what yeh did for me – in the Carron,' said the

Wildcat. 'But to them, what yeh did in thon raid could still be seen as a ruse – report back, destroy us from within, even. We've had such in the past. Maybe even now…' His voice tailed away. He sat up straight – hunter alert – and put a finger to his lips. Someone was passing by the bender and seemed to pause at the opening before moving on.

'But there's something yeh should know,' he continued, in a quieter voice. 'I understand from the harriers that the Morok are desperately hunting a stranger, an Albin. If it's indeed yeh, yeh ought to know that there's a price on yer head, and maybe a sharp postillion already set up in Erintor to stick it on. Yeh know,' he snorted, 'that that's where the Morok leader has set 'imself up – as the new Marcher Lord of Erainn.'

Instinctively, I put my hand to my neck. I hadn't been imagining things – the Morok *were* after me, and indeed, I'd almost been caught.

'What do your friends say about me – all this?'

'I was to interrogate yeh. Establish the truth. Find out who yeh really are, and why they're after yeh.'

'I am simply what I say,' I replied, placing my hand on my chest. 'Tell them that.'

He went silent and held my gaze for a long time.

'So, you are the resistance chief?' I said to break the tension.

'No, no,' he laughed, picking up a long thin bone pipe similar to one Grandfather had brought back from Erainn. 'I'm just another renegade.'

'I was told you were a tracker-shaman – the best. And last night, at the funeral byre…you were like a…a hedge priest,' I said.

'Oh. I do a bit of that – the Wind Hares trained me in the priestly arts.'

'So, who then is your chief – who leads you?'

'She would be Cana. Cana-Din.'

That must be the female I had heard speaking earlier, the She-Eronn with the extraordinary hair, swaying robe and long silvery bow. She'd moved like a swan. I wished I'd seen her face. She was the one Romi had told me about; with the incredible eyes, who the Morok hated above all others.

'Where is she now? Will she be back?' I was sorry I'd not seen those eyes. Blue like the sky, Romi had said. My own eyes were blue, but more lake-coloured than sky-hued. My Eronn mother's eyes were truer, the blue of the pure bred; my father's Albin green. When I was being teased as a half breed with frog's eyes by my Albin age-fellows, my mother would try to console me by saying, 'Our eyes show who we are; they contain the secrets in our souls.' But as I didn't know any of the secrets in my soul, I doubted whether anyone else did. And secrets or not, I usually got the better of my age-fellows with my fists till I earned their respect. Then the teasing stopped.

Tiroc Og's response was terse. 'Careful what yeh asks the others. What I can tell yeh is that the Morok have tried to catch her many times. In the Terai forests, she's invisible. Outside them, she moves quickly between the bands to avoid being caught, though there's always those who'll be tempted to betray her. And every band has a spy or two. Anyways, for as long Cana is free, there is a chance of overcoming the Morok.'

'Why is that?'

'Because she alone can rally all the free tribes,' he said, rising to his feet. 'Enough now, Osian. It must look,' he added with a conspiratorial grin, 'like I have interrogated yeh properly by nows; though I must admit I knows as much about yeh – or as little – as I did before. Anyways. Remain here.' Then, striding to the entrance, he lifted the flap and looked out. 'I'll be back,' he said over his shoulder.

'But I…I cannot just sit here and wait. I must go my way,' I said.

He turned and said sharply, 'Go where, Albin? To yer doom in the wide Wicken marshes? Yeh don't know where yeh're going. The trail yeh've been on turns to nothing. I say, wait till the others get back – and we'll talk again.'

It didn't sound like his fellows were going to make much allowance for me – a stranger and untrusted. Some, like the Brach named Bran, and that Aguan, seemed positively hostile. Anyway, 'trust no-one' was the warning that still rang in my ears. The longer I sat in the bender, waiting for Tiroc Og to return, the more I found myself wondering whether I'd be best taking my chances on my own. After all, I'd got this far. I decided to go and see what was going on.

Collecting my weapons and shouldering my *papose*, I left the bender and began to pick my way down towards the lake. The water was shrouded in morning mist, but I had a clear view of the beach, and further along the waterline, where warriors could be seen retrieving dugouts from the reeds and taking them down to the water's edge. I counted ten boats in total with space enough for two in each.

Tiroc Og was in the shallows giving instructions as, boat by boat, the company embarked and paddled into the haze. The Brach was onshore arguing with another of his tribe, equal to his size. At one point their noses touched, their chests pushed out; and I thought they were going to fight, but the next minute they were laughing and slapping each other on the back. Eventually the other Brach embarked alone on a dugout and the one called Bran pushed it out and returned to shore.

Suddenly, from the top of the island came a sound like falling rocks. Bran and Tiroc Og reacted immediately, grabbing weapons, turning and running up towards the rock mound. Soon they were over the top and gone from sight. What was happening? Should I follow them? But the fog came in again, so thick I could hardly see my feet, never mind find anyone else's.

As I hovered by the shore, I heard two piercing screams from the top of the island. Chest pounding, I wheeled blindly, trying to get my bearings in the mist. Suddenly, two huge ghastly figures charged out of it towards me, bristling with weapons, bodies parting the fog, faces painted like ghouls; horned bone masks over their eyes, robes splattered with what looked like mud. It was red – blood! They came at me like timber wolves in for the kill. Island ghosts they were not.

'Yahl save me,' I exclaimed, grasping my sword in both hands and digging my heels into the shingle of bones and charred remains of Avalor's dead, about to join them.

Crouched low, sword thrust out in front, I waited for the attack, swearing that at least one of them would go down with me.

14

THE GUARDIAN

'Put down your sword, Albin,' commanded the nearest. The voice was familiar. Only then did I realise who they were. The "ghouls" were none other than Tiroc Og and Bran! Nonetheless, I only half-lowered my sword, transfixed by their horrible visages and bloodstained robes.

Their warpaint was crude, clearly done in a matter of moments, but scarily effective. The Wildcat's face bore two thick stripes, one black, one blood red, twisted across his mouth and mask and across his forehead. Another pair of stripes, bright yellow, spread out from his nose like cat's whiskers. Bran's face was smeared dark brown with a single white stripe stretching from ear to ear across the mask. With the paint, beard and furs, he resembled a rampaging bear.

My heart was thumping. Those screams. The blood. They'd been killing. Who? Surely not one of their own? Tiroc Og had said the Morok didn't come here. He'd mentioned "spies" in the band. Had they uncovered such a one and subjected him or her to some horrid, ritualised death – hence the paint? I edged backwards into the water at the thought, my stomach clenching. Some here considered me a "spy".

'Don't be alarmed,' called Tiroc Og. 'We'll not harm yeh. But yeh must come with us.'

'I'm not going anywhere till you tell me what's happening… Why are you in warpaint?'

'We've learned there's a posse of Morok in Aguan small boats on the lake, approaching from the west – probably by now already beaching on the far side of the island. Two of their scouts landed in the night, and were hiding in the rocks up there. We made them think the island ghosts had come for them – hence the paint – and scared the truth from them, but couldn't let them live, for we are at war, and cannot show mercy to those who would bring us to our doom. There are too many more coming for us that have living souls to deal with. We cannot be here. The fates of those that enter this place with ill intent are already decided – ours are open handed. Stay here and yeh'll certainly die. Join us. That's all I can say.'

He turned away, Bran close behind, and they tore along the beach towards a bank of reeds, crushed shells flying up from their feet.

I'd little choice. I still didn't know enough about Tiroc Og's company, or their intentions towards me, to feel completely at ease, but I knew I didn't want to be around when the Morok arrived. Clutching my belongings, I chased after them and, with my lighter frame and younger years, quickly caught up.

'We have news for yeh,' panted Tiroc Og as I drew up alongside. 'News?'

'Seems the story yeh told us holds up, Albin,' he said without turning his head. 'For me, anyways. An Otar couple fitting yer description, an elder She-Eronn with an Albin male, were spotted a few moons past on the edge of the Terai, off the pilgrim way – part of a convoy going to the Norther Lands.'

My stomach gave a huge leap. 'An Aguan convoy?'

'No. I'm sorry, young 'un.' He paused for a moment. 'As Morok captives.'

'The Norther Lands – where were they being taken, then?' My kin – my parents! My heart was fluttering, part with joy that they'd been seen alive, part with rage that they were in the claws of the Morok.

We were now deep in the reedbed, parting the reed stalks and scrambling along wet shingle claggy with mud and wet marsh grasses.

'Rakhaus, in Kaliyag – the fire mountains,' he said. 'There to be enslaved.'

'Then, I must go,' I said, stopping in my tracks, shaking with rage. 'You must show me the way.'

'Yahl's sake, don't. Stop, Albin!' he snapped. Bran, who'd pushed through the reeds ahead, must have overheard for he shouted back, 'If he's going to slow us, leave him behind.'

Stung into action, I caught up with them and shouted over, 'The Morok'll surely keep my kin alive, though?' My voice quivered as I ran.

'Depends how useful they are,' Tiroc Og replied, racing forward. Bran was ahead in the reeds somewhere, shouting for us to hurry.

We came to a small clearing in the reed bank where Bran was tearing apart a huge pile of cut reeds. Tiroc Og joined in, removing the last of the stalks to reveal a large-bottomed, unpainted dugout, longer and sleeker than the others. I recognised the swift craft, similar to the type the Barod made for summer races back home, but with no totem, just a pair of snake eyes on the prow.

From another pile of cut reeds Bran pulled out a large sack of what looked weapons and a bundle of bender skins and poles. He threw them in the boat, grabbed the prow and proceeded to drag it, unassisted, in the direction of the shore. We followed through the gap the giant Brach was forging through the reed mass and quickly reached the water.

We were once again in the open – and exposed. The fog had lifted to reveal the top of the island. Moving quickly, Bran rearranged the piles on the boat for sailing and lifted out two sets of paddles. Tiroc Og threw his weapons and long *papose* into the boat, his eyes darting between it and the rockpile behind us and, breathing hard, asked me, 'What skills do yer kin have that the Morok could make use of?

Rakhaus is where they make their weapons, and I'm wonderin' if that's why they were taken.'

'My father, Faron, was smith to the lake-land tribes in Alba,' I replied, catching my breath. 'Horseshoes and knives, that kind of thing. My mother did fine workings – ornaments, rings and bracelets, which she traded for cotton cloth and dried foods and spices from across the Great Lake. Would these be of use to the Morok?'

'Ah. We don't really know what they're making – but I'm told Morok don't have tooling skills themselves, so the answer would probably be yes. Anyways, put yerself and yer arms aboard.' Then he barked, 'Bran, now.'

Bran heaved the dugout into the water and held it steady as we boarded, Tiroc Og taking position at the prow, myself in the middle between two piles of goods. Bran pushed the boat away as he jumped in and speedily began to paddle.

'Where is it that we go?' I spoke.

'Ye'll find out soon enough,' Tiroc Og replied as he commenced paddling. The boat shot into the open water like an arow.

Suddenly a bolt hissed out of the air and thwacked into the side of the boat. Another flew past our ears. Another whizzed past, narrowly missing my face, then another which hit my *papose* with such force the boat shuddered, but the bolt did not stick, and bounced harmlessly into the water. My companions paddled furiously, and we were soon in midwater and, I'd have thought, out of range.

Indeed, Morok troopers were now lining the beach, firing bolts that fell well short. But suddenly I spotted something different – a long-feathered arrow flying low across the water and heading straight for Bran's back. Extraordinarily, it was moving in slow motion, as if I was seeing it from a place outside my body. 'Watch out,' I screamed as I jumped to my feet, causing the boat to rock wildly. But just as the arrow was about to strike, I swung my sword at it and, even with the boat tipping to one side, managed to knock it clean out of the air. Then, just as suddenly, real time returned, and I was aware of Bran and Tiroc Og righting the struggling craft and taking it well clear of all Morok fire. I resumed my seat, dazed by what had happened. It was if my companions had seen nothing, so intent were they on paddling. I wondered if they'd even seen what had just taken place – and my part in it.

Half-way across, but still in view of the island and the Morok horde on the beachline, Tiroc Og suddenly got to his feet. 'Bran, keep steering away,' he said and, facing the island, threw his arms in the air and shouted, 'Yahl be with you, my brother. Take them!' Then putting his conch to his lips, he blew into it three times, though strangely it made no sound. Resuming his seat, he took up his paddle.

Take them? Perplexed, I stared at the shoreline, thick with Morok troopers buzzing like a swarm of wild hornets around boat craft they were launching into the water. Who on earth was the Wildcat addressing and why had the conch made no sound?

The answer was not long in coming. A plume of steam swirled out of the rock mound and rose high into the air, twisting and writhing like a serpent. I squinted, unsure what I was seeing. Was I imagining things – hallucinating? A ghostly face with huge empty eye sockets and flaming beard and hair streaming in every direction had formed out of the steam. The mouth was cavernous and from it issued a wail like a soul in agony that thundered and echoed across the lake, sending violent waves upon the water and chilling me to the bone.

'What on earth…? Did you…?' I spluttered, staring at Tiroc Og's conch. 'Did you call that up?'

'It's Hyndar the Watchling,' he replied without turning, his face calm, his paddle moving quickly to steady the boat being rocked in the sudden swell. 'He's the island spirit. He looks after Avalor, helps with the passage of the dead to the ancestors. He abides – if that's the word for such as him – in a hot cave under them rocks at the top of the island. We offer painted stones and the like for him to admire. He eats only warm dead flesh and…' he paused '…if the flesh isn't dead, he'll make it so.'

'But he's not real,' I said. 'I can see right through him.'

'Ah. He's real enough, but a half-life, caught between the worlds.

143

Part Manu, part spirit. He's harmless to all except those that disrespect the Isle of the Dead. To them, he's a cruel and merciless foe.'

I gaped, horrified and curious, as clouds of Morok bolts descended upon the Watchling and slipped through the ghostly form as if through a veil of mist before dropping harmlessly to the ground. The Morok horde then swarmed up to the mound, screaming and brandishing swords, maces and spears.

The gigantic ghoul roared – a sound so piercing the lake water rose again and banged against the sides of the dugout. A pair of huge smoky arms with clawed hands rose from the Watchling and descended towards the Morok. Their front lines continued to charge towards the rock mound, but many broke rank, running in all directions, hurling their weapons to the ground.

'I wouldn't look,' said Tiroc Og, steadying the boat before paddling forward at a more measured pace. 'Yeh'll not want to eat for days.'

But I'd already seen. As the Morok threw themselves at the smoky form, they were torn apart, their tortured screams resounding across the lake, their limbs and heads thrown back into the melee of those fleeing in terrified panic. A sickening red blood-soaked mist rose like a fountain from the island. I could no longer look on and turned away, stomach churning, then leaned over the side of the boat and retched.

Tiroc Og and the Brach paddled on, taking us out of open water into a narrow creek with alder and willow branches hanging low on either side. I tried to quiet my stomach with deep breaths, horrified by the realisation that the whole time I'd been on Avalor that monster had been present and – I shivered – watching for signs of disrespect.

'He'll leave none alive. Take comfort from that, young Albin. Sadly, there's plenty more where they came from,' muttered Tiroc Og.

As I calmed, I wondered about him again. Who was this character that conjured up astral bodies from a funeral pyre, and could summon a creature able to destroy half an army? Here I was, worrying about being seen as a sorcerer – when I was with the real thing. Was it in fact because of him that I was able to do what I did – suspend time and save his friend from certain death?

He was the real sorcerer here. But if he could do such things, what was to be my fortune, my mission, in his company? Not chance, or fate, or my own choice, or the shining stone – was it he that was in control of my destiny, he to determine the outcome of my mission?

15

A CONFESSION

We made camp that night in a shallow reedy cove in a shelter formed by fallen trees, one of which arched over us to form a roof. It was better, warmer, than any bender. Tiroc Og produced some dried fish, placed it in a pot, added powder and, very quickly, the tree shelter was filled with the scent of river fish and marsh mint. I eyed my companions, still wondering about them and their true motives for adding me to their burden. My gaze fell on Bran rummaging in his huge bearskin *papose*, who, with a grunt of pleasure, pulled out a sharpening stone and gleefully set about filing the edge of an already razor-sharp knife – the same that shortly before had taken at least one Morok life, and who knew how many more. Yet the joy in his face was that of a small child discovering a new toy. Tiroc Og, seated cross-legged across the fire from me, caught my gaze and rolled his eyes. I couldn't help but laugh.

The stew ready, bowls were passed and the three of us ate and drank in comfortable silence, each to our own thoughts – what had passed, what was passing and what was to come. My companions, clearly hardened warriors, showed no sign of trepidation, of the anxiety I felt. For despite my newfound confidence, my determination to succeed, I still felt fearful, and a little ashamed of my weakness.

Afterwards, Bran put down his bowl, tidied away his sharpened arms, rearranged his *papose* as a pillow, lay back and was instantly asleep, his huge frame rising and falling as he snored in eruptions like a small volcano. Tiroc Og had lit his pipe and was sitting quietly, contentedly smoking. I lay awake, gazing at the fire, seeking solace for my troubled soul in the warmth and sunglow of the burning coals.

After a long pause, the Wildcat asked again about my purpose in making such a dangerous journey, in such dangerous times. I repeated what I'd already told him, but he looked impatient and demanded, 'That's all? Nothing else?'

'What else would you like me to say?'

I tried to look as though I'd nothing to hide. But what could I tell him?

He shrugged, eyed me severely, but said nothing. As for my secret – the shining stone – how secret could it now be? He'd seen it, I was sure, and reacted to it, as if he knew something about it. But I felt I was not ready to tell all, not yet.

'All I desire is to get to Rakhaus and find my kin – if, indeed, they be there. And the help I seek from you is how to get there.'

'On yer own yeh'll not make it,' he said, shaking his head.

'What then am I to do? I must try.' My chest tightened at the prospect of what lay ahead. But what choice did I have?

'There are ways,' he said. 'But for the time being yeh have to keep with us, be one of us, and take orders.'

He gave me a stern look, expectant. Waiting for more explanations perhaps.

How was I to respond? His fading warpaint, wet from sweat and smatterings of marsh mud, made him look even more devilish than before. *Take orders* from a sorcerer? Really? But I hadn't exactly been doing fine on my own – hadn't even managed to cross the river; and I had no idea what to do, where to go next, if indeed my kin were prisoners of the Morok. And now guidance, the help I so needed, seemed to be on offer, conditional though it seemed.

'You mean become a bandit, like you?'

'Put like that, yes, I suppose. Become a wicked outlaw such as I.' He laughed, shook his head, toyed with the simmering pot, added herbs and powder then ladled the infusion high in the air, so that some fell on the coals, causing steam to rise and turn to droplets in the cold night air. When they landed on Bran he stirred, sniffed and sneezed and resumed snoring, louder than ever, mouth wide open. Tiroc Og reached over, rolled the Brach onto his side and placed his *papose* behind him as a bolster. The great warrior moved easily at his touch, and the snoring became soft breathing.

'It's not such a bad life,' he said, sitting back down and lifting his pipe. 'At least yeh'll be well fed. And yeh'll get to kill more Morok. Yer good at it.'

I resisted the temptation to tell him that, though I'd been trained in the warrior arts, I'd never killed anything but game before a few days ago; indeed, I'd been shocked by what I'd done – ashamed of the bloodlust that coursed through me.

'Yeh can leaves whenever you likes,' he continued. 'Be it on yer own head. But if yeh stay, yeh must follow us that know where we are, and trust in how we choose to deal with things. Think about it.'

What could I say – do, even? I'd no map. I didn't know the terrain, or what further terrors lay beyond; I had no idea how to get to Rakhaus or how I was going to rescue my kin if they were there. And so, I sat back, contemplating the offer, listening to Bran's soft breathing. Of course, I wanted their help. But I couldn't let my goal be sacrificed for anyone else's mission – no matter what. In the silence that followed I looked deep into the fire while Tiroc Og smoked and periodically poured his scented infusion over the hot coals.

Suddenly, he spoke up, his tone sombre. 'But know this, if we are to go further from this place with yeh, there's something I must know, young Osian, that yeh haven't been telling me. Indeed, my brothers insist on me asking yeh this.'

'Oh, yes?' I lifted my head. I'd been half expecting it, and now there was no backing away from the truth.

''Tis about thon moon-shaped stone in yer *papose*.'

'Yes, Tiroc Og, what of it?' My heart beat fast. What could I say? He'd seen it; I could hardly deny its existence.

'It bears the mark of the Morok,' he said gravely.

'This I know,' I said, thinking of the barbed maces and aber-axes carried by his warriors. 'But so too do some of the arms of your company.'

'They is won in battle though. How did yeh come by it? Did yeh steal it – kill Morok for it?'

I looked down. He sighed, took a long puff of his pipe and said, 'Consider this. My brothers and sisters fear – because of it – yeh might be a Morok spy, a very clever one.' He leaned forward, eyes glinting in the firelight, and waved his pipe in a circle. A perfect disc of yellowing smoke spiralled up into the air to join the steam escaping from the pot. The green stone at his wrist sparkled and winked.

I stiffened, feeling again the penetrating presence, the power of an *Akari* who talked to birds and summoned half-lives. Did he already know what the stone was?

'How did yeh come by it?' he said again. As he spoke, the steam and smoke gathering in the roof space coiled and twisted into a familiar shape – a pair of high-set eyes, a wide mouth. I gasped. It was a face from the totem carvings outside my family home – the visage of Otrec, the Mother, totem ancestor to the Otar tribes. With hollow eyes she looked at me. 'Speak,' she seemed to mouth.

'What...?' I exclaimed. Then the vision was gone. I drew breath and dropped my shoulders. My resistance was slipping away. The great ancestor had given her blessing – I could talk. A burden was being lifted.

I looked into Tiroc Og's eyes. 'I found myself in a cavern in the Karst...'

'Yes...' He sat back, relief on his face.

'I witnessed a shining crescent-shaped object being smothered in black webbing by a beast, then branded by two of a tribe strange to me.

I mean, I didn't know what they were at the time, but I've since learned are called Krol – Morok priests.'

He nodded, with a knowing look. 'Go on,' he said.

'Then, later, I found it…the stone…in the flood. I don't know how it got to be there or who it belongs to. I was drawn to it; given no choice but to rescue it. Seeing the mark, I was reluctant to keep it, yet could not rid myself of it. I know I have to protect it – till I find out what to do with it. This, all this, I can't explain to myself, never mind anyone else.'

'What makes you so sure it's the same object you saw in the cavern?'

'It shone like sungold and moonsilver when I first saw it and,' – I gulped – 'like a babe to its mother it cried out for help. To me. It called to me. Then later, when I retrieved it from the river it was because I'd spotted a shining crescent shape on the water, the very image of the object in the cavern, shining like a new moon warmed by the sun. It drew me to it; I had to rescue it. As I said, I had no choice.'

He stared at me, frowning. 'D'yeh know what it is yeh found?'

'What it was – what it is now…I…no. I have no idea. It does not shine on the surface, but my instincts tell me that inside its dark shell it still shines. And because it made me think of sungold and moonsilver, I have named it from sun and moon. *Sol-Lon*, *Solon*, the shining stone.'

He seemed to start at my choice of words, a momentary twitch, and quickly tapped his pipe on a stone, refilled and relit it. Then he had a faraway look, as if dragging something out of a memory store – or from another place, maybe an inner space where *Akaris* went for inspiration. I knew somehow not to disturb him, and I let my own gaze drift to the twists of smoke playing about the roof of the shelter, forming little shapes like small beings, seeking escape through tiny gaps in the wood.

'As ye'd expect, the Morok have some claim to what yeh have, this stone, this *Solon*, as yeh calls it,' he said at last, smiling at the word *Solon*. 'I believes it might be this they've been searching for up and down river – and now yerself with it. Frantic they are – desperate to find it. If yeh retrieved it from the flood, they Krol must have lost it. Two of 'em were spotted by the harriers with a dark crescent shaped object nearing the ferry point just as the helm was blowin' up, and not seen again. Drowned, probably.'

'Yes. I too gathered this. A robe like one of theirs was also in the floods. But what of Gwion? Was he with them?'

'We don't know where he is, or what happened. The Krol were probably trying to get passage across the river. He'd never have agreed to it in a storm.' He paused, seemed to reflect on something for a moment, then added, 'Those that might have known something – where he is – if he's alive – are dead now. Yeh yerself bore witness to it.'

'You mean Hiron's kin?' There was a lump in my throat. 'That's why the Morok were there? They were looking for what I had – what the Krol had lost – or for Gwion, or both?'

'Hiron's father and Gwion were close friends. Same elder group. The Morok will have known that.'

'The stone – the *Solon* and me – we're a danger to others, then,' I said, aghast. I remembered Hiron kneeling beside his kin, grief-stricken, and tears sprang hot to my eyes.

He touched my arm lightly. 'Calm yerself. Yeh're not responsible for anything those devils get up to. And we're guessing, anyways. The raid may have been just a random assault. Them raiders were drunk; might not even have been following orders. As fer a danger to others,' he continued, 'if yeh mean us, then no. We're no more at risk from the Morok than is our wont.'

'The *Solon*. D'you know why they want it so badly?'

Tiroc Og shook his head. 'Can't help yeh there, young 'un. Whatever it is, however yeh came by it, yeh needst be cautious. And my brothers'll be wary of you whilst yeh have it.'

'What do *you* think I should do with it?'

'That would be for yeh, only yeh, to decide. But I thinks yer life would not be in this place without it.'

'What d'you mean?'

He hesitated. 'It's maybe brought yeh danger – but also luck. Anyways, who of us can argue with our destinies?'

'I don't understand.'

'Yer *Solon*, as yeh calls it, whatever it is, as long as yeh have it it's part of yer *almadh*, yer destiny. Yeh said it called out to yeh. Maybe yeh were meant to find it, it's *yeh* that's been found, like the grasses find the sun, for reasons I cannot guess. Anyways, if the Morok want it, then it's best it's with yeh – anyone but them.'

More riddles! He relit his pipe and said, 'No more talk now. Drink yer *tai*.'

I sat back, relishing the *tai*, sweeter and more perfumed than normal. My mind buzzed with questions, but they didn't find a voice. I gazed at the fire, blanket over my back, watching the smoke trails from Tiroc Og's pipe disappear into the ether.

Whether it was relief at overcoming my close encounters with death, surviving so many strange happenings or just the warmth of the shelter and the *tai*, strangely, I felt I'd arrived at some kind of fixed point. For the first time on my journey, I felt comfortable in myself, what I was doing here, where I was and now, comfortable in the company of strangers.

This puzzled me, for my prospects didn't look great. Here I was, holed up in a desolate marsh, in the company of a pair of desperadoes, whose attitudes to me I'd yet to really comprehend. Yet they'd helped me in many ways and I realised that rightly or wrongly, despite my suspicions about their motives, their suspicions about me, I felt safe with them.

The scent of Tiroc Og's pipe smoke sent me drifting back to my younger days. I remembered Grandfather sharing pipes with Aguan traders who came every springtime. While they had their grown-up talks, I'd be sent outside to feed their wagon mules with carrots and fresh hay, and this allowed me to stay up for late-night fireside tale-telling and sea shanty singing. Later, deep in the night in my room, I'd hear laughter and shouting over games of *skim* coming up from the kitchen below that lasted till dawn. I remembered how the air hung for days after with the intoxicating whiff of *baco* and of fermented *aki*, the "crazy juice" the traders brought with them.

The thoughts of home made me realise what it was that I felt now, with Tiroc Og and the sleeping Bran. It was as though I was with family.

I began to feel woozy, and my head slumped. Dropping the *tai* bowl, I lay back on the reed straw.

'Rest, Albin, rest,' I heard a voice say, and between my closing eyelids I caught a glimpse of Tiroc Og peering into my empty bowl. 'Rest the sleep of Yahl. Leave yer worries to the creatures of the night.'

I shivered, and something deep and comforting was placed over me. 'My father's fur,' I heard Tiroc Og mutter softly. 'It will warm yeh. 'Tis enough.'

He continued to speak, but I didn't hear what was said; his voice had become a rhythmic cadence that weaved in and out of my drowsy consciousness, slipping into my dreams. I slept, yet was vaguely aware, as if through a cloud, of Tiroc Og rising to his feet, addressing the *sidhe* then bowing towards something on the floor.

With my dream eyes I followed his gaze, and saw he was somehow interacting with my *papose* where it lay nearby. It had become transparent, and inside it the familiar crescent shape of the *Solon*.

It was glowing.

16

TO TRISULDUR

I was being carried. I heard oars swishing through water. I was being brought home. Water birds hovered in hopes of scraps of fish or of succulent water-snails rejected from the nets of the fisher families. But not this terrible day.

There'd been an accident – a life and a boat had been lost. I'd been pulled out of the water by one of the Beaver tribes from the dam town at the end of the lake. Someone was no more. Someone close to me – who'd kept me alive in the water, but at the cost of her own life. I was freezing and needed a roaring fire to warm me from the water chill.

My mother was grieving – keening, crying out. Everything had changed.

I made myself wake. 'Grandfather,' I yelled, tearing the rug from my face, jumping up and rubbing my eyes.

It was a bad dream, an anxiety dream, one I'd had so many times before. I'd been too young when the accident happened. The only way I remembered it was in my dreams, for my kin never talked of it. My lost sister with the sky-blue eyes. I only remembered the eyes. My mother's eyes. It was all too hurtful for them. So, I never asked. Their pilgrimage to Arkesh had partly to do with it. An atonement for allowing such a thing to happen to one of their young. Yet, my life she had saved.

My eyes were heavy, like from a long sleep. When I finally opened them, I was in a marsh creek, twisting among sulphurous mudflats dotted with pockets of green mist. The character paddling the Barod dugout with his back to me was not Beaver tribe. It was Tiroc Og, who looked over his shoulder and smiled without breaking his paddle stroke.

'Ah, Osian,' he said. 'Awake at last. I'm sorry I'm not yer grandfather.'

A grunt came from behind. I turned to see Bran, paddling calmly, a gentle smile revealing his broken teeth. There were water birds. Three marsh harriers flying a short distance ahead, dipping their heads this way and that.

'What's going on?' I mumbled.

'We're on the way to Trisuldur. Yeh had a touch of marsh fever. We left the lakeside shelter two nights since, carried yeh on board – don't worry, yer things too,' Tiroc Og replied.

But, though barely awake, still shaking from the bad dream, I *was* worrying. Where was my *papose*? Ah, just there, beside my knees under the rug. My weapons lying to the side, neatly stacked. 'Marsh fever?' I asked. 'Two whole nights?'

But he didn't reply. I couldn't believe I'd slept for that long, couldn't even remember having fever. I'd felt fine when I first lay back in the shelter; my wounds had been healing. Conscious of everything… until I drank the Wildcat's brew.

Had I been given a sleeping potion? The *tai*? Was I wrong to have trust in them?

But drugged or not, marsh fever or not, I felt refreshed, invigorated. I'd only lost a day; for, judging by the light, it was barely noon. I was perhaps wrong not to trust them.

We'd left the creek and, entering a low-lying pool enclosed on three sides by banks of reeds, came to halt beside a mound of alder scrub. We disembarked and Bran dragged the boat onshore.

'Remember the time and place, brothers,' said Tiroc Og. 'On

155

a winter's day, mid-way between the rising and setting sun, look for the mound shaped like a pony. There's its tail.' He pointed out a line of reeds going from the mound into the water. From where we stood, with the risen ground as body and the high reeds as mane, the whole thing did indeed suggest the form of a squat horse. At his signal, we lifted our packs and weapons, then, after covering the stores and small armoury with skins, Bran single-handedly lifted the dugout into the heart of the reed bank, upended it and laid it over with cut reeds.

Pronouncing the job satisfactory, Tiroc Og mumbled a blessing to the spirits of this place, rubbed his hands and led us over the bank till we came to a vast expanse of sulphurous mudflats amidst a myriad of slow running creeks. There we moved forward in single file between two creeks, Tiroc Og ahead, me following, and Bran behind. It was a silent, gloomy place, but at least there was no sludgy snow, and we saw no marsh devils or other beasts. I was told we needed to move quickly to make up lost ground – maybe my fault, though nothing was said of it. The others would be waiting along the route.

I remembered seeing Trisuldur marked on Grandfather's sketch map as a *trisul* – a trident spear with three prongs, meaning 'three ways'. It was a crossway of old between the territories where travellers and pilgrims could procure hospitality and meet fellow wayfarers. To all the tribes, crossing points like this, along with hilltops and the meeting of rivers, were sacred places where gods and spirits were said to confer with worldly souls and, at the shrines there, assorted hedge priests and mendicants often made homes. At the bigger conjunctions on pilgrim ways, large benders were used to create covered markets where the faithful could trade cowries and moonsilver for trinkets and souvenirs, and pilgrims could find shelter. Trisuldur was one of the largest such conjunctions, famed across all Manau.

The ground underfoot was hard packed mud, and we moved forward quickly at Tiroc Og's relentless pace. Catching my breath as we rounded a bend between two treacherous-looking pools, I asked, 'Where are we now? What goes for the name of this dreadful place?'

''Tis the Flatlands,' replied Tiroc Og. 'All being well, we meet the others at sunset, then we all makes for Trisuldur together.'

'Have we crossed the river?' I asked, unsure of my bearings, unable to remember much of the detail in Grandfather's sketch.

'Long time since.'

Of course – it would have divided into marshes and creeks as it ceased to be a single watercourse. I had no memory though of crossing these, but I supposed we must have when I had been asleep. It was strange to think that after my failure to cross the river, it had been done without me even knowing it. All in all, I must have covered thousands of leagues since I'd left the Karst. For although the landscape was far from the rich azure pastures I'd dreamed of, I was finally in the "golden" pilgrim lands, Erainn proper, a place that, instead of being favoured by the gods, looked like somewhere that had been abandoned by them.

After a while, Tiroc Og hung back, allowing Bran to go in front, and indicated a willingness to converse. The harriers were no longer with us. I presumed he'd sent them on ahead. 'Tell me of Trisuldur?' I took the opportunity to ask. 'Are there Morok there?'

'Yes. They've closed the pilgrim way at that point, isolating the forests of the Terai, the shrine at Arkesh and the coast to seal Erainn and cut off Cana-Din and her allies. What was once the pilgrims' market there has been turned into a stockaded fortalice – only half-built, I understand – but the harriers tell me they've sent out a supply chain from their main camp at Erintor with an army of troopers to re-enforce it. They are bringing materials to extend the walls and dig spiked trenches, but fer some reason there are no slaves in the convoy, so works will be done by the Morok – which is usually badly. Nevertheless, once the fortress is complete, Cana-Din's renegades will be trapped between the sea and the Wicken marshes, with access to Clachoile blocked off to prevent her teaming up with any sympathetic free tribes.'

'Clachoile – that's Brach, Bear tribe territory. There are other tribes there too?' I asked.

'Sideag – the Grey Wolf – and some others, smaller. Some Catton like me; Barod – Beaver, of course; and Aguan too.'

'The Brach and Sideag tribes can't be happy about any of this, surely. I know they fought the Eronn, the Marsh Wars, over free access to the pilgrim ways. But surely this is worse.'

'Yeh'd think so. But these are things better asked of the Brach theyselves,' he said, nodding forward to our companion, now in close hearing.

''Tis indeed curious,' Bran said, joining the conversation. 'My tribe seem blind to the evils of the Morok. 'Tis a shame that is upon my fathers – and it weighs much upon my soul. I finds it hard to accept our fathers' allowin' Morok free passage along the pilgrim's turnpike, all the way from Erintor and across the edge of Clachoile, the way yerself might have come in better times. No-one uses the turnpike now 'cept the devils themselves.'

I felt a lump in my throat – the very route my kin would have been following if they ever got that far!

We pushed onwards, each in our own thoughts, striding across thick mats of grass, reed tussocks and rushes.

The other renegades, I'd learned, were waiting for us, encamped beside a creek, having been able to move all the way upstream in their dugouts to the meeting point. We'd taken a longer route in the supply boat. Leaving this at Pony Island was part of Tiroc Og's plan. We – some of us anyway – might need them on the return from Rakhaus.

As I walked, I contemplated how any remaining tensions between myself and my companions had largely lifted since my "illness" – if that's what it was. Had it to do my accepting my dependance on them? More likely, now that I'd unburdened my secret, Tiroc Og had found a way to re-assure them about me. I was no threat to them – maybe even useful to their cause. The giant Brach also seemed less scary to me, and his manner lighter. There was a kindliness in his voice, too. I felt more accepted – and more comfortable with them.

'Not much further now, chief,' Bran said, pointing at a clump of alders overhanging a wide creek. As we neared, I saw a group of beached dugouts and a huddle of benders like the ones on Avalor. The others were already there, milling around at the water's edge. Seeing us arrive, they waved and cheered. The marsh harriers were there too, perched on the roof of the largest bender. Two dugouts were sent across for us.

And so, by nightfall, I once more sat around a renegade campfire, in the inner circle of two rings of warriors. Hot food was prepared and conversations flew back and forth, among them Bran's telling of how I'd saved him as we left Avalor. It was then I learned he'd been aware of the arrow that flew at him, and that I'd deflected it. Admiring glances and friendly nods were coming my way. I'd proved myself as a warrior by saving Bran – but, engagingly, received some jests for doing exactly that!

The warpaint on the faces of the renegades was cracked and faded, making them look less formidable. Some played *skim* while we waited for victuals. Others talked and laughed. Some were pensive, silent. Yet the campfire brimmed with excitement. We were near to Trisuldur and, I was told, the biggest test of the company to date. But I detected no fear – this was a group of hardened warriors, clearly relishing the prospect of the battles to come.

I sat between Drion, distributing bowls of steaming food with his right hand, eagerly assisted by Bran and the other Brach – who had the name in him of Bron. Their own bowls were twice the size of all the others, but then, so were they! Tiroc Og was not present. When I asked after him, Bran explained with a wry smile that he was 'feeding the harriers'.

Intrigued since Avalor by the different tribes and individuals within the company, but so far feeling wary of being seen to be too inquisitive, I took the opportunity of being among them to finally ask. I whispered to Bran, 'I know the tribes but not the names of you all.'

'Well,' Bran replied in a whisper. 'I'll give yeh the main ones, but yeh'll never remember 'em all. Even I sometimes gets mixed up with who's who, and the bands switch round so much – we 'ave some of Cana's and she has some of ours. As fer all the clan names, we rarely use 'em, so can't tell yeh those.'

'Yes, that would be helpful. At home, we don't use the clan names much either.' This was often an area of great confusion. My clan's name was An, my mother's clan name, for the custom among the souther

Otar tribes, the Albin and the Eronn, was to inherit this from the female rather than the male line. Yet, across the tribes, we would be formally addressed by our father's first name – hence I was Osian An of Faron, and my father Faron An of Annan, adding the clan name An. All very tedious I used to think, though I'm sure there's reason in it.

'Who d'yeh want t'knows first?' he asked in a whisper.

I pointed out the two nearest on the far side of the fire. A pair of striking looking Wildcat who'd been sharpening knives with stones and comparing them, but who were now settling down to a game of *skim*, played across Manau with small red stones and sometimes for moonsilver. Both were male, and stocky like Tiroc Og. One was taller than the other, with sharp green eyes, and a yellow mane slightly greyed and braided at the back. He too had a green stone at his wrist like Tiroc Og's – which I'd been told indicated seniority. The other's mane was heavily matted; his face, though deeply scarred, seemed to carry a permanent smile.

'Those two Wildcat over there at *skim* – the bigger one is Ganoc; he's the best tracker we have – after the chief himself. The other is Sanic. Always smiling. A good tracker too. Don't be fooled by his size; he's the most dangerous fighter in our midst – after me,' he said with a chuckle.

'The tall Eronn watching 'em, there to the left of Sanic, is Lakon, a fine warrior. He and Ganoc lead the company when Tiroc Og is not about. Differin' tribes – but brothers sworn in blood.'

There were two She-Eronn sitting at the back, deep in conversation. I'd noticed them before with their unmistakeable long tricoloured Eronn manes, bundled behind their heads with cord. Behind their faded warpaint they were strong in face and, chatting away in the firelight, looked graceful in their movements. I thought of my brief view of Cana-Din, sensing her great beauty and powerful presence, and wondered if they also had her eyes.

'Thon She-Eronn,' Bran muttered, catching my gaze. 'Don't really know 'em or their names. They're new to the company, joined us on Avalor fer the first time – came late at night with Lakon, just back from the Terai with some new weapons Cana-Din's devised. Thon old

Eronn,' he added loudly with a guffaw, 'is Drion. You already know him from his terrible cooking.'

Drion, hearing this, smiled in response and ladled a tiny amount of stew into a bowl and signalled for me to pass it to the Brach. 'Your diet starts now, you great oaf,' he said.

'I take it back, oh wise one,' Bran responded, returning the bowl. Drion filled it to the brim, rolled his eyes and half whispered to me, 'Ask the great hairy beast how he lost his teeth, young Albin. Go on.'

Bran grimaced. 'Ha. I'd still have 'em if it weren't fer 'em bloomin' bones yeh leaves in yer soups.' Drion grinned back and showed an empty ladle as if to say 'no more for you,' to general laughter.

Between mouthfuls, Bran pointed out two Brach on the other side of the fire; young, eager looking, smaller than Bran, both with fearsome bearskin collars and headdresses. Sitting with them was a Brach as big as Bran. 'Though them two brothers comes from rival clans, they're like two peas in a pod.' I noticed the broader of the two waving a fist at the other, who brushed it away, laughing. 'Beside them is Bron. He's my twin. I'm the older – by one *hora*.' *Twin?* Goodness, there were two of them! He was the one who left Avalor in the solitary dugout, only slightly less imposing in frame than Bran. Lighter in colouring, but just as fearsome in his bearskin furs complete with claws and grizzly brown bear headdress. He beamed when his name was mentioned and gave the friendliest smile I'd seen yet. The other two Brach, Bran didn't name.

I pointed to a small group of three sitting furthest from the fire, deeply engaged in some kind of a heated discussion. One, a grizzled male older than the others, had a long grey pleated beard and a mane tied back inside a huge fur coat made from the skins of grey wolves, complete with heads and feet. I couldn't see the faces or gender of the others as they were both hooded against the cold night air. They also wore canine furs, one was bright red, the other more muted in colour. 'And those?' I asked in a low voice. 'Wolf?'

'Ah. Yes. Sort of. The name in the greybeard is Ranig. His friend was killed at the last raid on the Morok. He's a Sideag, Grey Wolf from Clachoile, now our only one. He has killed more Morok than anyone

I knows. There'll be a lot more of 'em dead by the time he's finished, I tell yeh. Them two wi' him are Rideag, Red Wolf from the Wester country. One of 'em is half Rhuad – even has the red hair o' them but, thank Yahl, not the long nose! Gimin is the name in her. She's our best runner. And our best archer. Can hit a leaf with an arrow a league away – a Morok at two. More on target than Tiroc Og hisself.'

A Rideag–Rhuad female – I was intrigued. I tried to peer over the heads of the Brach to see her. Just at that moment one of the Rideag stood up. And I knew it was her, her hood falling back to reveal a long mane flowing across the loveliest face I'd ever seen. As I stared she began to move away, her hair swirling in the firelight, a deep scarlet, bright against the more muted red of her canine furs. I saw in her something of Reyn, slender like a fox, yet strong like a wild dog, and strangely, as her form merged into the night, I felt as if I'd known her from before. If I had, it could only be from a former life, as Grandfather might have suggested, but my mind was playing tricks with me. My brief view of her had fixed hold of my attention like a vice.

As I stared after her, for the very first time in my young life, I recognised in myself an instinct as deep as an Albin lake. The mating instinct! Yet it was hardly possible, all this from a fleeting glance at a female from a tribe I did not know – and, I understood, a fearless killer! What on Yahl's earth was happening to me?

'I recognise the Rhuad,' I said, lamely trying to hide my reaction, gesturing to three Reyn-like figures, fox furs glistening bright red in the firelight, sitting silently beyond where Ranig and his companion Red Wolf sat. One was female, and fox-like in her face, with the long nose and sharp eyes, not like Gimin, apart from her mane, sharing her looks more with the young Rhuad at her side. Brothers and sister, I wondered.

'Ah, the long noses. Jokers the lot of 'em. Beware,' Bran said, his voice loud enough to ensure they heard. 'Don't believe anything thon lot tell you – unless it's in battle, and they're tryin' to save yer skin.'

The Rhuad grinned at me as their names were mentioned. I thought yes, they did have a mischievous look. Maybe I'd get the chance to ask them about Reyn – maybe they knew him? I smiled back and nodded formally. But because by that time I was imagining Gimin staring into my eyes like the vision of Erin in the Log Marten's fire, the names passed me by. "Pone" might have been one, but I was unsure.

'Now who's left – they that are not here?' muttered Bran. 'Well, there's Yamis and three other Barod around somewhere. Probably out collecting wood. Yeh'll see 'em later. Yamis is a good sort, help yeh with anything, can do just about everything, would kill fer yeh if yeh needed.' I smiled at this. I'd noticed the Barod in Avalor, had heard someone address him. He had a brown mane, was stout in shape with great muscular arms and no doubt had the strength of the stones, like the Barod in Alba, who excel at all the practical things, boat building, house building, repairs and making useful things from whatever bits and pieces are lying around. Back home the Beaver tribe were our greatest friends and I'd spent many a happy hour in their great hovels built on stilts over the water, treated to fish pie and goat's milk seasoned with honey and lake herbs. I felt warmth at the knowledge that there were Barod in the company – that they were on our side.

Finally, Bran turned towards the creek, frowned and grunted. 'Then…there's them Aguan – Aridh and Garidh. Mercenaries, they is. Kills for moonsilver. But Tiroc Og says they're useful so. Garidh is with Tiroc Og in his bender at this moment – talking boats, no doubt. Don't know where Aridh is. Funny sort, he is. Good fighter but never talks; grumpy, but maybes 'tis the cast in his eye makes him look that way.'

I knew the one. Sullen, always hooded, who'd been shooting suspicious glances at me earlier. Yes, one of his eyes did look skewed somehow. Even when young I always had trouble telling one visiting Aguan apart from another, though there were small differences between their blue-dyed robes and manes, and the shell wristbands were of different colours. Their curved swords and the curious long knives – made, I'd been told, from the bones of sea monsters – held at their waists, always aroused my curiosity. Romi, the She-Tarsin, sported similar weapons – but then she'd sailed Aguan ships.

'That's it, I think, and me and the chief of course.' By the time he'd finished I'd forgotten some of the names already. But not the slender

Wolf–Fox in the name of Gimin. She'd reappeared at the fire and was laughing at something her Rideag companion had said. I saw her glance in my direction, her eyes a steely grey that glowed in the firelight. I felt a quiver in my throat. Suddenly feeling breathless, I looked away, but sensed her eyes following me, burning into my soul.

More steaming bowls of stew were passed around. Bran handed his back to Drion. 'More, eh?' said the elder Eronn to him. 'Watch yeh don't break the rest of yer teeth,' he said with a chuckle. Others laughed, but, I noticed, warily. Making fun of Bran, twice the size of all of them, was a delicate matter. Examining his bowl, Bran turned to me and said in a loud whisper, 'I forgot to add, Albin, a thoroughly miserable lot they all are too – more so if I crack their heads together.' A hail of bits of stew landed on his head and shoulders.

The laughter died away as we ate, the humour of the moment replaced by soft conversation.

'I'm already struggling to remember names.' I said to Bran, between mouthfuls of warm flat bread and tasty fish stew.

'Yeh wills after a while, Osian,' he said. 'Meantime, the ones yeh needs remember are them that gives the orders: Tiroc Og, Ganoc and Lakon.'

As we ate, I looked around again at them one by one, studying the individual characteristics of each – the differing types of furs, robes and headdresses, and the warpaint, some faded, some freshly applied – each different, each in its own way. Their scarred visages and healthy frames alone would put the fear of Yahl into any that crossed them. Such strange and powerful company I was in.

I found myself gazing again at Gimin sitting opposite, gaily chattering with her friends.

'Didn't yeh hear me? Cougar got yer tongue,' said Bran, making me jump. Absorbed in my thoughts, I hadn't been aware he was talking.

'Sorry. What?'

'What think yeh of our fare, Albin? Yeh'll be used to fish, I suppose?'

'Fine, fine…' I said, flustered. In truth, I hadn't thought about it at all. The stew was good, though – rich with aromatic herbs, swollen millet and root vegetables. At home, we were so used to fresh fish that dried fish, when we got it, always seemed like poor fare. But in this place, it tasted like nectar, and far better than some of what I'd managed to scavenge or been given along the way.

Bran asked me about my homeland, and how much the Albin, so much cut off from the other tribes by the White Mountains, knew of what was going in Erainn. I told him that back home we had not experienced the Long Winter affecting these parts, though our last two springs and summers had been untypically cold and we'd had little sun so our harvests had been poor. But it was not like it was here – and we were anyway used to long winters, with much snow and ice, frozen lakes and slender winter feed for the Barod goat herds. Otherwise, little was known about what had been happening across the mountains, for the news bringers – Aguan traders – had not been seen for two whole springs. That was until the ones came who escorted my kin for their supposed *yatra*. It was hard to believe that my kin hadn't known of what had been going on before they set out. Their Aguan escort would have been fully aware of Kahl and his invasion – if perhaps not the full occupation, with all its terrible implications. Did Grandfather not know about this? And if he did, why had he said nothing to me about it?

Drion was now handing out the last bowls of stew from an almost empty pot, the shiny stone at his wrist glistening in the firelight. I asked Bran how he'd lost his arm and was told it had happened in a raid upon a Morok camp. Drion, then a fine archer, had managed to save the life of the Barod Yamis, but a Morok, seeing that Drion had spent his last arrow, managed to land a sword blow on the brave Eronn, severing his bow arm. He'd have died, but for Yamis risking everything to carry him clear from danger. After that it was down to Tiroc Og's potions and healing skills. Only then did Drion become the main cook to the company, as he could no longer shoot a bow, taking the role at the fireside of one of the Barod. I gazed at the brave Eronn, feeling pity for his wound but admiration for his actions and, as before, sensing a deeper connection with him. Although he was at least twenty winters older than I, I sensed we would become friends.

Following the meal, a bone quaich of *aki* was passed around. I declined, as always. I had no taste for the bitter "falling-over" liquid, brewed I knew from potatoes rejected from the dinner table and fermented with pine sap. I had always been told that it fortified the body, but in my young experience it seemed to make its drinkers aggressive when taken in large quantities.

Tiroc Og appeared back at the campsite accompanied by Yamis and the two Aguan, Aridh and Garidh. Behind them followed two Barod, one of them female, pulling sledges piled high with arrows wrapped with sticky cloth and smelling strongly of pitch. Walking to the middle, the Wildcat stood by the fire, warmed his hands and looked about, waiting for quiet. He was about to address the company.

As one, they ceased what they were doing, and silence fell. I gazed around at their faces as they waited for him to speak, noticing the deep respect in their expressions. He was not just their guide, their tracker. This was someone they would follow to their deaths. Their *Kaif*, their chief.

'The crossways of Trisuldur, as yeh'll know,' he said, in a commanding tone, 'is the last open link 'tween the Souther, Easter and Norther Lands. If it's broken, there's a risk we becomes separated from the Terai and Cana's band – and any support she might get from the free tribes. Fer once the territory is ringed with fortalices and patrols, the Morok conquest of Erainn will be complete. It will be isolated like a tall rock in the Karst desert.'

General murmuring followed. Drion held up his one arm.

'Drion, you have a question?'

'Only this,' he said. 'I understand from the Albin that the Rhuad recently held a great gathering of the Wester land tribes. Do the harriers know the outcome? Will the Red Fox, the Red Wolf and their allies rise against the Morok? Or will they be neutral, abandoning their ancient Eronn friends to extinction?'

I glanced over at the Rhuad who seemed despondent. Gimin looked angry and was shaking her head ominously.

''Tis my understanding,' Tiroc Og replied, 'that the Fox, Wolf and other Wester tribes were courted by the Morok at the Kwakwakam, and though there was dissent amongst the tribes,' – here I thought of Reyn – 'after their council, the great chiefs agreed to remain neutral.'

There were shouts of 'shame!' from the company. One of the Rhuad spat in disgust and uttered a fearsome curse. I heard the word *yeel* repeated – cowardly.

''Tis their terrible headdresses,' piped up Bran. 'Can't see their noses fer their eagle feathers.' There was general laughter, but the Rhuad grimaced and squirmed, not amused.

'Judge not the wisdom of elders. And these are our old friends,' Tiroc Og said gently. 'They may be playing for time. If Cana-Din wins over the Brach and Sideag, the Rhuad and Rideag may yet come onside, if only out of rivalry – of this, I'm sure. Especially if they suspect the Morok might look to the Red Lands for its riches of *riggid*, the red fire gold. My friend, Reyn's father, and the other chiefs have lived for too many summers to not know this.'

So, Reyn was indeed a prince, one day to succeed his father, for the Rhuad High Chief was a king, the only monarch in all Manau. Of Reyn's inclinations I was in no doubt. If only he was in a position to lead.

I observed the Aguan standing slightly aside, watching the proceedings. The one called Aridh caught my gaze but quickly turned away; the other was impassive, eyes downcast. These were fighters for hire, from a tribe of collaborators. If these two could be hired by the renegades, could they not also have been hired by the Morok? Even if not, their allegiances could surely switch at any point, and the company have an enemy – a spy or spies - in their midst. Why would Tiroc Og, with all his Wildcat cunning, tolerate such a risk? Something about his trust in them – or maybe it was just them – made my flesh creep.

Tiroc Og, fingering the totem carvings on his staff, spoke on. 'The harriers have seen the Morok supply force coming. 'Tis huge indeed – a long line of Aguan wagons loaded with weapons; and there are armour plated chariots carrying Morok archers readied for any attacks.'

'What are the enemy numbers, chief?' queried Ganoc. 'What are we up against?'

'Well, my friend, 'tis good to know indeed what's facing us. Truth is, there's only a score or so troopers at the fort, 'n' three or four Ferok with them. But...' he hesitated, 'in the supply wagons and the chariots... there are many hundreds.'

Ganoc's face showed no surprise, nor trace of fear. He simply nodded. Behind me, though, I heard some mumbling. But it wasn't of dissent or concern. It was about how easy it was to kill Morok – and who'd kill the most! The confidence was extraordinary. We were a tiny party, no more than two score odd in number and, no matter how skilled, what were our real chances against such a large force with their defences and chariots? Brave talk indeed...but perhaps it was only talk.

'Hear my plan,' said Tiroc Og. 'We leave here about two *hora* afore first light and make our attack on two fronts – striking the supply force on its approach, just when it leaves its night camp, and assaulting the fortalice afore the relief gets too close. So, we'll divide into three parties, under myself, Ganoc and Lakon. Sanic is to go with Lakon so there's a Wildcat in each party fer the harriers to pass information between us. Ganoc's party are to use our newest weapon, Cana-Din's firelogs, laying them on the pilgrim trail coming from the west across the flatlands. The idea is to force the wagons and chariots off the causeway into the creek mud and make them useless. Escaping Morok will be open targets fer our bolts and arrows.'

Ganoc, seated on the outer circle with Tiroc Og's other trusted lieutenant, the Eronn Lakon, raised his bow and smiled. I noticed for the first time the green stone flickering at his wrist – which I presumed, like Tiroc Og's, was an indication of his status in the company.

'Firelogs,' I whispered to Bran, 'what are those?'

'They're like our own firesticks, only better, producing not just smoke, but explosions. I've not seen what they can do – yet. But I've heard the stories. Cana-Din has some renegades who do nothin' else but makes 'em, I hears. With luck we'll see – or better still, hear,' he cackled and pointed to some goatskin bags at Ganoc's feet. Bundles of red sticks protruded from them, the visible ends about the width of a bender pole, a long thick waxen taper leading from the end of each and wrapped around the stick.

'Lakon's party,' Tiroc Og continued, 'will go east and around past the fortalice and come in from the north to attack the defences from the rear, the weakest point, where the palisades are half-built and can be broken in if possible. My party will approach from the front. Ganoc's attack will be first, then Lakon, then mine. If we can keep to this sequence and time it well, we'll create most confusion among the Morok – and hopefully they'll believe our forces are bigger than they actually are.'

Lakon grinned on hearing Tiroc Og's instructions and gleefully held up his bow.

'All of yeh in Lakon's group, there are outlying traps with spikes that are poison tipped – a dreadful, painful, slow death. The harriers with yeh can spot 'em and hopefully point them out. 'Tis unlikely the Morok would put a watch outside the fort but take care in case they do.'

He paused for questions, but there were none.

'I'm hoping,' he continued, 'some of the devils will leave the fortalice as soon as they hears the attack on the supply chain. That's when we'll mount a direct assault on its front, 'n' fire flamin' arrows over the palisades. This is the signal for Lakon to break in through the far side. The harriers will fly between us and warn the Wildcats if anything is amiss. All being well, brothers, the enemy'll be runnin' around like trapped rabbits not knowing which way to turn.'

At this there was loud cheering, and many stood, waving their weapons, and I too felt the blood rising within me.

'What about the Albin?' said someone. I looked behind me. It was Garidh, one of the Aguan.

'For those of you left in any doubt,' snapped Tiroc Og, 'Osian is one of us. Remember, Bran's life is his. He has a life debt with our bravest warrior—'

A voice interrupted, 'Shame on the Albin!' to general laughter. Bran growled and jostled with his immediate neighbours. Tiroc Og joined in, forced to laugh, but added, in sombre tone, 'Make no mistake. The Albin is young, but a proven warrior – I have seen him kill. He is swift and deadly.'

I lowered my head. When I lifted it, I noticed Aridh staring at me. This time he didn't look away. It was me who averted eye contact.

'Osian will stay with my group,' said Tiroc Og. 'The rest of you go with your fellows, as is your custom. Watch out for Morok scouting devils. Lakon, Ganoc – when yeh're within half a league of the fortalice, send out yer harriers to let me know yer positions and yer readiness. We'll wait for the explosions from the trail, then three blasts from me,' – he held up his conch – 'will signal the start of the frontal attack on the fortalice. Any questions?'

There were none.

'One final thing. Bring yer benders with yeh. After Trisuldur, if Yahl is with us, we will meet again to plan our next move. Drion is to leave us. He'll go east along the creeks, then take a safe route known only to the Eronn and meet up with Cana-Din in the Terai.'

'So, who'll be feedin' us?' grunted Bron. It was the first time I'd heard Bran's brother speaking out.

'Why yeh, of course,' replied Tiroc Og.

'What!' exclaimed Bron, amidst a chorus of 'Ugh, spare us!'

'Yeh should've kept yer mouth shut,' said Bran, slapping his brother on the back. Bron growled and clattered his sword in its sheath.

'What about Cana-Din herself?' queried one of the She-Eronn with silver and purple warpaint stretched across a deep scar in her brow whom I'd learned was called Iona. 'Won't she be joinin' us for the fun at Trisuldur?'

'Cana-Din is in the Terai, on her way to assault the Morok's easternmost fortalice. Afterwards, it is planned for her to journey to Clachoile, to meet with the great chiefs of the Brach and the Sideag. Drion will go with her. She knows what we are planning, and will join us at some point if she can. She – we – cannot fail.'

At this there were shouts of 'We shall not fail!'

Tiroc Og smiled at this, then, raising his arm, expelled a deep breath and chanted aloud: 'I invoke the great spirits, guardians of forest, wood, stream and mountain, to ride upon our shoulders on this day. We are the fleet-footed, the sure-armed and the pure of heart. The enemy are craven, weak-hearted and cowardly. They are to be crushed by the might of Yahl's chosen warriors. Our spirit is strong, our hearts are brave. Yahl go with us.'

'Yahl go with us,' repeated the company. Then he spoke again, but this time not as shaman, but as chief. 'Brothers, sisters, yeh know the plan – 'n' yer duties. There are enough of us, and we are warriors enough to deal with what lies ahead. Meantimes, get some rest. Again, remember, we leaves two *hora* afore sunrise.'

We rose from the fireside and made for the benders. Bran showed me the one where I was to rest, sharing the space with him and Tiroc Og. But our chief didn't join us at first. As I lay down my head, I heard him outside in whispered but animated conversation with another, a little away from the bender. I recognised the dialect of the one he was speaking to, but not who it was. It was one of the Aguan.

17

THE SIEGE

We rose in darkness, took hot rations prepared by Drion – our last from him – and packed our belongings for the final approach to Trisuldur. Then, just as we were about to embark on the short journey back across the creek, Drion stood before me, muttered the blessing of Yahl the way an elder does, and gave me his hand.

In that moment, I again sensed a deeper connection, as if parting from him was more like a separation from one of my own – a dear uncle perhaps, but closer. Yet I had to wonder if we really would ever meet again. Given the enormity of the task we faced, against such odds, what possible circumstance could that be?

On the far side, we secreted our boats amongst banks of reeds and from there went on foot, splitting into the three parties – Ganoc in a north-westerly direction; Lakon towards the northeast; while Tiroc Og's party, made up of me, Bran, Garidh, Yamis, the She-Eronn Iona, the Grey Wolf Ranig and the young male Rhuad Pone, carried on due north. One of the harriers hovered just above us, scouting for danger with its sharp eyes.

As night became day we made swift progress through the flatlands, leaving open mud plain for dense willow carr overtopped by clumps of alder and the occasional stand of birch and pine. After a while, our harrier indicated danger to Tiroc Og – in the peculiar way they had of communicating – pointing out a thin column of smoke some short way ahead. I could easily see that this was not a skilled hunter's fire, but yellow–white, easily seen even in semi-darkness. As we neared, Tiroc Og sent the harrier up to get a better view. I saw a faint flickering of firelight on its wings, as we crouched in the scrub waiting for it to return.

'Morok,' whispered Tiroc Og when the harrier reported back. 'They're burning damp wood. Just a small party – scouts, maybe, easy prey. Garidh, Ranig and Yamis, yeh go left. Iona and Pone come in from the right. Osian, Bran and I will approach from the front. No signal needed. They won't expect it. Just attack when yeh're ready.'

I followed Tiroc Og and Bran as we crept soundlessly through the trees, bows and crossbows mounted. But when we got there, it was all over. Three Morok lay sprawled on the ground, stone dead, the remains of their breakfast scattered at their feet, blue feathered Aguan bolts protruding from their backs. Ranig greeted us with a bundle of Morok bolts in his arms. Yamis triumphantly held up a Morok belt studded with daggers and wrapped it around his huge waist. 'What kept yehs all?' he said.

Iona and Pone arrived just after us, looking disappointed. Though quick to trawl among the dead for weapons, their faces showed distaste for the scene before them.

''Tis a cruel deed that had to be, brothers,' said Tiroc Og, confirming my own thoughts, 'though yeh shoulds have spared one fer interrogation. They'll be from the fort no doubts – an outer watch, maybe. It would have been good to know more about the place, the defences.'

Garidh – responsible, it seemed, for all the kills – curled his lip. 'They heard us approach and were about to use this,' he said defensively, holding up a long, twisted ram's horn, the dark mark of the Morok cut deep into the bone. Casting it to the ground, he muttered, 'Would 'ave been heard for leagues around.'

'Ah, Garidh, maybe well 'tis done,' Tiroc Og muttered, but unconvincingly.

Ranig shrugged and said, 'Garidh offered to scout ahead. 'T'was all but over when Yamis and I got there.'

'What do we do wi' 'em, chief?' Bran gestured towards the bodies. 'Don't want ravens circling and attracting attention.'

'Yamis, Ranig, throw 'em in the creek, up against the side,' responded Tiroc Og, kicking traces over the Morok campfire. 'Put mud and rushes over 'em. But maybes pick up that Morok horn, Bran. Bring it with yeh. Could be useful.'

Later, with Tiroc Og striding ahead through the trees, I was prompted by Garidh's kills to again ask Bran about the Aguan fighters.

'They's jus' killers, Osian, as I said afore. Do it for the pleasure, and the moonsilver, of course, any 'scuse.'

'Can they be trusted – their loyalty?'

'Not by me, any rate,' he replied. 'Don't like thon Garidh much – don't understands why Tiroc Og spends so much time wi' 'im.'

'What about the other?'

'Aridh. Can't really speak fer 'im. Thon bad eye of his came about in a fight with Bron – they were drunk on *Aki*. Bron wouldn't hurt a friend. T'was an accident, but Aridh's shy anyway, wary of everyone – that's why he's always on the sidelines. The injury gives him a severe way. Yeh have to remember where he's looking isn't always what he's looking at, if yeh knows what I mean.'

Suddenly something sounded in the distance – a heavy rumbling. Tiroc Og raised an arm, bringing us to a stop. Placing two fingers to his lips he made a bird sound – barely audible. The harrier alighted on his arm, bent towards Tiroc Og's mouth, then flew off.

Tiroc Og signalled 'prepare weapons'. The bird came back, squawked in his ear then departed to the west, in the direction of Lakon's party. Tiroc Og then lifted his conch, blew three blasts, hefted his sword, pointed it and started forwards.

As one we started to run. My legs were shaking, and I felt fear, but in the faces around me I saw only steely determination – tensed shoulders, even fierce smiles – ready to fight, to kill, to win! As I ran, I became aware of warm tremors radiating from the base of my spine, where the *Solon* rested in my *papose*. My fear dissolved.

Suddenly a shower of bolts appeared in the sky ahead of us, but quickly became entangled in the treetops and clattered uselessly down through the branches. Some landed among us, but their force was already spent. None followed. We halted by a thick stand of old pines. The rumbling became louder – closer. But no more bolts flew up.

Tiroc Og looked puzzled. 'Them bolts were meant fer us. The conch call will have drawn their fire, but they don't know where we really are. From the sounds of it, their reinforcements are closer to the fortalice than I thought. Iona, here,' he said, giving his conch to the She-Eronn, the swiftest runner in our party. 'Take this towards Ganoc's party till yeh sees 'em, then blow it, a quick triple blast to let us know they're alright, only one blast if there's a problem. Take care fer spike traps. Then get back here. We'll stick up ahead fer yeh – at the tree edge jes' before the fort.'

He waited till Iona had gone, then said, 'Brothers, we needs go in. We should have heard Ganoc's firelogs by now. Maybe he didn't have time to lay 'em. We can't wait. We'll destroy as much as we can afore the wagon train gets there, then withdraw for a separate strike. We'll attack head on – and hope Lakon's ready on the far side.'

We moved stealthily forward. Soon, through gaps in the pine canopy, the top of the fortalice came into view. I made out a high wooden palisade bristling with Morok firing random shots off into the trees and yelling chaotically at each other; their bolts lost in the thick foliage. Judging by their missiles, they didn't know where we were – yet. Or, with our limited numbers, who or what we were. The way a conch call echoes and bounces always makes it hard to tell where exactly the sound is coming from.

The lower part of the fortalice was now visible through the trees. I could see a huge double gate in the central column; above it a watchtower with three tall figures moving around the top. Towering over the column was a platform on a single pole, a lone Morok on lookout.

'Those three in the tor are Ferok,' Bran whispered to me. 'The ones that gives orders. They're mine. I'll have thon stupid devil in the crow's nest while I'm at it.'

Still moving forward, our position undetected – no missiles coming our way, we neared open ground littered with stumps and branches where trees had been cleared. But crossing it would put us in the open – and in range of Morok bolts.

Tiroc Og signalled. 'Stay low,' he urged. 'Wait.'

We crouched behind the last line of trees. My chest pounded with anticipation, the excitement building in my blood. And again, that small tremor in my lower back, and a gentle calming in my head. I felt my senses sharpening, my vision clearer, my hearing crystal sharp, so acute I could hear the hearts of my colleagues thumping with ardour, on edge, impatient to begin. I felt no fear, only a quiet confidence in myself and, I hoped, shared with my brothers and sisters in arms.

Suddenly from the west came a thunderous booming crash, like a hundred trees falling at once. A pall of red smoke rose into the sky. Then another explosion. Stars wheeled across my vision – fiery arrows dropping out of the sky. In seconds, the marsh forest bloomed with flame.

Tiroc Og turned to us and grinned. 'The firelogs. Ganoc made it after all. Blow the devil horn now, Bran.'

The Brach lifted the twisted Morok horn to his lips and, with a grimace, blew hard. It sounded harsh, grating, doom-laden, like a funeral peal. Hearing it, the guards on the fort battlements, already in commotion, started dashing around even more furiously.

Bran spat and laughed. 'The devils think 'tis their own scouts over here. But they'll know something's wrong. They'll be confused. Hopefully they won't know which way to turn.'

Meanwhile, Iona returned with Tiroc Og's conch, passing it to him with a look of triumph. Still, we waited and watched.

The gates at the base of the watchtower suddenly flew open. Troops of Morok poured out and began running west, towards the explosions. Amidst the throng, I saw four long chariots bristling with archers harnessed to strange looking four-legged creatures in heavy armour. A Ferok rode in each chariot, cracking a whip at the beasts as they hurtled past the racing ground troops.

'What in Yahl's name are those?' I whispered to Bran, pointing at the chariot beasts, the like of which I'd never seen. From the tops of their heads protruded spiked horns trailing black ribbons. Jagged metal plating covered their sides and rear.

'They is a kind of wild boar, Osian. See their tusks,' he answered.

The chariots and followers disappeared into trees to the west. A single Morok emerged from the fortalice, darting around nervously and beginning to close the gate.

'This one's mine, 'tis our moment,' said Tiroc Og. He fired a single bolt. It thumped into the guard's chest, pinioning him to a half open gate, his head hanging down. Bran fired another, striking the lookout on the crow's nest, sending him toppling backwards.

Over the fort flew two harriers, circling once, twice, three times.

Tiroc Og sounded his conch. The answering call came immediately. Lakon was in position. Another explosion pierced the air. A cloud of smoke poured into the air at the back of the fortalice while from within came yelling, screaming, horns blowing. 'We go in. Now!' Tiroc Og commanded, raising and dropping an arm.

We raced across the open ground, dividing to either side of the gate, and entered the fort unchallenged. There we found a scene of total devastation. Lakon's party was already inside, cutting and stabbing at a clump of Morok troopers. Dead Morok lay everywhere. A mist of blood-tinged smoke hovered in the air. The rear palisade was wide open; the whole back of the fort just a blasted burning ruin.

The watchtower itself was unharmed, as were the east and western sides. Suddenly, Morok came tumbling out of a room on the right and ran towards us, screaming and waving maces and swords. I claimed my first with a bolt fired from the shadow of the gate, then two more as they struggled to load their weapons. Looking for another target, I saw Bran ahead of me taking out three more with a single swing of his staff – no longer the gentle giant but a savage killer, living up to his frightful bear-like visage. His sword finished off two more; another was felled by a knife in the belly.

I paused for breath – astonished at the one-sided slaughter taking place before my eyes. But there would be no quarter, no Morok was to be allowed to escape. The injured were being finished off – toppling like broken trees. Soon, none remained alive. I caught sight of Gimin gazing around at the smouldering ruins; her graceful form at odds with the sea of carnage around her. Lakon's party was everywhere, busily suppressing fires, smothering flames and smoke with anything at hand – including Morok corpses.

'Bran, Morok horn. Over here. Quickly,' commanded Tiroc Og. Bran threw it over. Three vibrating blasts followed. Tiroc Og cleared his throat, spat and shouted, 'Bran. Iona. Close the gates. Lakon, go with yer party out the back, run through the woods along the line of the western trail, find Ganoc and give 'im any help he needs. Yamis and Pone, yeh stay at the rear of the fortalice – jes' in case there's any livin' devils in the woods beyond. Rest of yeh, get up on these palisades, keep out of sight and ready yer bows. Osian, come with me.'

I followed him to the base of the watchtower where we scrambled up three rickety ladders to the top. From there we had a clear view of the old pilgrim turnpike winding through the forests, clearly marked out by a line of smoke and blazing wreckage, fleeing Morok and terrified boars, some with their harnesses and armour ablaze. Silhouettes of our warriors shimmered on the edge of the inferno, manes and arms flying furiously in the red glow, dealing death into scatterings of panicked Morok.

Tiroc Og looked at me and grinned. 'That's the end of that supply chain. Ganoc's firelogs did the trick. Nothing there will survive now. But them chariots that left the fort'll soon be back.' He grinned widely. Extraordinarily, everything was happening just as he'd planned. The Morok force had been divided into three. Two sections had been wholly destroyed, the last about to fall into a trap, summoned back by their own horn. I smiled in admiration. Tiroc Og's cunning were allowing him to overcome forces far superior to his own.

'Close the gate, Bran,' he shouted. 'Here they come. Everyone on the palisades below, keep yer heads down and make no noise.'

We crouched and watched through slits in the timbered walls as a chariot packed with Morok screamed out of the forest and shuddered to a halt at the gate, directly beneath us. Two more followed, pulling up behind it. The Ferok in the lead vehicle jumped down, sniffed the air and yelled for the gatekeeper. When there was no response, he bawled commands at those behind.

Archers poured from the vehicles, formed a line behind them and began arming longbows – the first I'd seen in the ranks of the Morok. Their drivers remained on board, struggling to control their beasts. 'Don't let 'em hear yeh even breathe, Osian,' whispered Tiroc Og. 'Keep still and watch.'

The lead Ferok looked around, clearly bewildered. The fort was deadly quiet. It must have looked to him just as his chariot train had they'd left it. But where was the gatekeeper? And why did the air reek of smouldering timber and burning pitch? Turning his head in every direction, he sniffed the air, clearly unsure of the source of the burning (for a light wind coming from the west was bringing with it smoke from Ganoc's fires.) The boars were unsettled, stamping the ground and snorting, probably smelling the slaughter within, Morok blood. He looked nervous but waited, undecided –what to do.

I felt a crawling, prickling sensation at the base of my spine. At any moment a volley of poison arrows could be coming our way, over the top of the palisade and through the gaps in the posts.

Then the boars in the lead chariot spooked. One of them reared up, causing the others to panic, throwing the lines of archers and the other chariots into confusion.

'Attack!' screamed Tiroc Og suddenly, jumping to his feet and firing an arrow at the Ferok in the lead chariot. I followed with my crossbow aimed at the second chariot. Then, along the battlements beneath us, renegade heads popped up and began shooting arrows flaming with pitch into the mass of Morok archers. Disoriented, they crashed to the ground, dead or dying, their bodies peppered with bolts and flaming arrows. The boars were in a frenzy. The armour of the lead beast in the first chariot was on fire, causing the others to tear away from their harnesses, overturning the vehicle and, if he was not already dead, crushing the driver beneath it. The middle chariot was aflame, its beasts trapped between the blaze and the palisade walls, its driver lost in the melee. The third chariot broke away, its lead boar screaming in agony, arrows poking from the thin armour on its back. It tore into the woods, out of control, as its driver, unharmed, screamed and wildly whipped at the terrified beasts as they tried to tear themselves from their harnesses.

'Bran. Take Osian and the swift-foots, Iona and Gimin,' Tiroc Og shouted down. 'Deal with that chariot before it meets any outlying Morok. I'll go with the rest to Ganoc. Be wary. Make sure nothing lives – including the boars. When you're done, rejoin us here.'

I was flattered to be sent with Iona and Gimin; that Tiroc Og really thought I could match their pace. Leaving the watchtower to join them, Bran and I scrambled down from the palisades and pelted out the gate, passing renegades already outside stripping weapons from the corpses. Then we were in the wood, following a trail of smoke and the screams of the terrified pig. I was going as fast as I could, Bran and I barely able to keep up with the swift-foots, who were probably pacing themselves for our benefit.

Our pursuit ended in a clearing where we found the chariot overturned and one of the boars lying on the ground screaming in agony, flames pouring round its head. The driver and the other beasts were nowhere in sight. I saw then that the beast's "armour" wasn't, in fact, metal, but painted wood strapped tightly to the poor creature and now burning furiously. It was a ghastly sight. I felt for the beast – its suffering as a victim of Morok warmongering. Bran ended its misery with a single thrust of his spear.

'Shall we go after the other boars?' suggested Iona to Bran.

'We'll never catch 'em now,' replied Bran, looking around the clearing. 'More important we find the driver. He can't have gone far on foot. We'll split up, cover three directions, meet back here in one *hora*. Iona, you go that way,' he urged the She-Eronn, pointing west. 'I'll go east. Gimin, you take this brand and Osian with you – there.' He pointed south; into the trees from where we'd first seen the fort. 'Take care of 'im,' he added with a chuckle.

Gimin took off through the wood, and I followed. The scrub was thick, hard to see through. Suddenly, Gimin stopped and whispered, 'Over here,' pointing to a trail of broken twigs and rushes on the ground. Cautiously, we moved forward, swords in one hand, knives in the other.

The forest was deadly silent. I felt the back of my neck prickle – there was danger near. 'Look at this,' she hissed, pointing to an area of flattened scrub that narrowed at one point. 'See there – where he's tried to hide his tracks.' We carried on, easily picking up the trail. After a while she stopped at a very dense thicket, knelt down, fingered a broken branch, sniffed it, and recoiled. 'Blood. A two legged. Ferok!' she said, wincing. 'He's injured, won't be far. We'll catch him now.' We scouted around, but the trail went no further. Where did he go? (How had we lost it?)

As we stood uncertainly, wondering which way to go, I heard a soft rustling sound behind me.

'Get down,' Gimin hissed.

I wheeled about. A ghostly figure, blood pouring down his face, stood feet away from me, crossbow raised and aimed. Suddenly I felt a surge of power – emanating from the base of my spine, coursing through me. Quick as thought, I dodged aside, but too late, I heard the snap of a bolt then the whistle of an arrow passing my ear. Something crashed into my lower back like a sack of stones. I was sent flying across the clearing. My head struck something with a sickening crack that rattled through my body before the blackness came. Last thing I saw was the bark of a tree sliding away from me. Many trees.

A red mane grazed my face; someone was speaking gently; their breath was hot. I was too drowsy to see who. I drifted away and then back, the pain coming in waves. I was lifted up. I heard someone panting close by, followed by running sounds.

Then nothing.

18

THE GILDENARK

I woke in a windowless room with wooden stakes for walls, a broken timbered opening to one side. From beyond came chanting and a scent of smoking herbs. I'd been wrapped up in my blanket, with my *papose* settled under my head. My lower back burned, and my head throbbed. When I tried to move, a jolt of pain tore down my spine. I felt a dressing on my head, and a thick bandage around my waist.

Then I remembered.

The assault on the fortalice, the chariots on fire, the squealing boars, the frantic hunt for the Ferok in the forest, Gimin's warning, the bolt fired directly at me. It was too close – mortal range. No-one could survive that.

Yet, somehow, I had.

I stumbled to my feet, grabbed my *papose* and staggered to the opening. I was back in the fortalice, in some kind of courtyard room, the area beyond littered with rubble, broken and burned timber and abandoned Morok weapons.

I went outside. Immediately to the right was another room; within was the familiar form of Tiroc Og seated by a fire, back to me, chanting rhythmically. An iron pan bubbled over the flames. Thin trails of steam rose from it, forming tiny ghostly shapes that hovered briefly before dissolving up into the roof space. I stood and watched, waiting for my moment. Then, with a half turn of his head, he slowed the chanting, and with a loud 'Hah!' clapped his mitts before reaching down for his pipe and filling the bowl. Without turning right around he said, laughter in his voice, 'Don't mind me practising my magic tricks, Osian. It's all right to stare. Yeh don't have to hide in the reeds this time.' Lighting his pipe, he poured some powder into the simmering pan and said, 'Come, join me by the fire.'

I shuffled over to the fireside and squatted, the effort painful, my head rattling with every step.

'How's the back?'

'Sore. But how—?'

A shout came from beyond, and laughter – warriors boasting, drinking *aki*. I heard Bran's roar among them, louder than any.

'The fortalice – where yeh are,' Tiroc Og replied, 'is ours. Well, it is 'til we fire it. All the Morok that were here are dead now. Yeh almost joined them. The Ferok in the woods. Remember?'

'Yes. He fired at me – surprised me.'

'Well, the devil's dead.'

'How?'

'Gimin.'

'She has my life!' I smiled inwardly at the thought of being indebted to the beautiful Fox-Wolf. 'Where is she now? I need to see her,' I blustered, trying to rise.

'With the others,' he said, with a disapproving tone, such as my aunt might have given me once upon a time. Were it not for the steely cat-like glimmer in his eyes, I would have said that he was gently mocking me. Then, he added, more matter of fact, 'She and Bran brought yeh back after she'd finished off the Ferok devil. As fer yer life, well, yeh have to thank the fates – or more likely,' he paused, his tone becoming serious, 'thon thing in yer *papose*.'

I looked at him blankly, then remembered. I'd turned away just in time as the Ferok's bolt was loosed and it hit my *papose*.

'The *Solon*?'

'*Solon, Sol-Lon*. Yes, 'tis indeed a good name, a good name,' he murmured, stretching out the word. 'A sun and new moon, in one.' He continued muttering to himself, other words I didn't catch, in *Askrit*, the old language which I knew well, but rarely spoke, as at home we used it only in its written form. One word I made out from his mutterings was *Sunar*, which meant 'dawn', and which we used in morning prayers. I knew it could also mean 'hope' and 'new beginning'.

'Anyways,' Tiroc Og spoke up, tapping his pipe against the wall. 'However, yeh survived – yeh did! 'Tis only my tribe that's supposed to haves nine lives. Not yers! With yon thing at yer back, as it were, yeh must be half-way through a Catton's list by now.' He burst out laughing.

I smiled grimly. Ridiculous though it seemed, he was right – the impenetrable shell of my strange acquisition had kept me from certain death. But to have been able to dodge a direct crossbolt hit at that range I must have moved – or been moved – at a speed faster than flight itself. (The whole thing was incredible, defying explanation).

'Yeh've been out for a full day, young Albin,' he continued. 'Gimin said the blow was severe. Said she'd never seen anyone take an attack like that and yet live to tell the tale. Thon dreadful bolt bounced off yer *papose* like it was a stone, forcing yeh 'cross the ground like a tree being felled, before yeh hit an actual tree with yer head. She said the terrified look on thon devil's face when his dart didn't go through yeh was somethin' to behold. The shock quickened his end, for he just stood there shaking, unable to move till Gimin put him out of his misery. Said he almost looked relieved as he left this life.'

I picked up a piece of kindling and toyed with some smoking cinders that had fallen out of the fire-circle, slowly taking in this information.

''Scuse me one moment, Osian,' he said. 'I needs go out and set a watch.'

He left me pondering. This was the second or maybe even the third time my life had been saved in a most unlikely way. Was this it, or would there be other interventions? Gingerly, I took up my *papose* and with shaking hands I took out the *Solon* and rolled it over. Incredibly, the Ferok's bolt had left no mark on the shell; although there was a slit at the base of the *papose* where it had pierced its thick hide. Gingerly I placed it back in its nest, as baffled as ever.

Tiroc Og returned as I was rubbing my head, part puzzlement, part pain. 'This dressing. Was that you?' I spoke.

'I used a willow bark salve. The pain'll go soon,' he replied. 'Ye'll be fine in an *hora* or so – for we'll have to leave here before morn. Meantime, yeh hungry?' He moved the pot that was over the fire and replaced it with another. I nodded, head pounding, but less so. I was indeed hungry, far more than sore. Whatever was cooking smelled like pork. I tried not to think of those poor beasts that had pulled the Morok chariots.

'So Ganoc's firelogs worked in the end?' I queried.

'Apparently they exploded right under the chariot wheels. The devils inside were all torn to pieces though hogs and mules were seen running into the woods in a bad way – easy food for the wolves and ravens. Lanoc said no Morok escaped 'n injured were let to live in these cruel times. Ganoc brought back some Morok weapons and a few Krol and Ferok robes that may proves useful. The horrible dry stuff they live off, that smells like it was dug out of a plague pit, *petican* they call it – ugh – that's all gone.'

'So, what happens next? Where does the company go now?' I felt a pinch of anxiety – for whatever they were planning, my own mission came first. I was still resolved to go on alone if necessary.

'I've heard from Cana-Din,' he replied. 'Gwion is alive, but a prisoner in Rakhaus. She's in Clachoile, at an assembly of the High Chiefs and clan leaders of the Brach, the Sideag and the lesser tribes of the easter territories. We're hoping they'll agree to help mount an assault on the island. Old Amon, the Brach High Chief, despite what Bran may think, is our best chance. He goes back a long way with Gwion. So, there's hope. We go forward with hope in our hearts.'

It was what I wanted to hear. I felt my heart lurch. 'Rakhaus.'

'Yes. Rakhaus, Osian. Yer coming, I take it?'

'Of course,' I beamed. 'Nothing would stop me.'

'Yeh know it's possible yer kin might not be there…or worse…'

I nodded. 'But I have to look.'

He gave me a sidewards glance. 'Of course, it may not be what is *wanted* of yeh.'

'I don't understand, Tiroc Og.' I stared at him.

He waved a finger at my *papose*. His words in the shelter, 'It's yeh that's been found,' rang in my ears. And I knew what this meant. My curious find, the shining stone, had a purpose of its own; for this it was keeping me alive, for this I couldn't rid myself of it. Like the shaking dancers at *jagar* – the midnight vigils in Alba when the wild spirits are drawn into the worshippers' bodies by the backwards echo of the *huruk* drum – I felt I'd become possessed. Not by a spirit, but by an object – if that's what it was.

A long silence followed. Tiroc Og emptied, refilled and relit his pipe, then sat back and puffed smoke rings over the fire. I gazed after the smoke. I was getting used to the tracker's manners; his bouts of quiet contemplation, his sudden questions, his pipe smoke.

Later, when we'd eaten, I lay back against the palisade wall and waited, for I knew from his manner that he was going to question me again. Indeed, after a short while, he set down his pipe, folded his arms and said, in a tone that was soft but firm, 'First off, Osian, I needs understand more about thon thing in yer *papose*. If it is to be with yeh then we must be sure it is with *us* too – and not likely to bring down harm on our band. This time,' he added with emphasis, 'I need yer full story, the stuff yeh've already told me, not just about yer *Solon* as yeh calls it, but everything from the very beginning. We've all night – we can drink *tai* while we talks. 'Tis surely a night fer truth tales.' He smiled, leaning his head towards the outside, where the warriors were still boasting and laughing. 'Unlikes them out there,' he said, 'I only wants to hear truths.'

'Then truth you shall have,' I said. 'Where shall I start?'

'From the very beginning usually works,' he said, twinkling.

I collected my thoughts, then began to relate the whole story of my journey from Grandfather's parting words in Alba to the point when I'd arrived on Avalor. My previous reluctance to talk about the *Solon* had all but disappeared – with Tiroc Og, at any rate – so I told him again of my encounters in the Karst cavern and at the river, down to the finest detail. I also described crossing the White Mountains, meeting the Red Fox, the Marten and Romi the She-Tarsin, and I relayed my encounter with the comical Morok couple and how I came to recover my hunting bow and sword, 'stolen from me by who or what or how, I do not know.'

Tiroc Og listened closely, querying occasional small details of my journey, including the weather, the state of the river, types of tracks on the ground, muttering from time to time, 'Ah, yes. Ah, yes,' while puffing and periodically refuelling his pipe. When I'd finished, he said, 'Thinking about it, thon beast in the cavern would have been a *Xthone*, an earth dragon. It'll have been used by the Morok fer that stuff it makes, so they could seal yer *Solon* for some reason – to secure it, hide it from its owner, but most likely to make it safe fer them to carry.'

'Why would it do that?'

'In exchange for something.'

'What?' I answered.

'Live victims.'

My stomach turned over. The pile of bones, the stream of blood. Who or what poor creature had been sacrificed to that beast to enable it to produce that horrible unguent?

'That stuff it makes – that web – is deadly poisonous to the touch. No doubt that's what made sick yer Krol, the Morok priests. 'Cept when it's dried,' he added. 'Then it's really useful. The old shamans used it like a rubbing stone to heal wounds – but never raw. And it can't be cut, fired or smashed. Not by any means.'

'Yeh didn't try to open it, Osian – to crack the shell?' he queried, looking into my eyes. 'Do yeh still feel no desire to see, to find out if yeh could open it?'

'My instincts were that it should remain hidden – even from me.'

He stood and placed more kindling on the flames. 'The problem we have with it is that the others have seen what it can do. They know it has the mark of the Morok. In their eyes, it might be a tool of theirs – an accursed thing with evil intent.'

'It does seem to have intent. "Evil." I don't know. It certainly feels alive.'

'Sorcerous, yes, and alive, though perhaps not like yeh and thon trees out there, but beyond nature – a kind of being that is dangerous, toxic even in its raw state, 'cept perhaps to its rightful owner, whomsoever or whatever that mights be.'

'It heard it call out – in the cavern, like a living thing. When I saw it again on the water, it shone through its shell. It is a life indeed, but, you are right, more than that. It lives, shines even, through me… through the elements – thunderstorms, the earth, the water, the trees, even the air. It mostly sleeps but wakes when danger is near. I see a flash, then time slows and space shifts. All are frozen. And I can act, fight, for myself – and for it.'

I paused, then. 'But, you think its a curse, a danger to us, family, friends – the company…me?'

'Now that, I don't know. It's not of this world and has a hold over yeh that's not of this world. How that follows through is anyone's guess.'

I shuddered, thinking again of the *jagar* dancers who, when possessed, were able to do all kinds of extraordinary things – walk on hot coals, speak in strange tongues, even heal the sick. I'd heard they could fly, although I'd never seen that and always doubted it. They acted in these ways because they were under the control of another, a shaman or a spirit. They were not themselves. Was it that kind of a hold it had over me? But then, I'd not done anything that hadn't been my own decision – even the killing. Or was that even true? Had the *Solon* been acting through me without me knowing it?

'And something else,' he said before I could comment. 'Thon storm the night before yeh found it was the worst I ever remember. It was almost as if the very gods were enraged, unleashing their anger in a fury of water and thunder and helping yer *Solon* get away from the Krol, free from the clutches of Kahl's Morok.'

'Maybe I should throw it in the marsh waters. Let the marsh beasts take it, let them have its devilish force and drown any curse in it.'

'No, no, my friend. It is not for you to decide such a thing.' Abruptly, he flung the contents of his pipe into the fire, rose to his feet and pushed past me to the open doorway. At the threshold he stopped, looked out into the night, then turned and said, 'When yeh found it. Did anyone – anything – see yeh taking it from the water?'

'Since you ask, I *did* feel I was being watched. But I'd had that feeling before and seen nothing. I did check – but no.'

'Not even a high flying Skarag?'

'No, not that I was aware of.'

He came back to the fire, casting a sideways glance at my *papose*, lying against the wall, the slight bulge at the base visible in the firelight – the shining stone, the *Solon*.

'There's many already knows yeh have it – too many, maybe.' He gestured to the outside. 'And there's Ferok eagles that can fly to great heights and see at great distances, even through cloud.'

I gulped. If this was true, then I probably had been seen. And I was pretty sure that the *Solon* and I were being hunted. 'Why would the Morok want such a thing?' I asked.

'For its power – or powers – whatever they be, or whatever the Morok think they be, which could be differin' things by my way of it. But there's one thing of which I'm certain. It found ye. Yeh didn't come by it by accident. Osian, my friend, yeh *are* its carrier of choice – 'tis part of yer *almadh*, yer destiny. And as long as yeh bear it, it'll seek to protect yeh – till it doesn't need yeh any mores.'

'And then what?'

'Ah, that's fer the gods to know and us – yeh – to find out.'

I squirmed and sat erect, my heart pumping furiously. The walls felt very close around me.

He leaned over and patted me on the shoulder. 'Ah, young Osian. Don't take it so. None of us really know why things are done to us. But there'll be reason in it. The reason of the gods.'

'So, what should I do with it?'

'Yeh must carry on with yer mission, 'cos that may well be its mission. It is yers now, until 'tis lost or claimed by another that it accepts. Yeh are taking it into the enemy's territory, into the very heart of it, but it must be kept out o' their claws...even if...'

'Even if...?'

'Yeh die in the attempt.'

My insides felt weak and watery; my legs shook.

We lapsed into silence. Tiroc Og seemed wrapped in contemplation. But after a while, he said, 'Yer *Solon*, yer shining stone, reminds me of an old story.'

'Oh, yes?' I was hungry for explanations, understanding of any kind.

He blew a single ring of smoke and watched it hang in the air. 'But first...' Then he stopped, his expression deadly serious as if he was about to reveal some terrible truth.

'But first...?'

He laughed. 'We'll have some *tai*.'

Outside, except for the watch, our companions lay asleep in their blankets around the embers of their cooking fire, and the only sounds were of their snoring – mostly the big-chested Brach and Barod. Inside, I gazed at the fire in silence, waiting for Tiroc Og's tale, and remembering vividly the last one I'd been told.

After a while, he added wood to the fire, put more *tai* to boil, then sat back and asked, 'Do you know, Osian, the stories of the *Gildenark*?'

The *Gildenark* sagas were old fireside fairy tales, comforting and reassuring. I smiled expectantly at the thought of hearing one of them again – if that's what he was planning.

'Yes, my grandfather's favourite was *The Gildenark and the Nightingale*. I remember liking the sound of the words. And, of course, we had nightingales in the woods around the lakes at home. If I listened to them, it helped me sleep.'

'Yes,' he answered, 'there are many such stories. Did your grandfather ever tell yeh about the *Gildenark itself*? Did he say what it was?'

'Grandfather said it was invisible, like a spirit, but it made itself known through the song of the nightingale, a song that enchanted all who heard it, helping the sleepless and soothing the sick.'

'Hah. Very good. There is wisdom in such stories, wisdom indeed,' Tiroc Og said, stroking his chin the way cats do (when they shift position). In the soft firelight, he had a real look of the cat totem on the hilt of his sword. He was wily predator, yet compassionate with it.

'Of all stories, what made you think of those of the *Gildenark?*' I asked, prompting a telling. I wrapped my blanket tightly around me in expectation of the soothing sleep that might follow.

'Because yer *Solon* brought it to mind – a thing with power, little understood, that exerts its will through others,' he said, his tone matter of fact.

I felt a chill at this, and huddled closer to the fire. He poured out the tea, his eyes following the steam in the cups as it rose into the air. I half expected one of his *Akari* tricks with smoke. Instead, he started the story, commencing with the opening words of the tale tellers. *'If all were told…'*

He continued, trance-like, rhythmic and slow. *'Long after the Icetime, there came once again a cold and darkness upon the land. The ancestors gathered together and asked Yahl to give them back warmth and light. Yahl said to them, "Yeh have fire, yeh have water, yeh have earth and sky, and the sun that goes around it. What more can I give yeh?"*

"But we are unhappy," they replied. "The sun is weak. Our young ones are cold and hungry, our crops do not grow, we cannot find the fishes in the waters or the small game in the hills and the trees. We need more light, more heat."

'At this, Yahl boomed and flashed great lightning forks at them so that they scattered in fear. They'd dared to question the Creator, to doubt the great plan. But after some time, Yahl realised that this was harsh, so he looked into the world and indeed found that something was wrong. So, he called them from their hiding places and said, "There is a world beyond yers – it is the mirror of yer world. Without it yer world would not be in balance. I have looked into this world, and I've found that something from

the time of creation, a special thing, is missing from it. This will explain the darkness in yer world, a kind of hole such as a burrowing creature might make. I don't know how this came to be – but I am going to have this special thing remade so it can be restored to the mirror world. This means, once finished, it will also be in yer world, though not visible. It will restore the balance between the worlds and clear the darkness. Think of it as a talisman."

'"What will be its nature," the ancestors asked, "this talisman that will be made here but will not be here?"

'"That yeh'll find out," Yahl answered. "First, send me two of the very best of yer Farae, Otar smiths of sungold and moonsilver. One must be of the Eronn who care for the holy places, and the other must be of the Albin who dwell beyond the holy mountains. Place these Farae, with their tools, upon the great slanted rock in the desert, in the space between day and night on midwinter's eve, and I will show them how to build the talisman. They will be gone for a full six moons. And during that time yeh must all wait. Pray for success, and for their return."

'This the ancestors did, and by the morn of midwinter's day, it was seen that the Farae were indeed gone. But six moons later, on midsummer morn, they were nowhere to be seen. They had not returned. Many more moons passed over and still no sign of them. The ancestors became troubled and feared they'd been let down by the Creator. The world remained dark and cold. Yet, they'd little choice but to keep believing, and so they kept praying.

'Then, miraculously, at dusk on midwinter's eve, a sudden shaft of moonlight revealed that the Farae were once again upon the great slanted rock. They came off the rock and explained that they'd built something at the Creator's request out of beams of the sun and the moon. It had a name, the Gildenark. And they said that although it would be in our world, it had the properties of the mirror world, and was thus invisible. It will be known through its voice – a sound of great beauty that straddles the worlds and can be heard both night and day. The sound you will hear is a song, the call of the nightingale, the little bird sacred to the God of the Wood.

'Then, at dawn on midwinter's day, for the first time in many moons, the nightingale was heard to sing again, first in the sacred wood of Arkesh, then elsewhere. And the ancestors saw that the sun began to rise higher in the heavens. They made garlands for the two Farae and offered sacrifices to Yahl. From then onwards, there was indeed light, and warmth, and plenty. The ancestors were happy and gave thanks to Yahl.'

Tiroc Og signalled the end of the story by lying back and pulling his blanket up to his chin. But I didn't feel sleepy, and wished to question him why he thought the *Gildenark* reminded him of the *Solon*. I knew the tale well but had enjoyed hearing it again in such a different voice. It was very alike the version told me by my grandfather – except in one respect – who the Farae were. First, I asked about this.

'Tiroc Og, I'd always known that the Farae were Otar, the greatest smiths in all the tribes. But I never knew that one was Eronn and the other Albin. Is this always the case – in all tellings?'

'Always,' he replied, 'I'm surprised yeh didn't know. The names in them were Sol and…Lon.'

'What!'

'Yes, I know – yer choice of a name for the shining stone. Funny that,' he said, stifling a yawn. 'Maybe yeh'd been told and had forgotten – a chance thing though, yeh coming up with that name.'

But his over-casual response suggested he knew it wasn't just chance. I looked at him quizzically. I'd certainly never heard before the names of the Farae before, just as I'd never known they were Otar of different tribes. Was there more to it that he wasn't telling me, some direct connection between the mythical *Gildenark* and the very real but just as mysterious *Solon*?

Then, as so often before, it appeared he'd read my thoughts, for he said, 'No. I doubts if it is what yeh think,' and laid back against the palisade wall. 'I was just reminded of the old story, that's all. Though there is an odd thing – since the coming of the Long Winter no nightingale has been heard to sing in Erainn. Anyways, sleep now. We'll talk again in the morning.' He rested back and closed his eyes.

I too lay back and placed my head on my *papose*. But my head buzzed with questions and sleep did not follow. I had got into the habit of opening Aehmir's little book when sleep failed me, so I pulled it out and came straight to 'Fall not into weakness. Arise like a fire that burns all before it.'

I wondered if the *Solon* was, like the *Gildenark*, a force for good – not just for me but for the free tribes. As it had strengthened me, could it help them arise from their weakness, so that they could open once again the pilgrim ways? Could it help bring back the call of the nightingale; banish the darkness afflicting the holy lands.

Was this its destiny – its true purpose? (Then I slept).

I woke in the night to the sounds of commotion beyond the wall. The warriors were awake, busy breaking camp. Some grumbled loudly about the early hour, some complained of sore heads. But there was laughter too – jostling and the rattling of weapons, the folding of benders, the scrape of knives and swords on sharpening stones. I sat up.

Tiroc Og was still asleep, and the little *tai*-making fire was out.

Suddenly, Bran charged in, shook Tiroc Og awake and said, 'Come quickly, chief. The harriers are back.'

Tiroc Og leapt up as though he'd never been asleep and hurried outside with Bran. Before I'd even got the chance to rub the tiredness from my eyes, he was back and stuffing his blanket, pipe and utensils into his long *papose*.

'What's happening?' I muttered, yawning and stretching.

'Collect your things, Osian,' he said. 'We're leaving.'

'Why the hurry?' I said, realising this would mean we were going without breakfast.

'The harriers brought new messages. There's a large Morok force on its way here. Coming from the southeast, upriver from the coast in small Aguan boats. They know we're here, and what we've done – it was all seen by high flying Skarag – and the Morok are already in the near creeks. We needs be gone – and quickly – if we're to get to Rakhaus alive! Ganoc has already put firelogs in place on the four sides of the fortalice.'

My chest pummelled, all thoughts of sleep and breakfast gone completely. At last, I thought, I was going to Rakhaus. Whatever its terrors, there lay all my hopes of finding my kin – if indeed they still lived. I stood and began to bundle up my blanket. 'I understood Rakhaus to be impregnable?'

'There are ways in. And I know them,' he said in a way that didn't invite further questions.

'What if Cana-Din cannot persuade the Brach to join us?' I asked, lifting my weapons and hoisting my *papose* onto my shoulder.

'Then, Osian, we'll just go in alone.'

I looked at him, unsure whether to believe this or not. Catching my gaze, he shrugged and grinned ruefully.

We walked out together. One group of warriors were already gathered ready for departure. Others were making last minute adjustments to their weapons and packs. Occasional glances and smiles came my way. No doubt news of my miraculous escape from the Ferok had already spread around the camp. Gimin was conversing with Iona, who giggled when she saw me (and nudged her companion's shoulder.) Thankfully, Gimin didn't look over, for my cheeks were burning.

'Tiroc Og,' I said, as I tightened the weapons on my belt. 'I have one more question.'

'Yes, Osian?'

'Why is Gwion so important that you would risk the lives of all your friends?'

'Ah. Of course,' came the reply. 'You don't know. Why would you? But Gwion is not just our friend. He is Gwion-din.'

'Gwion-din?' I looked at him blankly.

'Sire to Cana-Din,' he responded.

'Ah! I understand,' I said, not taken wholly by surprise, for I'd well-learned on this adventure that there were already wheels within wheels, and something else too – that nothing and no-one here was ever quite the way it or they seemed.

Tiroc Og then said something which left me wondering even more.

'Yeh know about Gwion, yer grandfather and my father?'

'Yes, that together they brought an end to the Marsh Wars, guided by Aehmir – the Wind Hare. I have Gwion's sword,' with a glance at it, poking above its sheath at my waist belt. That was when I noticed, almost for the first time, the tiny insignia separate from the other carvings on the hilt – a conjoined moon and sun! A *Solon* sword!

'Did yeh also know that he was not just a wise elder?'

'Well, he was ferry keeper to the tribes.'

'In more ways than one. Think of what a ferry keeper does. He is someone who makes crossings, who connects worlds, the past to the future, brings souls together, and binds.'

This was a little too vague for me. I shrugged but didn't respond.

Then he smiled at me. 'It should come as no surprise to yeh that old Gwion isn't quite what everyone thinks.'

'What do you mean?'

'It's not his real name.'

'So, who is he?' I queried, wondering if this was something Grandfather knew.

'I cannot say.'

'But you do know?'

'I have been pledged to secrecy by my father on this matter. Suffice to say, his importance to us all – to the freedom of the tribes – is greater than yeh can possibly imagine.'

Before I had the chance to take this in, even reflect on anything Grandfather might have indicated about him – even how he'd lost his sight, which I'd meant to ask – Tiroc Og raised his sword for attention.

'Gather, comrades,' he commanded.

As they drew around, he lowered his sword, shouldered his *papose* and said to Ganoc, 'Are the firelogs in place, brother?'

'Safely set on all sides of the fortalice,' replied Ganoc, holding up a bundle of arrows wrapped with pitch-soaked bandages. 'Lakon and I will fire them with these from a safe distance. Go. We'll be quickly on yer heels.'

Nodding approval, Tiroc Og smiled broadly and said, 'Do it well, brothers. Aim high and true.' Then, raising his sword, he said aloud, 'To Rakhaus, we will now go, my friends. Trisuldur was a success, but small in measure. Now we face our greatest task. But we go with brave hearts and right on our side. Death to the enemy that follows and all those that come. May the ancestors bless our journey. May Yahl and great fortune go with us.'

As one, the company raised their swords and bows and repeated the refrain, 'May Yahl and great fortune go with us.'

And thus, we set off.

EPILOGUE

CARYN

'That will have to do for this night, Caryn,' I said, putting down her father's chronicle and rising to bend over the log basket, 'for I'm tired.'

'You can't stop there, Guardian,' she responded, suddenly alert, shaken from her trance by my movement. During the reading I'd stolen occasional glances at her and had seen her quick mind continually trying to put together the many threads of the story, guessing their interconnections, and no doubt piling up the many questions that would follow – who, what, how.

'Wait till the end of the tale afore you ask any questions,' I said insistently. 'Anyways, my old eyes are too weary with the reading to go on with it all now – and when we get to the end, the *very* end, there will be different questions.'

The howling blast had banked ice against the window, leaving a tiny gap. Through it, a single star wavered in the moist night air – a brief calm in this season of wind and hard snows. I was glad I'd doubled the roof timbers earlier in the year, securing our little cabin against anything the storm gods could throw at it. I thought back to the deep-blue-skied summer days when we did the work – Yamis's son, Kamis, lifting timbers up to me as he skipped over sun-kissed roof beams, trying to impress Caryn and shouting, 'Look at me! I'm Iskar, Skraeling King of the North!'

The only cloud in the firmament back then was that we'd heard nothing of Osian or Bran; no messages had come to us from across the Broken Sea. And now, still nothing. We'd been busy in the time since, making cheer as best we could – stacking the cellar with rosy apples, pears, pumpkins and marrows, loading jars of fruit preserve on the shelves, filling oak barrels with salted butter and cheese from Yamis's goats and loading sacks of oats on the floor. I glanced up at the tall stone chimney breast, hung with dried fish and game for smoking, and I knew he'd be proud of all our works. I had hope still in my heart that her father yet lived and would return before long. He had to. But as yet another new moon faded into old, so too my hope was fading with it. And I could feel my own time drawing in like winter's bane.

Caryn was quiet, running the red stripe in her tresses through her fingers; wondering, no doubt, if Gimin, the lovely Wolf–Fox in the story, might be the mother she'd no memory of. The truth of that, of course, would become clear in the full course of the story. Not till then.

'So, Guardian,' she said, shifting her gaze, her eyes shining, 'in that jar is the *Solon* – the shining stone – and that's why it can't be opened. It won't allow us!'

'Ah, Caryn. I've never seen inside, never been told what it contains, other than that in it is a memento of sorts from your father's journeys.'

What else could I say? For I really didn't know.

She looked at me quizzically. Though she knew I'd never tell her an untruth, her horizons had been widened beyond our safe little life here, and she'd have understood from the story that nothing is ever quite the way it seems. She must feel now that she'd entered a strange new world brimming with magic and mystery, at its heart the heroic, dauntless father she loved so deeply and, because of things in that world, might never see again.

'You're not scared – troubled by anything you've heard?' I queried, retrieving the largest log from the basket, the night log that would keep a low flame alive through the cold darkness.

'Goodness no,' she declared with a laugh. 'Remember, *I'm not a kid anymore!*'

I laughed with her. Yet I'd seen her shiver and wrap her shawl tight during the ghost scene in "the fall", seen a tear fall when Osian described his vision of Erin in the Log Marten's fire, then seen her tense when he'd been under attack. I'd seen her shed a tear when he was in danger – nearly killed, seen the shock on her face as Bran, who she'd only ever known as a kindly, cuddly giant, was revealed to be a fearless, frenzied killer. I'd also seen her glance over and mouth my name when Osian described meeting Drion – me.

There was much for her to wonder over, to query, and yes to be troubled by. But nothing compared to what was to come – to what, as Osian's tale develops, she'd find out about her mother – and who she, Caryn, really was.

As we prepared to retire, I saw her glance again at the jar. Her sky-blue eyes were as radiant as ever, but in that moment, as the night log smothered the flames, I saw them darken. A shadow passed across them.

And it had.

To be Continued: Tales of the Q'alix #2

Remembering

Chas, Connie, Dixie, Alan and our beloved wildcat Monty